GIRL

UNDER

GLASS

A NOVEL BY
GINNY RORBY

Black Rose Writing | Texas

©2024 by Ginny Rorby
All rights reserved. No part of this book may be reproduced, stored in a retrieval system or transmitted in any form or by any means without the prior written permission of the publishers, except by a reviewer who may quote brief passages in a review to be printed in a newspaper, magazine or journal.

The author grants the final approval for this literary material.

First printing

This is a work of fiction. Names, characters, businesses, places, events, and incidents are either the products of the author's imagination or used in a fictitious manner. Any resemblance to actual persons, living or dead, or actual events is purely coincidental.

ISBN: 978-1-68513-420-4
LIBRARY OF CONGRESS CONTROL NUMBER: 2024934613
PUBLISHED BY BLACK ROSE WRITING
www.blackrosewriting.com

Printed in the United States of America
Suggested Retail Price (SRP) $21.95

Girl Under Glass is printed in Garamond Premier Pro

*As a planet-friendly publisher, Black Rose Writing does its best to eliminate unnecessary waste to reduce paper usage and energy costs, while never compromising the reading experience. As a result, the final word count vs. page count may not meet common expectations.

OTHER BOOKS BY GINNY RORBY

Like Dust, I Rise

Freeing Finch

How to Speak Dolphin

Lost in the River of Grass

The Outside of a Horse

Hurt Go Happy

Dolphin Sky

DEDICATED TO

Teresa Sholars
For her commitment to the ecology of her community
And the planet.

GIRL

UNDER

GLASS

"They tell us that plants are perishable, soulless creatures, that only man is immortal but this, I think is something that we know very nearly nothing about."

–John Muir

"It's never too late to become who you might have been."

–Unknown

"A Colorado State University scientist has reengineered plants so that they can detect explosives, air pollution and toxic chemicals. Plants fixed with custom-made proteins in biologist June Medford's lab signal the presence of potentially deadly vapors by turning white from green. Military and federal Homeland Security research directors Wednesday said they envision wide applications for the genetically modified plants positioned in buildings, war zones and cities where terrorists could set up covert bomb-making factories.

–...from *The Miami Herald*, February 2011

"What is a weed? A plant whose virtues have never been discovered."

–Ralph Waldo Emerson

"Did you know that trees talk? Well, they do. They talk to each other, and they'll talk to you if you listen. . . . I have learned a lot from trees: sometimes about the weather, sometimes about animals, sometimes about the Great Spirit.

–*Walking Buffalo*

"What's crazier—plants speaking, or human's listening?"

–Richard Powers, *The Overstory*

PROLOGUE

The black paint on the steel door bears the marks of the attempt to break the padlock. A bit of bloody skin sticks to one of the silver scratches. The only sound comes from behind the padlocked door. Barely audible scratching, muted by the walls, the wire arms of an old polygraph drift calmly across the paper that rolls lazily through. Nothing like the frantic scrapes of last night, now buried beneath layer after layer of printout folding over on itself onto the floor.

Behind the door is the concrete room that forms the back wall of the greenhouse. If whoever tried had managed to open the door, he would have found the polygraph, an old Dell Toughbook laptop, a laser jet printer, an overflowing shelf of botany books, and a gas chromatograph.

The front door to this greenhouse is standing open, letting damp air seep in. There are signs of the struggle that took place. The gravel flooring has been stirred to expose the weed mat beneath it. Potted plants are tipped over. A few have been knocked off the potting tables onto the floor, root balls exposed, dirt everywhere. Pieces of the philodendron in a hanging basket to the right of the steel door, lie scattered on the gravel floor. Unseen behind its basket, wires from a hole drilled in the concrete wall, dangle.

A fat, black and white cat sits beneath a hidden drawer in the potting table next to what might be mistaken for a crumpled pile of laundry. Except for the shock of white hair standing out in all directions around the bloody hole in the side of an old man's head.

A young girl comes up the driveway on her bike. She leans it against a rusting old Dodge truck and walks toward the greenhouse. "Gen," she calls, expecting the cat. "Who left this door open? Hobby? Where is everybody?"

CHAPTER 1

Kelsey McCully twists strands of limp brown hair around her forefinger as she waits for the lady behind the Rite Aid pharmacy counter to find her mother's prescription. She peers at Kelsey over the top of the shelf she's searching. "M-A-C?" Same as she asked last month.

Kelsey rolls her eyes. "M-C." Same as last month.

"Levothyroxine?" the clerk shouts.

"I don't know the real name."

"For her thyroid?" Her voice is loud.

"Yes." There's a line behind her, and Kelsey feels their eyes on her back. She stops twisting her hair and puts her hands in her hoodie pockets.

Ronald, the pharmacist, looks up from pill counting. "How's your mom, Kelsey?"

An insincere question if there ever was one. She wonders what he'd say if she told him the truth? Would some do-gooder in line behind her call Child Protective Services, while the others, fearing involvement, scattered? "Fine," she says.

"Glad to hear it."

Ronald always asks. Kelsey always lies. Her mother worked here five years ago and was fired for showing up drunk for her shift. No one really cares how she's doing, and Kelsey hates him for pretending he does.

"Found it. And her Lithium refill from last month." The woman comes out from behind the shelves shaking two bottles like maracas. "Medi-cal, right?" Drawing everyone's attention to their finances.

Kelsey glares at her. "Yes."

Resentment balloons in her stomach. Every month, it's the same. Her mother hasn't set foot in Rite Aid since they fired her. Not only does Kelsey have to keep track of her mother's prescriptions, she has to endure picking them up, and dealing with this idiot employee every time.

"Birthday?" the clerk says.

Kelsey glances at the growing line behind her. "Two, twenty-two, oh six."

The clerk laughs. "Not yours, dearie, your mother's."

Behind her, someone clears their throat impatiently.

Of course, her mother's. Kelsey just wants out of here. "Four, fifteen, seventy-eight."

The clerk hunts and pecks Lydia's birthdate into the computer. "Right you are. Receipt's in the bag." She crooks a finger at the next person in line.

Kelsey's friend, Brie, who's been guarding their bicycles, grins when Kelsey comes out and tosses the bag into her basket. "Sorry," Kelsey says. "That woman in there is an idiot."

Kelsey only met Brie a few months ago when she and her parents moved up from the Bay Area. She doesn't know much about her except that her dad's a lawyer and her mother is busy, Brie said using air-quotes, "volunteering." Kelsey thinks they hit it off because they both recognize miserable when they see it.

Brie nods toward the store employee whose butt-crack shows every time he bends to reset the pots tipped over by the last night's gusty winds. They watch him pick up a lone gardenia and put it back on the plant stand.

"My mother tried to grow a gardenia once." Kelsey smiles at Brie. "Think I should give her another shot at it?"

It takes Brie a second to get what Kelsey means. "I'll cover you." Brie pushes her bike in front of Kelsey's.

When the clerk turns to pick up another plant, Kelsey straddle-walks her bike over to the gardenia and presses her nose into the single, sweet blossom. She feels light-headed and her heart thuds. She sniffs the white flower again, turning her head slightly to sneak a peek at the blue-vested employee. He's holding a fuchsia, about to rehang it, but his attention is fully on a woman crossing the parking lot in high heels.

Kelsey snatches the gardenia, jams it into her bike basket, and rides away. She shoots across the parking lot toward the tire store and out onto the sidewalk. She speeds past the Motel 6 before slowing and circling back to peek around the corner. Several minutes pass before she sees Brie ride out of the drugstore's parking lot. Kelsey heads back toward her. Brie shouts something, but a passing logging truck drowns her out.

"What?"

"Go!" Brie looks scared.

Oh my god. Kelsey does a 180 and pedals as hard as she can toward the motel's rear exit. She bounces over a speed bump and nearly falls as she makes a sharp left onto the sidewalk behind the motel. Jerry Curtis, a Fort Bragg cop she knows all too well, stands in the center of the sidewalk with his hands on his hips. She tries to steer around him, but he catches her handlebars, stopping the bike so suddenly, the gardenia flips out and lands right side up against the motel's rear wall. The bloom pops off and drops near the tip of Jerry's highly polished boot. The prescription bag lands in a puddle left by the drip system.

Kelsey tries to act innocent and confused. "Geez, Jerry, you scared me." She retrieves the bag and wipes the wet side off on her sleeve.

Brie pedals out of the motel's rear driveway, sees them, and turns the other way.

"Nice gardenia." Jerry picks up the flower, sniffs it, and jams it behind his badge.

"I bought that for my mother. She's been sick."

For a split second, she sees a look of pity on his face. Maybe he'll let her go again. Jerry not only knows her record, he's a neighbor. His back fence is across the alley from their garage. Close enough to know way too much about their lives.

"I bet she would have liked it." His smile doesn't reach his eyes.

"Yeah. They're her favorite." She sees Brie stop by the rear wall of the Savings Bank to watch.

"Gardenias don't do well here," he says. "Too cold, I guess."

"Well, I gotta go." Kelsey tries to twist the handlebars free.

Jerry keeps his grip firm. "Sure, Kelsey. I just need to see the receipt."

Heart thundering, Kelsey slips off her backpack and pretends to look for it. Her hands shake as she checks inside the prescription bag, then pretends to scour the sidewalk. "It must have blown out of my basket."

"Uh huh. Well, I'm afraid we'll need to check with the store." He's looking past her.

Kelsey turns to follow his gaze.

The Rite Aid clerk jogs up the sidewalk toward them, his belly bouncing like a beach ball. "There were two of them," he pants.

"I'm afraid the other one got away," Jerry says. "Take the plant, and leave me your name. You'll probably be called to testify."

"Not a problem. I'm sick of these kids ripping us off when they've got more money to pay for stuff than I have."

Jerry nods. "Tell me about it."

Kelsey swallows over and over, trying not to cry. "I won't do it again, Jerry, I promise. Mom really has been sick."

That look of pity is there again, and gone as quickly. Should she try telling him she took it as revenge for firing her mother and leave out that it was five years ago? He won't care that the stupid clerk asks her the same questions every month when she picks up her mother's prescriptions probably because Kelsey and her mom aren't important enough to remember from one month to the next.

"Sorry, Kiddo. I told you last time, no more passes."

By last time, he means a few months ago when she and Brie got caught shoplifting at Racines, a stationery and art supply store. Kelsey'd seen Jerry pull up out front, and put back the cute cat diary she was about to snatch, but she didn't have time to warn Brie, who had a calligraphy kit for beginners in her backpack. Brie's father "knew people" so only Kelsey got in trouble when Jerry drove her home and told her mother.

Jerry takes her mother's pills out of the prescription bag and reads the label. "My wife takes this. Pretty common, I guess." He puts the bag back in her basket. "See you in court, Kelsey. Maybe a few weeks in juvenile hall will change your tune before it's too late."

CHAPTER 2

"You do these things because of me, don't you?" Her mother stands in front of the bathroom mirror as Kelsey works to comb out the snarl at the back of her mom's head from too many hours spent sleeping in her recliner.

"Why do you say that?"

They have to be in court at ten this morning. Since the day Jerry brought Kelsey home and told her mother she'd been caught shoplifting again, Lydia has made this about her parenting skills, or lack of them. "I'm a crap mother." Her voice quivers like she's on the verge of crying.

"It's not about you, Mom."

Kelsey's most recent crime has tipped her mother into a state of depression again. It's eight-thirty and Kelsey has brought Lydia a second watered-down Bloody Mary. She's been trying to keep Lydia sober enough to walk and talk, but hopefully tipsy enough not to make a scene in front of the judge.

Kelsey puts the comb down. "There's still a small knot I can't get out." She holds the knotted strands above her mother's head for her to see in the mirror. They look eerily alike and yet unrelated. Kelsey's hair is a mousy dull brown, her mother's a graying shade of dishwasher blond. Kelsey's eyes are green, her mother's are pale blue and perpetually red-rimmed and bloodshot. They both have pug-noses and a gap between their front teeth.

Lydia's sad eyes meet Kelsey's. "I don't suppose you remember sitting on the edge of the sink to let me brush your hair?"

Kelsey wishes she did. "Did I wear barrettes?"

Her mother brightens. "I think so. Pink rabbits."

"I remember. With their legs outstretched like they were being chased."

Lydia takes her drink from the lid of toilet tank, tilts her head back, and drains the glass. "Go ahead. Cut it all off. What do I care?" She holds the empty glass up to the light, and shakes the ice cubes. "Need another one of these first." She turns to leave the bathroom too quickly and catches the doorframe to keep from falling.

•   •   •   •   •

The bailiff calls, "All rise," when Jonathan Lehan, the Mendocino County Juvenile Judge enters the courtroom. Kelsey pulls her mother to her feet and keeps her steady with an arm around her waist. After Judge Lehan takes his seat, Kelsey sits and tugs Lydia into the seat beside her.

"Well, which is it? Stand or sit?" Her mother's voice slurs.

She'd tried to keep her mother out of this by intercepting the notice to appear in court, but three days ago the woman from the Mendocino County Juvenile Probation Department came by to make sure her mother knew about Kelsey's court date. She'd come late in the afternoon, but Lydia managed to appear lucid. After the woman left, Lydia fixed herself another vodka and water and had a good cry over the fact Kelsey was in trouble again. A half an hour later, she turned on the television, and seemed to have forgotten all about it.

"Young Lady," Judge Lehan say.

"Yes." Kelsey stands. Lydia starts to get up, too, but Kelsey puts a firm hand on her shoulder to keep her down.

"It's yes, your Honor."

"Yes, your Honor."

"I've read Officer Curtis' report and heard the testimony of Mr. Jennings from Rite Aid and have reviewed your record. This is your second arrest for shoplifting—"

Kelsey glances at her mother for a reaction, but Lydia's eyes are closed, as if she can't bear to watch.

"—which means, incidentally," Judge Lehan is saying. "You aren't very good at it. And you've been picked up three times for truancy. That's quite a record for—" He looks at paperwork. "—a thirteen-year-old." He puts down the file, folds his hands, and glares at Kelsey. "You're nearly fourteen. In spite of the recommendation of Ms. Rontero of the Juvenile Probation

Department, I am loathe to send you to Juvenile Hall, but I see no other way to get through to you."

Kelsey picks at the chewed skin around the nub of her thumbnail.

"Look at me."

She sucks on the inside of her cheek and looks up at the judge.

"I want to hear your excuse."

"For which thing?"

"The one you're here for now," Judge Lehan snaps.

"My mother's—" Kelsey whispers, and glances at her mother. Lydia has dozed off.

"Speak up."

"—been sick. She likes flowers."

"So, you stole one for her." The judge's voice rises. "Would a stolen gardenia have made you feel better, Ms. McCully?"

Her mother's head comes up lazily, and she blinks at the judge.

"Say, 'No, your Honor,'" Kelsey hisses.

"No, your Honor." Her mother smiles dimly.

Judge Lehan studies Lydia. "How are you feeling now, Ms. McCully?"

Kelsey turns to whisper the answer, but her mother says, "Not well, your Honor."

"What's the problem?"

"Gout," her mother answers.

Kelsey coughs to cover her astonishment. Her mother doesn't have gout.

"Uh huh." The judge stares at Lydia, before turnings his scary gaze on Kelsey. There is absolute silence in the courtroom.

He studies her for a moment, then opens her file again. He shuffles papers, stopping to read sections, while Kelsey's heart thunders and blood whooshes in her ears,

"Here's the deal," he says suddenly, causing Kelsey to jump.

"I see in the file you'll have your fourteenth birthday in less than seven months, so I'm giving you one more chance—six-months' probation and 300 hours of community service. That means every day." He shakes his finger at Kelsey. "Starting tomorrow, every single day after school, and all day on weekends, you will work for Dr. Jonathan Hobbes. The bailiff will give you his address. Is that clear?"

"A doctor?" Kelsey says.

"He has a PhD in botany. You've got six months to grow some flowers for your mother." He writes something in Kelsey's file and hands it to the clerk. "Kelsey."

"Yes, your Honor."

"If I hear you've missed a day or caused Dr. Hobbes one minute of trouble, you *will* go to Juvenile Hall. Is that clear?"

Kelsey nods.

"Yes, your Honor," Judge Lehan says.

"Yes, your Honor," Kelsey repeats.

"I never want to see you here again."

"You won't sir. I promise."

"That's what you said the last time."

"I mean it this time."

"You had better, young lady. You are headed down a dead-end road."

CHAPTER 3

According to the directions the bailiff handed Kelsey, the doctor's place is almost directly across the Pudding Creek river from her middle school. The new school year starts on Monday, but today is Saturday. Nervous about being late, she gives herself thirty minutes to get there.

It's mid-August. Locally known as Fogust. Kelsey rides back streets through fog so dense it's hard to see two blocks ahead. At the river, she dismounts and walks her bike across the narrow, traffic-y Pudding Creek Bridge. To her left, the old train trestle's braces look like a line of spiders crossing the gap between the cliffs of Glass Beach, once the city dump, and a motel perched on the other side.

One night, during another of Lydia's "down times", as she calls them, her mother got emotional talking about the trains that used to carry logs from the harvest sites at Ten Mile River to the Georgia-Pacific mill in Fort Bragg. After the tracks were removed from the trestle, logging trucks replaced the train. At that point in the story, her mother teared-up and fixed herself another drink. Kelsey thinks it was because Lydia's father, a logging truck driver, died when his truck rolled over taking a sharp curve too fast on Highway 20. Lydia was the same age as Kelsey is now. Four years later, her mother died, leaving Lydia to raise her younger sister—an aunt Kelsey can't remember having ever met. Watching Lydia dab her eyes made Kelsey wonder if raising her sister used up all her mother's child-care capacity.

On the other side of the bridge, the hill that runs east past the recycling center is so steep she's forced to push her gearless old bicycle to the top. Once there, she stops to catch her breath. The fog's so dense she can't see the ocean, but she can hear waves tumbling and crashing against the cliffs.

Kelsey rides back and forth parallel to the winding river looking for the address. On the second pass, she sees a mailbox with only a four-digit number. All the others have five. She looks at the address the bailiff gave her and sees four of the five are a match.

Just about every house in Fort Bragg has rhododendrons in the yard, but this long, rutted driveway is lined on either side with the tallest rhodies Kelsey's ever seen. The ground beneath them is littered with blossoms too dried up to recognize what color they were in spring.

The end of the driveway opens up onto a gravel parking area. An ancient, turquoise, rust-encrusted Dodge truck crouches in the weeds that grow around its tires. She doesn't see a greenhouse which, according to the directions, is where she's most likely to find Dr. Hobbes.

Her bike doesn't have a kickstand, so she leans it against the rear bumper of the truck and walks toward a long, low building covered with a tangle of sweet-smelling honeysuckle vines. Its shape suggests it might have once contained horse stalls, but there's only a single door. A carved woodpecker with a broken beak serves as a knocker. The two dirty glass windows on either side of the door are boarded-up from the inside. Dead insects form a pyramid between the wood and the glass. Kelsey finds a gap and cups her hands against the glass. Only darkness.

To her left she see an arbor covered with tiny pink roses. Beneath it lies a fat, black and white cat lolling in a puddle of sunlight. As she approaches, it opens one eye, scrambles to its feet, and runs toward her.

Because of her mother's allergies, the only cat in Kelsey's life is the black Kit-Cat clock in their kitchen, with its creepy, bulbous white eyes clicking side to side with the passing seconds. Kelsey's never had so much as a goldfish, but she loves animals and squats down to meet the oncoming cat. To her astonishment, the cat jumps into her lap, stands on her knees, and puts a paw over each shoulder. It's yellow eyes stare into hers before it buries its face in the crook of her neck and begins to purr. An ache oozes like water into the cracks left in her defenses. For no reason she can grasp, she thinks of her father—a man she's never met—and feels the sting of tears. She strokes the cat's back and it purrs louder. She shifts a little under its weight, and the cat tightens its grip around her neck. Kelsey cradles its head and presses her cheek to one soft ear. If she ever needed a hug, this is the time, but the strain of its weight starts to make her leg muscles quiver. "I'm going to have to get up." She tries to disengage, but the cat holds on.

She pushes herself to standing with a free hand and carries the cat to the front door. She uses the broken woodpecker to rap on it. Odd, tuneless music floats in the air, but she can't tell from where. No one answers. She tilts the cat's chin up. "Is anybody home?" She kisses its cheek and puts it down.

The cat rubs against her leg, then waddles, tail up like a tour guide's flag, down the side of the building, pausing once to see if she is following. They cross under the rose-covered archway. Beyond, she spots two huge greenhouses made of glass panes set in aluminum. Between them, is an open shed. Dozens of begonias, blooming in shades of red, pink, orange, yellow, and white, hang from the beam that supports the roof of the shed. During one of her mother's "up-times," Lydia bought a coral-colored begonia, then watered it so often its stem turned to mush and the flowers fell off.

Kelsey opens the door of the closest greenhouse, even though the sign on it says *No Admittance*. The moist, muggy building is filled with orchids. A ceiling fan makes lazy, squeaky circles, and another fan directly above the door rattles noisily.

"Anybody here?" she calls.

Through the opaque glass wall of the second greenhouse, a shadowy figure moves slowly down the row between shelves of plants. Music, accompanied by the sound of dripping water like ones her mother used to play when "her spirits needed lifting" drifts from inside.

The cat nudges open the door to the second greenhouse with its head, and squeezes in. Kelsey follows. The back of this greenhouse ends at a concrete wall in the center of which is a steel door painted black. To the right of the door, a large tinted window reflects her fog-damp, windblown image. Lydia insisted she dress appropriately—as if this was for a job interview and not to avoid jail time. Now she looks like she slept under a bridge.

An old man wearing a bathrobe and bedroom slippers is removing a root-bound plant from its pot. His white hair sticks out in so many directions it looks like he stuck his finger in a light socket. He turns when the cat meows. "Hey, old boy." He picks it up, then sees Kelsey. "Who the hell are you?"

"Kelsey McCully."

"McCully?" His brow creases in thought. "I used to know a McCully." He looks at her. "Well, what do you want, McCully?"

A fuchsia in a basket hangs near her right shoulder. "The judge sent me." Kelsey lifts a white blossom and peers at its purple center to avoid seeing his negative reaction when he realizes who she is and why she's here.

He shakes a trowel at her. "Make some sense or get out." The blue-veined, paper-thin skin of the hand holding the trowel has scabbed-over sores on two knuckles.

"I wish I had a choice." The blossom comes off in her hand. Her breath catches. "Oh. Sorry."

Dr. Hobbes watches as she lets it fall to the ground, then looks up at her. "Aha," he says. "You must be my newest delinquent."

"What'd you do to your fingers?"

He looks down at his hands as if he hadn't the foggiest notion what she means. "These?" He wiggles the last two fingers of his left hand, which move as a unit since they are wrapped together with black electrical tape. "Broke 'em a while back."

"Did a doctor wrap them like that?"

"I wrapped them like this. It's nine-thirty. What are you doing here so late? The day is practically over." He's smiling down at the rumbling cat in his arms.

"It took me a while to find this" . . . *dump*. . . she wants to say, "place," she says. "Your mailbox is missing a number."

"Is this what I can expect—you showing up when it's nearly too late to get anything done?"

"I had to ride my bike clear across town," she snaps.

"Watch your tone, girly. I'm your last chance, so you better keep your nose clean."

"Yeah, well, Juvie might be better than hanging around here."

"You ever been in Juvie?"

"No, but I've got friends that have. They say it's not so bad."

He puts the cat down and waves a hand like he's shooing flies. "Well, if you think it's such an Eden, get on out of here. I don't need this crap."

He's called her bluff. Kelsey squares her shoulders and sucks the inside of her cheek. If she walks out, it's juvie for sure.

The cat walks toward her along the edge of the potting table like an eight-ball with legs. When he reaches her, he stands, put his paws on her shoulders, and rubs his chin against hers.

For a moment, Kelsey closes her eyes and strokes the cat's head. As long as this nightmare comes with this cat, she'll survive it. She opens her eyes and she sees Dr. Hobbes watching them. He's smiling until he sees her looking at him. "Ah hell's bells." He shrugs. "Genera likes you. You might as well stay."

Don't do me any favors, Kelsey thinks, but, for a change, she keeps her mouth shut.

"Start by sorting those pots." He sweeps his hand the length of the potting tables. Beneath each one are piles of pots in all sizes, hundreds of them, maybe even thousands.

"Where do you want them to go?"

"I don't want them to go anywhere. Just sort them."

The drippy music stops.

"Sort them by color, size, shape—what?"

"Hell, I don't care. Make them look neater." He scoops up the cat and shuffles toward the steel door in the concrete wall. He hunches over and squints to see the numbers as he dials a code into the bottom of a padlock. When it falls open, he glances back at her. "Those pots have been there for years, so watch out for black widows." He grins. His teeth are Day-Glo yellow and crooked. "You know what those are?"

Duh. "Spiders."

He's set her to a fool's task as her mother likes to say—meaningless work, like digging a hole, and filling it in again.

"See that jar?" He points to an old applesauce jar with a filthy, worn-away label.

"Yeah."

"Put the earwigs and brown slugs you find in there."

Kelsey's nose crinkles in disgust. "Earwigs pinch and slugs are slimy."

Dr. Hobbes smiles. "And your point is?"

"I don't want to touch them."

"Then don't." He taps the side of his head. "Use something to pick them up with." He squints at her. "Do you like plants?"

"They're okay. Why?"

"Just asking." He pulls the steel door open. "What's your favorite subject in school?"

She kind of likes biology, but she isn't going to tell him. "Lunch."

"Figures. Watch her," he says to the cat before stepping inside and closing the door. She hears a bolt slide shut on the inside. To the right of the door is a tinted window. Her reflection stares back at her, sad-eyed, wet and windblown. She considers giving him the finger, but he could be spying on her. Then that mushy music starts again.

•   •   •   •   •

By five-thirty, tired and hungry, Kelsey decides she's done for the day. The afternoon fog has seeped far enough inland to reach the greenhouse. It's going to be a cold and wet ride home wearing only a thin jacket.

She sorted a few hundred pots by size, and left them in neat rows under the potting table ranging from the very smallest to pots trees must have come in. The only good to come from this is the laugh she and Brie will have when Kelsey tells her how she spent her Saturday.

"I'm leaving now," she yells at the bunker door.

There's no answer.

She steps to the window, cups her eyes, trying to see inside this bunker of his. She hears faint scratching, but nothing else.

"I'm leaving," she yells again, and nearly jumps out of her skin when he raps on the window.

"Is that goodbye?" *Idiot.*

Genera has curled up near one of the fans that keep the air moving in the greenhouse. He rolls on his back and starts to purr. She's rubbing his broad belly when she sees the empty applesauce jar. She'd forgotten the earwig / slug part of the task. "If he asks—" She kisses the tip of Gen's nose. "Lie for me. Tell him I didn't find any."

CHAPTER 4

Kelsey arrives home at six, damp and cold. She hangs her mist-covered jacket on the nail in the wall by the back door and shakes her head like a wet dog. In the living room, her mother looks as if she's been ladled into her chair in front of the TV news. Some guy is sitting in for Anderson Cooper, who's on assignment in Afghanistan.

Kelsey likes the sound of "on assignment." She'd like to be sent some place where things were different—totally different from this shabby little house with its ratty furniture and her mother splayed out most nights like a dead person.

"Hi, Mom."

Lydia doesn't wake.

Lydia's nest consists of a threadbare Barcalounger and a rusty, metal TV tray for her drinks and cigarettes. The rest of the room is taken up with a sofa the neighbors put on the curb with a "Free" sign on it when they moved away five years ago, a split and cracked leather hassock, and a coffee table from the State of the Ark thrift store. On the table is a half-finished jigsaw puzzle of a heart-breakingly beautiful little cottage built on the edge of a pond. Its windows glow with a warm, welcoming light. A mossy little stone bridge arches over the water which reflects an early evening sky. When Lydia found it at that same Botanical Garden's Pack Rat sale where Kelsey got her bike, her mother said it had always been her dream to live inside a Kinkade painting. Sappy, unreal, and unattainable, but for a few nights they worked on the puzzle together. Now, two months later, it is buried under stacks of mail order catalogs, a skein of ugly, multi-colored Rite-Aid yarn for Lydia's knitting, and three of her mom's precious photo albums. The newest thing in the house is the television they found three years ago at the Caspar Dump.

The vodka bottle is down three inches from the mark Kelsey put on it before she left this morning. Knowing how much Lydia drinks when she isn't watching lets Kelsey know whether or not it will be safe to leave and join her friends without her mother missing her. Tonight, it doesn't matter. Kelsey's staying in. The judge scared her this time, and it will be easier to stay out of trouble if she steers clear of the alley off Laurel Street and the kids who hang out there.

The judge was wrong about her not being good at shoplifting. She's stolen lots of things and not gotten caught. A couple of weeks ago, she and Brie traded in their worn-out sneakers for new Nikes, leaving the old pairs in the boxes so the clerk wouldn't notice a weight change. They walked out when he went into the back room to get a different size for another customer. Getting caught stealing the gardenia was bad luck.

Last night's grilled cheese sandwich pan is on the burner where Kelsey left it. "Dinner looks yum, Mom." She drops the frying pan into the sink with a loud clatter, and turns on the water.

Her mother stirs.

Kelsey's tired and hungry. She opens the freezer to find two small, freezer-burned Boboli pizza crusts, two bottles of vodka, a bottle of gin, a quart of vanilla ice cream, refrozen since the last time PG & E turned off their power, and a dented box of fish sticks. Kelsey can't remember whether the fish sticks pre-date the power outage or not. She chooses the Boboli.

There's a half jar of spaghetti sauce in the fridge and a package of government-issued cheese slices from the local food bank. She spoons the mold off the top of the sauce and spreads a clean layer on each pizza crust. She covers them with the cheese slices and tops them with a few of her mother's martini olives, which she pinches to flatten so they don't look quite so much like eyeballs.

Kelsey puts the first pizza in toaster oven and sets the timer. She waits with her elbows on the counter, chin on a fist. The light from the TV flashes and flickers across Lydia's sleeping face, softening and hardening her features, making her look like the younger version of herself in those photo albums, then grotesque.

Lydia sits up when the timer goes off. She blinks a couple of times, then turns to search for her glass.

"Hi, Mom."

Her mother looks surprised to see her. "Where have you been?"

"I just got home from work."

"You got a job? That's nice. Doing what?"

Court was only yesterday. Proof her mother doesn't remember she's been assigned practically a lifetime of community service.

"I'm helping an old guy in his greenhouse."

"How nice. I love flowers." Her mother yawns.

"The pay's not much, but he really likes me. I might get a raise after six months. Did you eat today?"

"I'm sure I did."

"I made us pizzas. You want one?"

"That would be lovely." Lydia finds her glass lying on its side on the rug. "And maybe you could rinse this out and fix me a little vodka and water. Would you mind? My knees are killing me."

"Don't you think you've had enough?"

"I do not." Lydia glares at Kelsey. "You know how hard it is for me to sleep."

Kelsey rolls her eyes. Between drinking all day and taking sleeping pills at night, Lydia is rarely awake. She replaces her mother's smelly ashtray with a pizza and takes the empty glass. Shag-carpet hairs stick to a Chapstick print of her mother's lips on the rim.

"Thank you, sweetie. Now just a little something to wash it down with, please." She smiles over her shoulder at Kelsey, then fishes out the remote from between her recliner's seat and the armrest, changes the TV channel, and turns up the volume.

Kelsey carries the ashtray to the kitchen and checks to make sure there aren't any smoldering butts before emptying it into the bag under the sink. At least she can get one stink out of her life.

She waters down her mother's drink and puts it on the TV tray next her mother's untouched pizza.

"Whoop-de-do." Lydia lifts her glass in a toast. "To your new job."

"Right. Whoop-de-do." The toaster oven bell dings. Kelsey's pizza is done.

One of the photo albums is open on the coffee table. Her mother likes to look through them and remember when she was young and happy. But the more she drinks, the more depressed she gets, until every picture reminds her of all that's gone wrong in her life.

Kelsey closes the album. "Why do you make yourself miserable looking at these pictures?"

"Shh." Lydia presses a finger to her lips. "*Jeopardy!* coming on."

Kelsey eats her pizza sitting on the floor with her back against the sofa. They watch the Saturday reruns of *Jeopardy!* and *Wheel of Fortune.* By the time *America's Got Talent* comes on, Lydia's slumped sideways in the chair, an arm draped over the side, tobacco-stained fingers brushing the carpet.

Kelsey sits with her legs are out straight, feet in a pair of socks with threadbare heels. As she watches an Indian dance group, she lifts her right leg and points her toes. "I have a nice arch, don't you think?" She raises her arms like the upbeat of wings.

Lydia's out cold.

"A beud-e-ful arch, dear." Kelsey mimics her mother's drunken slur.

Her mother's head has rolled to rest on her left shoulder, exposing the oily hair stain on the Barcalounger's headrest. When she starts to snore, Kelsey feels her face muscles tighten in anger. The night before they went to court, they'd had one of their many fights: Kelsey trying to get Lydia to drink less; her mom's ridiculous list of excuses, until, in a rage, Kelsey threw her mother's glass across the kitchen. Deep down she wishes she could make life right for her mother. She can barely stand how useless and impossible that wish is. Tonight, she refuses to get mad.

Kelsey gets to her feet and stands looking down at her mother. She picks up the remote and mutes the TV.

Kelsey hasn't seen Brie since her arrest the week before last, and Brie hasn't called. It's Saturday night. Kelsey is sure she'll be in the Laurel Street alley with the other kids. Brie's lawyer-father got her off. The blame for stealing the gardenia landed, as it should have, on Kelsey. Only fair. She wouldn't want Brie getting into trouble for something that was Kelsey's idea. Brie will get a big laugh out of how it turned out.

Kelsey gets her coat off the nail and shuts back of the door quietly behind her.

CHAPTER 5

Brie isn't on Laurel Street. None of the kids Kelsey usually hangs out with are. Will and Ryan, with their knot of spiky-haired friends, sit in the alley beneath the fuse boxes, smoking. It was Will who told her Juvie wasn't so bad. He's fifteen and has been twice. "Three hots and a cot," he'd said. Sadly, that actually sounded appealing. Someone else doing the cooking and not having to sleep with one eye open, worrying about her mother burning the house down with a forgotten cigarette.

She waves to Will, but goes straight to the pay phone outside the Headlands Café's back door to call Brie. A jazz guitarist plays inside the Café. She has to stick a finger in one ear to hear Brie's mother when she answers.

"I'm sorry, Kelsey, she can't come to the phone."

"That's okay, Ms. Jeffries. Please tell her I called."

"Kelsey—" There's a pause, then Brie's mom says to someone else. "It's no one. Go to your room." Her voice is muffled like she's pressed the phone to her chest. A moment later, Kelsey hears a door slam.

"Kelsey, are you there?"

"Yes."

"I'm sorry, but I'm not going to tell her you called, and I don't want you calling here again. You're just not the kind of friend we want for Brie." Click.

Stunned, Kelsey stares at the dead receiver. Inside the brightly-lit café, bodies move subtly in time to the music, then the shrill disconnect signal goes off. People seated near the screen door turn. She slams the receiver into the cradle, crosses the alley, then circles back. If she had another quarter, she'd call back and tell Brie's mother to go to hell.

"What's happening, Kels?" It's Will's voice, but it takes Kelsey a second to see that he and the others have moved across the alley and now sit in the shadows with their backs against the Café's wall.

"Nothing."

"Come hang with us." The light from the windows falls on three pairs of sneakers. Smoke from their cigarettes rises in wisps, like ghosts.

"Not tonight," she says

Will gets up and comes toward her. "I heard you gotta do time with old Doc Hobbes."

"Yeah. So?" Kelsey's not into the punk-goth-whatever look Will and his buddies are into, but Will is a heart-stopping, *Good-Girls*-star-Manny-Montana-good-looking.

"He's an okay guy," Ryan says from the shadows. Will kicks Ryan's leg.

"How do you know him?" Kelsey asks.

"Been there, done that. What'd they get you for?"

"None of your business." Kelsey mounts her bike.

"Damn. Testy, ain't she?" Carlos says.

Rather than ride down the dark alley, Kelsey turns toward the lights of Franklin Street. Before she can launch herself, Will grabs her handlebars. "Don't go, Kels. I'm tired of these losers. I've got some good weed."

"No, thanks." She tries to back out of his grip.

Will straddles her front tire. "Why don't you want to hang with us?" His upper lip curls in a way that makes him look amused and a bit scary at the same time.

"'Cause I gotta go." She twists free.

"You sure ain't being very friendly." He grins, then suddenly looks past her and gives a jerk of his head. The three boys scramble to their feet and disappear down the alley.

Kelsey glances over her shoulder. A cop car has turned onto Laurel Street. If it's Jerry, she'll be in for it. He told her to stay home and out of trouble. She hops on her bike and power-pedals down the alley, expecting to pass the boys, but they must have ducked into one of the garages that line the dark, narrow passage. As she nears Redwood, she looks back to see if the cop has followed, and is caught squarely in his headlights as he turns into the alley. He drives slowly, his searchlight probing the garages and the spaces between buildings. Kelsey crosses Redwood and continues down the alley behind the Furniture Mart. She's furious with herself for coming out tonight. Why didn't she stay put for once?

If the cop is Jerry and recognizes her, he'll probably cut over to Franklin and try to catch her before she gets home. She crosses to the Purity Market's parking lot and stops behind a big SUV. A couple minutes pass before the patrol car noses out by the post office. She ducks down. When she peeks again, he's turning the opposite direction from her way home. She straightens and smiles.

"That's my car. What are you doing there?"

Kelsey jumps and turns to face the man approaching with a basket full of groceries.

"I'm not bothering your stinking car." She mounts her bike and rides toward home.

CHAPTER 6

Since Kelsey will have to go to the greenhouse pretty much for the rest of her life, she rides her gearless old bike to school on Monday rather than walk like she usually does.

She and Brie have one class together—first period Language Arts. After the call Saturday night, Kelsey's nervous about seeing her and isn't sure Brie will disobey her mother and still want to hang out.

In the hallway, outside of class, a girl Kelsey doesn't even know bumps her, knocking Kelsey's books to the floor. "Oops, sorry, Jailbird." She turns to her friend and laughs. "They shouldn't let criminals come to school."

Juvenile arrests aren't listed in the paper like adult ones are, so Kelsey's momentarily taken off guard. Someone must have seen her with Jerry, or going into court with her mother. Nothing stays a secret in a small town. She lifts her chin and gives the girl the once-over. "I hear there's a bacon shortage. I'd keep my head down, if I were you." The girl's friend guffaws, and slaps a hand over her mouth.

In class, Brie sits at a back table with Lauren, who, though pretty, rich, and popular, seems to like and collect misfits. Josh, another member of Lauren's band of losers sits with them. Kelsey likes him. He's always been nice to her and can be funny when he's in the right mood. She also feels sorry for him. He's tall and twig-thin with thick black hair and a smile full of straight, white teeth she'd kill for, but he's even more of an exposed nerve of a person than she is. His voice and hands tremble when he's called on in class, and he tears up easier than most girls. Lauren's gentle with him, like he's an injured animal.

Brie glances up from examining the tips of her hair for split ends and grins. Kelsey takes it as a conspiratorial grin and smiles back.

Lauren sees her, waves, and moves her backpack off the fourth chair at the table. She gets up and gives Kelsey a hug. "Are you okay? Brie told us what happened."

"Yeah, sure. No big deal. I got sentenced to doing time in a potting shed. Might even be fun." Kelsey glances at Brie. "I hope you didn't get into too much trouble."

"Not much." Brie, who's a worse student than Kelsey, turns to copy what their teacher has written on the board. Kelsey watches her and thinks she may have misinterpreted the meaning behind Brie's grin.

"She told her parents, and the cop when he showed up, that she didn't know what you were going to do," Josh says.

"Shut up, Josh." Brie glares at him. "What do you know about it?"

"It's okay. I'm glad you did," Kelsey says. "Your mom was pretty mad at me when I called Saturday."

Brie looks at her. "Was she? She'll get over it."

The bell rings and Miss Brown turns. "Let's get started."

Brie lowers her voice. "She's only pretending to pay attention to what I do. She's like really into politics right now. Me getting busted made her miss a rally or something." She rolls her eyes. "She'd be happier if they locked me up."

"That's not true," Lauren whispers.

"Enough, girls." Miss Brown taps a fingernail on her desk.

If Kelsey could trade places with anyone in the world, it would be with Lauren. Everything about her is perfect, from her home-life to her looks. Both she and Lauren have brown hair, but Lauren's is dark, straight and shiny; Kelsey's frizzes when it rains. Lauren has hers cut at a salon in Mendocino; Kelsey cuts her own, whacking off the sprigs that stick out. Lauren is shorter than Kelsey by a couple of inches, but Kelsey slumps. Lauren stands ramrod straight, so they look the same height. About the only thing they have in common is this class. The fact Lauren likes her, makes Kelsey feel she isn't really a terrible person. More than once, Kelsey has wondered why Lauren doesn't prefer the popular kids, but she's never asked.

• • • • •

At the greenhouse that afternoon, Kelsey stands for a moment in the doorway watching Dr. Hobbes talk to a vine that's in a basket hanging from the hook above the dark window to his bunker. Gen, who is at his elbow on the potting table, sees Kelsey, jumps down, and runs to greet her.

Dr. Hobbes turns. "Late again." He taps his wrist though he's not wearing a watch.

Kelsey picks up Gen and kisses him on the nose. "I go to school, you know. Were you talking to that plant?"

He smiles up at the vine. "And Phil here responds—in his own way."

I'm working for a loony. "Okay."

He crooks a bony finger. "Follow me."

Behind the slat-sided begonia shed are two large sinks—both full of water. On the counter beside them are stacks of medium-sized pots. A few dozen of them.

"Oh my God, you want me to wash all of these?"

"I do. Scrub them with that brush—getting out all the dirt—then put them to soak in this water." He points to the second sink. "It has a fungicide in it. Got it?"

"What's not to get?" She puts Gen down.

"Too bad that smart mouth's not attached to the motor running it." He taps the side of his head and walks away.

Kelsey wants to throw a pot at him.

She's washed about twenty pots when he comes back and fishes a few out of the rinse water to inspect.

"Not bad," he says. "Keep at it."

When she finishes, she goes looking for him. He isn't in either greenhouse, so she knocks on the steel door to his bunker.

He cracks it open and looks at her. "What do you want?"

"I'm done."

"What do you mean you're done?"

"I finished washing those pots."

"Really?" He squeezes through the crack in the door, blocking her view of the room's interior, like he's hiding some massive secret inside.

He takes her by the sleeve, pulling her along until she jerks her arm free.

"Finished, huh?" he says.

"Yeah."

"What about those?" He points to the rows and rows of pots she sorted yesterday.

"You expect me to wash *all* of them?"

"Not today." He smiles.

•　　•　　•　　•　　•

A little after five, Kelsey knocks on the steel door again.

"What?" he shouts.

"I've got to start for home."

He opens the door, wider this time. Kelsey hears the hum of machines and glimpses all kinds of equipment. "What's all that stuff?"

He glances over his shoulder. "None of your beeswax." He steps out and pulls the door closed.

"Like I care, anyway."

"Why'd you ask then?"

Kelsey doesn't answer. "It's after five. I'm leaving."

"How many hours will I have the pleasure of your company?"

"As of today, two hundred and ninety more."

"You've got a long row to hoe, girly, at two or three hours a clip—. "

"I did seven hours on Saturday."

"Whatever. You'll be registering to vote by the time you're done. How about coming Sundays, too, so we can get this over with?"

This Sunday, she, Lauren, Brie, and Josh have plans to go the beach if it's sunny. They're meeting for lunch at Denny's. Kelsey said she could go because she was pretty sure, since she skipped last Sunday, Dr. Hobbes doesn't know she's supposed to work both weekend days on. "I've got plans," she says.

"Really? What's more important than getting this over with?"

"Am I going to spend every hour washing and sorting those stupid pots?"

"If you turn out to be worth your salt, I might find something more interesting for you to do."

Kelsey sighs. "I can be here by two."

"Good. On your way, stop at Rite Aid and buy me a tomato seedling."

"I don't shop at Rite Aid."

"That's not what I heard." He smiles, and plucks a dead leaf from the vine that trails down one side of the bunker's window. "How you doing, buddy?"

Kelsey cocks her head. "You're talking to the plant again?"

"This is Phil." He rubs one of the vine's leaves between his thumb and forefinger. Phil, meet our new delinquent."

Kelsey circles the side of her head with a finger. "If you were smart enough be a doctor, how come you waste your brain studying plants? They're boring."

One wild, white caterpillar of an eyebrow lifts. "That's what you think. Stick around, you might learn something amazing."

She rolls her eyes. "Am I supposed to buy you a tomato plant with my own money?"

"Wait here." He steps into the bunker. A minute later he comes out and hands her a twenty. "Bring me the receipt and the change."

"Like, duh."

"Girly—" He gives her a yellow-toothed smile and shakes his head. "Knowing when to keep your mouth shut is a virtue you should cultivate— if you'll pardon the pun."

CHAPTER 7

On Sunday, Kelsey rides to Denny's with the tomato plant in her bike basket. She finds Lauren, Josh and Brie in the alcove outside the main entrance. Josh holds Lauren's backpack while she works the joystick on the claw machine full of stuffed animals.

"Which one are you after?" Being a thief herself, Kelsey has brought the small plant in with her.

"The elephant. I love elephants. Someday I'm going to India and ride one."

Josh bumps the machine, trying to knock a purple rabbit off the elephant's head.

Lauren digs in her pocket and comes up with a quarter. Josh gives her another.

"Is that a tomato?" Brie asks.

"Yeah."

"For your mother?" Brie's tone is sneery, then she grins. "Kidding."

Brie's been like this all week. Little cutting remarks, then laughing like it's a joke. She's always been unreadable. Not for the first time, Kelsey wonders if their friendship is only Brie's way of worrying her parents, someone she can sink in the muck with, while Brie's friendship with Lauren has the parental stamp of approval. She knows that's not the case for Lauren, who seems to befriend the people she likes, and for no other reason.

"It's for the nut job," Kelsey says to Brie. "Like he doesn't already have a greenhouse full of tomatoes."

Lauren feeds the two quarters into the slot. "One more try." She manages to get the tip of the elephant's trunk but can't free it from under the rabbit. They're still laughing at her frustration when the hostess comes to say their table's ready.

"What's the plant for?" Josh asks.

"I just told Brie. You weren't listening." Then to all of them. "I can't go to the beach. The whacko's got me working today, too."

"Poor you." Brie hooks arms with Lauren.

"That's okay," Lauren says. "We've decided to go to the movies instead of Glass Beach. While we were parking, we saw Will and Ryan drive by headed that way."

Kelsey gets the change of plans. Will and his cronies' favorite sport is to ridicule Josh.

Josh must see the knowing look Brie gives Kelsey. He says, "Don't skip the beach on my account. I've got things to do."

Lauren slaps his arm. "Are you kidding? The *Angry Birds Movie 2* just opened."

"At least you have a choice," Kelsey says. Either would beat what the day has in store for her.

The four of them follow the hostess past lots of empty tables to a booth near the kitchen and as far away from other customers as she can seat them.

"Are you going to have lunch with us?" Brie smiles at the hostess.

"Sorry?" the woman says.

"Are you going to sit with us?"

"No. Why?"

"Then let me show you where we'd like to sit."

"This will be fine," Lauren says to the hostess. "She's kidding."

"Am not."

"Sit, Brie, and shut up," Lauren says, because she can, and Brie will.

Kelsey didn't eat breakfast and is starving, but Lauren can't decide what she wants. An exhausted looking waitress hovers until Lauren finally orders a Club sandwich. Brie says she'll have the same, but without the middle slice of bread. Kelsey would love the Buffalo chicken tender sandwich, but she doesn't have enough money. "Go ahead," she says to Josh. "I haven't decided yet."

Josh says he really wants a Jenny's Giant burger from the little diner across the street. "If I get it over there, can I bring it in here to eat?" he asks the waitress.

"Don't be a dork," Kelsey says, before the waitress can answer. "Go get one if you want it, but eat it there."

"I don't want to go alone."

"He'll have a burger," Lauren says to the waitress. "Well done. No onions."

Kelsey orders the chicken tenders from the Starter menu, and a Coke.

While they wait, Kelsey crunches the paper covering of her straw down to a tight accordion, dips the straw in her Coke, and puts one fingertip over the end to seal in the liquid. "Watch this." She holds the straw tip over the pleated paper, lifts her finger and lets a drop of Coke hit it. The paper reacts like a worm stuck with a pin, wiggling and jerking. Lauren, Brie, and Josh laugh. They're trying it with their straw-wrappers when the food arrives.

Brie's Club comes with all three slices of bread. She picks her sandwich apart and removes the soggy middle slice from each quarter. "Want this?" she says to Josh, flipping the mayonnaise-soaked bread at him like a fish by its tail.

"Let me wash it off first." He takes the slice and drops it into her water glass.

"Gross." Lauren giggles.

"Want my parsley?" Kelsey says.

"Sure." Josh takes the sprig and drops into Brie's water glass, then he rips open a sugar packet and pours the contents into her glass with the bread.

"Give it a break, Josh." Lauren turns to Kelsey, who's blowing bubbles in her Coke. "We're going to a party out on Sherwood Road next Saturday. Want to ride with us?"

"How are you getting there?"

Lauren grins. "Brie's driving."

Brie glances around and lowers her voice. "Mom sent me to the hardware store to get a new house key made. I copied both sets of car keys while I was there. My parents have season tickets to the Orpheum. Whichever car they take to San Francisco next week for the play, we get the other one."

"What if we get caught?"

"We won't. It's like four miles out Sherwood Road. No biggy."

Kelsey laughs. "I hope they leave the Lexus." She takes a bite of her salad, and spits out the slice of cucumber that escaped her notice. "What time?"

"I don't know for sure. Early afternoon. I'll call you," Brie says.

"I've gotta work until five."

"That's okay," Lauren says. "It'll be going 'til all hours."

"What about your parents?" Kelsey can't imagine them letting her go.

Lauren grins. "They're taking Harrison to the Giants game."

"Then, yeah," Kelsey says. "I'm in. Are you going, Josh?"

"No way. I've got things to do."

"Like what?" Kelsey knows his calendar is as empty as hers.

"I just don't feel like it. Okay?"

"Okay."

By the time lunch is over, every water glass on the table contains the remains of their meals: a foil-wrapped pat of butter, pepper, globs of assorted jellies, parsley, the tomato off Josh's hamburger, even the lid to the saltshaker.

The waitress rushes toward them when they stand to leave. She stares at the mess they've made of the table. "What's with you kids?" She glares at Kelsey like it's all her doing. "I know you."

"So."

"I worked at Rite Aid with your poor mother. What would she say if she saw this?"

Kelsey shrugs. "We were just playing around."

Josh and Brie have gone to the register, paid, and are in the foyer feeding their change into the claw machine.

"I'm taking you to lunch," Lauren says when Kelsey gets to the register.

"Why?" Kelsey suspects everyone knows her mother is on disability, but they usually pretend they don't.

Lauren says, "To celebrate your new job."

"It's not a real job."

"I know. But it beats the alternative, right?" Lauren grins.

"I have money." Kelsey tries not to sound defensive.

"I know you do," Lauren said. "It's still my treat."

Before going to Rite Aid to buy the tomato plant, Kelsey went to Safeway and used her EBT card to buy packaged lunch meat. She paid for it, then went to customer service for a refund. When the clerk asked why she was returning what she'd just bought, Kelsey told her she was cutting back on nitrates.

"Okay, but next time it's on me."

"Deal," Lauren says.

At the door, Kelsey glances back. The waitress sits in their messy booth, with her elbows on the table, her face buried in her hands. Kelsey nudges Lauren.

"Oh." Lauren slips off her backpack and roots in it for her wallet. She takes out a five-dollar bill, walks back, and places it to the table, startling the waitress. Lauren says something, then begins stacking their dishes onto the waitress' tray. To Kelsey's astonishment, the woman stands, takes a dirty glass from Lauren, puts in on the table, and hugs her.

"We're forgiven," Lauren says when she comes back. "I told her we were sorry. She told me her husband died last week."

"I'm sorry, too." Everything about the woman reminds her of Lydia. The hump of her shoulders, her messy, graying bun, skin like balled up tissue, but Kelsey doesn't have the wherewithal to pity anyone else. She turns and follows Lauren out the door.

Josh has the elephant in the claw and is swinging it toward the chute.

The door behind them opens. "Does this belong to one of you?" The waitress balances the tomato plant's pot on an open palm.

Kelsey had put it on the floor under the table. "It's mine. Thanks." She takes it. "I'll tell my mother I saw you."

"You do that," she said, clearly disappointed that it's Kelsey's tomato and not Lauren's.

CHAPTER 8

On her ride to the greenhouse, Kelsey wonders if Brie would have mentioned the party next Saturday if Lauren hadn't invited her? She thinks of Brie and Lauren, and Josh to a lesser degree, as her best friends, but she saw Brie wince when Lauren invited her. Saying yes wasn't easy. Not only did it look like Brie didn't want her along, Kelsey tries not to leave home unless Lydia is passed out. Maybe she should have said no. It's not too late.

If her grandparents hadn't left them the house they live in, they'd be homeless. Kelsey's had a fear of Lydia falling asleep with a cigarette burning ever since she came home in the third grade to find the living room full of smoke and the carpet sizzling and sparking. The last thing they need is for her mother to burn it to the ground.

•   •   •   •   •

As if he'd been expecting her at the exact moment she rides up, Dr. Hobbes comes shuffling out to meet her, his slippers slapping against his heels. He takes the tomato plant and, without a word, carries it into the greenhouse. By the time Kelsey leans her bike against the truck, picks up and hugs Gen, Hobbes has placed the tomato in the middle of a cleared area on one of the potting tables. Three tiny green pots, each with a single seed lying on top of the soil, are lined up on his left. On his right, are two small cardboard boxes, two empty plastic one-quart milk cartons with lids, a clear glass dome, a petri dish, a mortar and pestle, an ice pick, a box of Strike-Anywhere matches, a plastic drinking straw, and a cotton ball.

She puts Gen down. "Whatcha doing?" She rolls the ice pick from side to side.

He's clipping a few leaves off the tomato. "Testing a plant's sense of smell. And leave things alone." He swats at her with the clippers.

"Ha. That's funny."

Dr. Hobbes gives her a raised eyebrow look. "You think so?"

"Duh. Plants can't smell."

Hobbes straightens and rubs his lower back. "I am a lucky guy."

She knows this will result in something sarcastic, but she asks anyway. "How come?"

"To have a botanical authority like you sent to *me* instead of to the hoosegow."

"What's a hoosegow?"

"Jail."

"You're a laugh an hour." She turns away determined not to give him the satisfaction of showing how curious she is about what he's doing, or that that stung. She crosses to where the hose is coiled, reads the schedule he posted, unwinds the hose, adjusts the nozzle to a light spray, and turns on the tap. She smiles to herself at the thought of the expression on his face if she were to whirl and soak him instead.

His bunker door is ajar. She glances in Hobbes' direction, then drags the hose over and waters the plants nearest it. All she can see is a long sheet of paper coming out of a machine and folding over on itself on the floor. It reminds her of the readout from the electrocardiograph her mother got the time she thought she was having a heart attack.

Out of the corner of her eye, she watches Hobbes set up his experiment, getting more and more curious, but only risking a look when his back is turned. She works her way around to the three little pots and askes, "How do you know which end of the seed grows up and which end grows down?"

"It doesn't matter. It will right itself." Hobbes looks at her. "Unlike a person headed in the wrong direction."

She thinks he says that to hurt her pride, but the joke's on him. For that to be the case, she'd need to have some pride left to be hurt. "Do you want me to poke these seeds into the dirt?"

"No."

"Want me to water them?"

"I do not, and if you're not interested in learning anything, go water in the other greenhouse."

Kelsey bites her lip. "Why are you so mean?"

"I—." For a split second his eyes look old and sad, then they spark again. "I mean it's up to you whether you want to do your time like all the others and get it over with, or take this opportunity to learn something."

At this moment, Kelsey hates him too much to admit she *is* interested in what he's doing. He makes it worse when a hint of a smirk-y smile starts in his watery, bloodshot, blue eyes, like he knows what she's thinking.

They stare at each other, until Gen waddles up, stands on his hind legs, and meows at Kelsey to be picked up. They both look down and smile. She does love his cat. It probably wouldn't kill her to try to make the best of a crap situation. She puts the hose down and scoops up Gen.

Dr. Hobbes turns back to his experiment. He uses a mortar and pestle to smash the tomato leaves he snipped. Kelsey's mother uses a smaller set to mash pills too large for her to swallow.

From a stained, nasty-looking coffee cup, Hobbes adds water to the mashed tomato leaves and soaks up the slurry with the cotton ball. He places the green, dripping wad in the center of a petri dish, and sets it aside.

"That looks disgusting."

Gen nearly drowns out her comment with his loud purring. Like that first day, he has his paws locked tightly around her neck.

"Not if you're dodder."

"What's daughter?" She's rubbing Gen's ear.

"Not daughter. Dodder." He presses one of three single seeds into its pot of soil, moistens it with a splash of water from his coffee cup, and places it under the glass dome. "D-O-D-D-E-R. Put him down and help me with this." He hands her the two plastic milk cartons. "Cut the bottoms off these in a straight line. My hands shake."

He's marked a circle around the bottoms of the milk cartons with a line of uneven black dots. She evens up the lines of dots he drew with the scissors, while he makes a hole in the side of the cardboard box with the ice pick. He presses the second little seed into the soil, waters it, and puts the box over its little pot.

"What *are* you trying to prove?" Kelsey hands him the milk cartons.

"That dodder finds its victim—" He makes air quotes— "by smell."

"Its victims?"

"Dodder is a parasite on many plants, but has a strong fondness for tomatoes." He pokes the third seed into the soil, and adds a bit of water. He strikes a match, blows it out, and places the hot tip against the side one of the plastic milk cartons, melting a circle in it. He does it again to the second carton. He fits one of them over the tomato plant she brought him.

Watching him, Kelsey picks up the straw lying nearby. She absent-mindedly scrunches up the paper covering.

"Give me that." He takes the straw and fits it into the hole in the cardboard box, and jams the other end of the straw through the hole he burned in the milk carton that's covering the little tomato plant.

He covers the cotton ball's petri dish with the second milk carton and puts the box over the third seed-pot. He places them close to each other, but doesn't connect them.

"Now what?"

"Now we wait to see if dodder can find its favorite victim in spite of the obstacles, and if it can be tricked by a cotton ball soaked in essence of tomato."

"How long will that take?"

"Cell phones, video games, always the need for instant gratification."

"I don't have a cell phone." She picks up the hose. "How can plants smell if they don't have noses?"

"Shall I dumb this down for you?"

"Don't tell me then. I could care less."

"Couldn't care less. If you *could* care less then you could care less."

"Whatever."

Hobbes dismisses her with a flip of his electrical-taped fingers and begins cleaning up around his experiment. On the left is the tomato plant she brought him under a milk carton next to a dodder seed under one of the boxes. They're connected by a straw. On the right, is the cotton ball under the other milk carton. It's next to the second dodder, but the holes he's poked in the box and the milk carton aren't connected.

"What about the dodder under the glass dome? It can't smell in there, can it?"

Hobbes smiles. "That's the control experiment. Which direction will that seed grow if it can't smell the tomato? Do you understand how we and other animals smell?"

"With our noses."

Dr. Hobbes holds up a finger. "One."

"One what?"

"Strike one."

"Okay. I don't know."

Gen jumps up and rubs his chin on the corner of one of the boxes. "Better not do that." Kelsey picks him up and kisses the side of his face. Gen licks her chin.

Dr. Hobbes' eyes soften. "Are you paying attention?"

"Yes."

"We have cells in our noses to detect airborne chemicals—scents—that relay the information to our olfactory nerves. A plant's sense of smell is a nose-less process, but still chemical. Has your mom ever put an unripe avocado in a bag with a ripe banana to get the avocado to ripen faster?"

"We can't afford avocados."

Dr. Hobbes blinks, but his expression doesn't change. "Ripening fruit gives off a gas called ethylene. A tiny amount in the air will cause unripe fruit to ripen. The more fruit ripening, the more ethylene in the air."

"How does that prove plants can smell?"

"They are able to perceive odors in the air. What would you call it?"

Kelsey shrugs. "So, what's going to happen with your little experiment?"

"You'll have to wait and see." He takes Gen from her. "On your way here tomorrow, use my change to buy a plant with big leaves—like a *Dracaena*. Ask a clerk."

"You've got a million plants with big leaves."

He grins. "I need a plant that's a stranger to the others."

CHAPTER 9

Kelsey qualifies for free breakfast and lunch at school. Their meals at home come from California's food stamp program, a once-weekly allotment from the Fort Bragg Food Bank, which is open on Mondays, Wednesdays, and Fridays, and what little is left over from her mother's disability check after the monthly expense for booze and cigarettes.

Lydia used to do the Food Bank trip, but too often forgot what day it was. Kelsey, when she got her bicycle, took over the job and goes on Wednesdays because it's less crowded than Mondays, and has better stuff than end of the week. Wednesdays are half-days at school, so she can go after seventh period, which ends at one, shop, get home, put stuff away, and still get to the greenhouse by three-thirty.

The first week of each month is set aside for USDA canned-goods. Last month Kelsey got a five-pound bag of rice, a bag of beans, a large can of beef stew, and one can each of corn and peas. All fit in her bike basket with room to spare. On the other weeks, she goes for perishables, which means whatever the supermarkets, the government, and the community donate.

This Wednesday, Kelsey gets there at a quarter past one and, though it's warm—by coastal standards—and sunny, she waits in line with her sweatshirt hood up. There are no shops that bring people to this end of town, but she keeps her head down and covered, in case someone she knows drives by.

The line moves wordlessly along, selecting from the assortment on the counter. She takes milk, eggs, a pint of vanilla yogurt, cheese, a box of cereal, and a pound of Thanksgiving French Roast coffee, her mother's favorite. From the rack by the door, she gets a loaf of bread, and takes a head of lettuce and a few apples from the boxes outside. When she turns, a heavy plastic shopping bag in each hand, she sees a kid standing next to her bicycle, which she hadn't bothered to chain to the fence. He has one hand on the handlebars and is looking over his shoulder—a snapshot of her bike about to get stolen.

"That's mine!" She charges him, bags swinging.

He runs, but Kelsey is furious. She jams the bags of groceries into her basket, jumps on her bike, and takes off after him. She bounces off the curb to follow him south on Franklin Street and rides right into the path of an oncoming car. The driver slams on the brakes, stopping with less than a foot to spare. It's Lauren's mother and Lauren's in the passenger-seat.

Her mother rolls down her window. "Kelsey, are you okay?"

"Yes, ma'am. Sorry." She turns to look in the direction the boy ran and sees him disappear into the Rose Memorial graveyard. "I—. Never mind. Sorry." If she could melt into the pavement, she would. Instead, she waves and rides away. Kelsey occasionally recognizes other kids' mothers shopping at the Food Bank, but the last person in the world she wants to see her coming away from there with bags of free food is Lauren. She's also the one person Kelsey trusts to never spread it around school.

•   •   •   •   •

Lydia got out of bed when she heard Kelsey come in with the groceries. By the time she finishes putting them away, her mother is in her recliner holding her knitting near the light, trying to pick up the stitches she dropped last night. A freshly made Bloody Mary sits on the TV tray. Kelsey has her hand on the back door knob, headed for the greenhouse when the phone rings.

"Will you get that, honey?" Her mother glances at her drink, then over her shoulder to see if Kelsey is watching.

"Go ahead, Mom. Don't mind me."

"Just answer the phone."

"Hey, Kels." It's Lauren. "I didn't expect to catch you at home. I was going to leave a message, but there you are." Lauren's voice always sounds happy, like she's smiling through the phone line.

"Sorry about scaring your mom." Kelsey says. "Where are you?"

"No worries. I had a dentist appointment, and—ta, da—! Mom said I could order a pizza tonight, but only if you'll come for dinner. Will you? I'm dying for pizza."

This is a pity call, but Kelsey doesn't care. She glances at her mother, who's holding the Bloody Mary to her lips with both hands. Tiredness washes over her. She turns away. "Yeah, sure. I'd love to."

This is the first time Kelsey's been invited for dinner. Every year, Kelsey's invited to Lauren's birthday party, but she's only gone to one—her eleventh. All the other times she made excuses, not because she didn't want to go, but because she couldn't afford a gift. Kelsey's a month older than Lauren. For Kelsey's eleventh, her aunt in Nebraska sent her a cross on a silver chain. Kelsey kept the chain, rewrapped the cross, and gave it to Lauren, who raved over it in front of the other girls. The next day at school, Lauren holds up her arm so Kelsey can see the cross has been added to her charm bracelet. A few days later, Kelsey got a Thank You note, which she saved though she's not sure why.

•   •   •   •   •

Kelsey arrives at the greenhouse to find Hobbes trying to start his truck. The hood is up.

"Where ya going?"

"No place, apparently." On the ground beside the front tire is a gas can and a potted plant with feathery leaves and yellow flowers. He gets out but leaves the door hanging open. "Come here." He carefully steps around the plant like it's poison oak. "Get in here and crank it when I tell you."

Kelsey climbs behind the wheel and, through the filthy windshield, watches him lift the gas can. The raised hood blocks what he's doing.

"Now," he shouts.

Thunk, thunk, thunk.

"Okay. Okay."

She climbs out.

"Watch the mimosa," he snaps, and slams the hood, then peers down at the plant.

"Don't you have Triple A?"

"I do, but I called them twice this month. They're going to cut me off." He's looking at her bicycle.

Kelsey follows his gaze. "What?"

"Even better," he says, picks up the plant, and carries it, an arm's length away, to where her bicycle is leaning against the arbor. "Take this plant for a bike ride."

Kelsey snorts a laugh. "You're kidding."

An eyebrow goes up. "When have you known me to kid?" He waits for her to right her bike, and carefully places the mimosa in her basket. "Don't touch the leaves."

"Why?" Kelsey eyes the plant suspiciously. "This isn't like stinging nettle or something is it?"

"No. I don't want you to alarm it. Just watch the plant and tell me what you see it do."

"You're certifiable." Kelsey gets on her bike and pedals toward the driveway.

"Watch the leaves," Hobbes shouts after her. "Watch the leaves."

Kelsey glances back at him and hits a pothole.

"Stop!" He runs—if his quick shuffle could be called a run—toward her.

Kelsey watches the spectacle of his attempt at speed, elbows out like plucked chicken wings.

"Ah ha. You see."

"See what?" She looks down. The mimosa's leaves have closed. "I didn't touch them," she says.

"I know. Hitting the pothole did it."

"Is that what you expected?" She reaches for the plant.

"Don't. Leave it there. Lean your bike against the truck and go water the tomatoes. I'll call you when I want you to do it again."

"Do it again? What are you trying to prove?"

"You don't need to know that right now." He waves her off.

Gen follows Kelsey to the greenhouse. She barely gets started watering when she hears Hobbes shout, "Come take the mimosa for another ride."

The mimosa's leaves have reopened.

Kelsey rolls her eyes.

"Watch the leaves this time."

She skirts the pothole out of consideration for her bike tires and rides out the driveway. It's not until she crosses the big weedy bump down the center of the driveway that the mimosa's leaves close. She turns around and cruises to a stop beside Hobbes. "They closed when I went over the center bump."

"Why do you think they do that?"

She shrugs. She is curious, but would rather die than admit it.

The look he gives her is one she's seen a hundred times. Dismissive. A hopeless case. The same look she gives her mother. He lifts the plant out of her basket and walks away.

CHAPTER 10

Lauren's beautiful old house sits on a large lot surrounded by fir trees. The backyard garden has a pond and half a dozen bird feeders. Kelsey goes through the gate and starts to chain her bike to the fence, then decides it will be safe in this nice neighborhood. Her bike was probably donated to the Pack Rat sale, where she bought it, by one of Lauren's neighbors. Kelsey leans it gently against the maple in the front yard.

When she rings the doorbell, she hears Lauren's little brother shout, "I'll get it," then footsteps running. He was five, maybe six, when she was here for Lauren's birthday party. He's seven or eight now, and tall for his age—unlike his sister.

"Are you Kelsey?"

"Yes, and you're . . . Harrison, right?"

He nods and steps aside. "She's here," he shouts. "They're all in the backyard."

She remembers these rooms from the birthday party. Everything soft and welcoming, with over-stuffed chairs and a fat-cushioned sofa. The day has ended foggy and cool; a fire blazes in the woodstove and an orange cat sleeps on the rug in front of it. As Kelsey follows Harrison, she imagines this is what the inside of a Kinkade house must look like. In the dining room, the table is set for five with real China plates, not paper, and cloth napkins instead of paper towels.

She steps onto the deck.

Lauren's mother and father are lying, side by side but feet to head, in a hammock on the deck, sharing a blanket, each with a book. Both wave.

Lauren sits at patio table rearranging Scrabble letters. "Harrison is winning. Come be on my side."

"Sure. How do you play?"

Lauren and her parents look at her and smile as if she's told a joke. Kelsey has embarrassed herself already.

"Forget this," Lauren says. "My room's changed since you were here last. Want to see it?"

Kelsey remembers how she thought it was the most perfect room she'd ever seen back then. How could it have gotten better? "It was so pretty before."

"It's more grown-up now." She takes Kelsey's hand. "Like we are."

When she was here for Lauren's birthday, her room had been done in shades of pink nothing like the brown shag carpet and cheap paneling on their walls at home. Now the walls are the color of butter, her furniture is white, and the carpet—a shade lighter than the walls—is so thick and soft it feels like crossing a cloud. The only thing she recognizes from last time is the framed poster of young ballerinas. Over the corner of the frame, Lauren has draped her old toe shoes.

Lauren sees Kelsey look at them. "Mom wanted me to be a ballerina, but I'm too short and my legs are too chunky."

"I wanted to be one, too."

"At least you have nice long legs," Lauren says. "It was Mom's dream, not mine. I hated taking lessons. Lessons and more lessons, even when I wasn't very good. Trips to the ballet in San Francisco to keep me motivated. I hated it." Lauren's eyes flash.

Kelsey blinks in surprise. She didn't think Lauren had that level of anger in her. She turns away. "What goes there?" She points to the empty nail in the wall, where she recalls another ballerina poster hung.

"I'll show you." Lauren opens the louvered door to her walk-in closet. Leaning against a set of shelves is a huge black and white photograph on canvas of a mother elephant and her calf. The sky behind them is dark with storm clouds. "It's too heavy for that little nail, but Dad hasn't gotten around to replacing it. Don't you just love it?"

To smile in appreciation is almost painful. But she does. "It will do until you get to India."

"Right." Lauren says. "My dream trip."

Even though it's just pizza, they sit together at the table and hold hands to say grace. Lauren's mother has made a big salad and insists they eat it before they have pizza.

After dinner, they invite Kelsey to stay and play Dominos.

"I'd better not," she says, though she never wants to leave. "Mom wasn't feeling well this morning. I'd better get home."

"Matt will drive you," Lauren's mother says.

"You don't need to do that, Mr. Wells. I rode my bike."

Lauren's mother glances out the window. "It's getting dark."

"Really. I do it all the time. I'm two minutes from here." The last thing she wants is for Lauren's dad to see where they live and decide, like Brie's mother, that Kelsey is an inappropriate friend.

•   •   •   •   •

The next afternoon, Kelsey turns into Dr. Hobbes' driveway and realizes, for the second day in a row, she's forgotten to buy him a big leafed plant.

The open padlock dangles from the bolt, so she knows he's in his bunker. Before knocking on the steel door, she pins herself against the wall so he can't see her if he looks out the window. Cautiously, she lifts the padlock to check out the combination. Four zeros. She nearly laughs out loud. That's the same as her bike-lock combination. Neither of them has bothered to create a code different from the one the lock came with. She knocks.

He opens the door. "There you are." He skips telling her "you're late."

"I forgot your plant again."

"Tomorrow's soon enough." He says it so nicely, she looks at him suspiciously.

"How are your dodder seeds?"

"They're fine."

"How's the mimosa?"

"Glad you asked. Time to take it for another ride."

Once again, he carries the plant out, holding it so the leaves don't brush against his arm. This time when she rides over the center hump in the driveway, the leaves stay open, but close when she purposely hits a pothole.

"It took hitting the pothole this time." She leans her bike against his truck and lifts the mimosa out of her basket.

"Aha. Progress." He takes the plant and crooks a finger for her to follow. He leads her around behind the greenhouse to an ancient, orange concrete mixer.

"What's that for?"

"You'll see. Do you like to bake?"

"No."

"Umph. I bet you wouldn't admit it if you were Betty Crocker herself."

"Who's she?"

"Never mind. Can you follow a recipe?"

Kelsey shrugs. The meals she fixes for herself and her mom only require she open a can or a box.

Against the back of the begonia house is a narrow storage shed full of gardening tools. He takes out a shovel and hands it to her, then a large blue bucket with a heavy rope handle. "See this?" He points to a hand-written recipe stapled to the inside of the shed door.

She stares at him. "I see it."

"You read, right?"

Kelsey throws the shovel aside and stomps off down the weedy path between the greenhouses. She slows. What happens if he lets her go?

"One call from me and they cart you off to the hoosegow, girly."

She turns, but doesn't want him to see that she's relieved. "I'll tell the judge I left 'cause you tried to molest me."

He stares at her for a moment, then still carrying the mimosa, he marches past her, bedroom slippers slapping his heels. "Come with me."

Her stomach flutters. "Where to?"

"Just come on. I want to show you something."

She follows him back to the bunker and steps inside when he holds the door for her. He pulls out a chair from beneath the desk, and puts a pad on the seat, Kelsey assumes so she wouldn't contaminate it.

"Sit," he says.

"Afraid I'll get your chair dirty?"

He's untangling wires and doesn't answer.

Kelsey plops into the chair. This is her first good look around the cluttered office with books and papers piled on his desk, including Gen's cat dish where a fly searches for a missed bite. There's something labeled a gas chromatograph on a table in the corner, a boom box and a stack of cassettes sits on the shelf above his desk, and another large machine is on a table under the window. A long sheet of paper with wavy black lines hangs to the floor. She thinks it must be to record earthquakes.

Her eyes are drawn to an applesauce jar on the shelf above the gas chromatograph. Inside, half a dozen earwigs circle, looking for a way out. Two small brown slugs have inched up the side. Next to the applesauce jar are two plants, each under a plexiglass dome. A glass tube connects the domes. "What *is* all this stuff?"

"Maybe I'll tell you later." He's gotten the wires separated. "I want you to wrap one of these tubes around you lower abdomen and another around your chest."

Kelsey jumps up. "I will not."

"They won't hurt you. They just record differences in your breathing."

"Why?"

"Because you threatened to lie about me. I'm going to show you how easy it is to detect when someone is lying. Do you know what this is?"

"No." Her stomach feels heavy.

"It's a polygraph, commonly known as a lie detector. I want you to see what happens when you lie."

What if he asks her how much she hates him? Especially right now. "I don't think so."

"I'm afraid you don't have a choice, Kelsey. I can't let you threaten me and continue to work here." He puts the things he wants her to wear on the table.

"I was just kidding."

"We don't have a kid-with-each-other relationship."

Tears threaten. "Okay." Kelsey sits. She feels her chest tighten as she puts one rubber tube across her stomach and another across her chest and kind of bungie-cords them in place. She rolls up her sleeve and Hobbes places a blood pressure cuff around her arm above the elbow and squeezes the bulb until it's snug. Lastly, he puts an Oximeter on her left forefinger. Since her mother had that heart attack scare, she's carried an Oximeter to track her oxygen levels in her bathrobe pocket.

"Pretend it's a game. You don't have to answer any question you don't want to. All you have to say is Yes or No. Okay?" He flips a switch on the machine and the paper begins moving. Four thin wire arms draw wavering lines along its length. "Keep an eye on the pens."

Kelsey watches the paper move slowly through the machine. The four arched arms draw wavy lines as the paper rolls past.

"Answer the first couple of questions honestly, so we get a baseline."

She nods, afraid of her own voice.

"Relax and take a deep breath." He smiles. "Is your name Kelsey McCully?"

"Yes." The pens' tracks remain calm.

Dr. Hobbes marks the paper opposite her answer. "I had a student at Berkeley named McCully."

"Is that a question?"

"Did it sound like a question?"

"No." The pens continue to drift.

"Do you live in Fort Bragg, California?"

"Yes."

"Have you ever been arrested?"

"No." Kelsey flinches like a jolt of electricity might be coming, then glances over and sees the pens rip from side to side on the paper.

"See there?"

"You made it do that?"

"I didn't. You did. When people lie, the body gives off electrical impulses that the body can't control."

"Ask me another question." Kelsey glues her eyes to the scratching pins.

"Are you old enough to vote?"

"Yes." Again, the pens sweep from side to side.

"That's really cool."

"Are you thirteen?"

"Yes." The lines sagged into their previous pattern.

"Do you like working here?"

"No."

The needles sweep from back and forth on the paper.

"It's lying. I hate working here."

The jagged lines continue, even darker.

Dr. Hobbes marks the paper and smiles. "It's just as easy to lie to yourself, you know."

"I like Gen, and the plants." The pens slide to the center of their columns and calmly trace their resting pattern.

"Have I tried to molest you?"

"No."

The pens remain calm.

Dr. Hobbes turns off the machine, removes the blood pressure cuff and the Oximeter. "I hope this makes it clear. You are assigned to work here, and you'll do what I tell you to do."

She slips off the breathing sensors and nods. She never would have said he tried to molest her. She's not *that* big of a liar.

•　　•　　•　　•　　•

Kelsey follows Hobbes back behind the begonia house to where there are heaps of dirt. Each pile is labeled in Hobbes' shaky handwriting: Fir bark, Sand, and Peat. The mounds are separated by two-foot board walls.

"Follow the recipe for the Propagation mix." He points to the second recipe from the top of tool shed door. "Put each ingredient in the concrete mixer. The peat will take the longest because you have to break it up until it's powdery. No lumps." He shakes a finger at her. "If you leave lumps, you get soggy globs and bone-dry places in the pots, so no lumps."

"Okay, okay."

Hobbes gives her a look over the top of his glasses, then puts the big, blue plastic tub next to the pile of fir bark.

"Were you a cop?"

"What?"

"Why do you have a lie detector in your office?"

"I use it to recreate experiments that were done decades ago." He hands her a one-gallon black plastic pot. "Use this to measure. Call me when you are ready, and I'll show you how to work the mixer."

The recipe calls for five gallons of fir bark, which, when she scoops it up, feels soft and warm; five gallons of peat, which comes tightly packed and takes forever to powder, three gallons of sand, which has lots of rock-hard cat droppings in it, and three gallons of dusty Perlite, which looks like tiny white Styrofoam BBs. To this she adds a handful of yellow fertilizer beads. She puts all these ingredients in the tub, then can't lift it to carry it to the mixer.

"Dr. Hobbes?" She knocks on the bunker window. "I can't lift it," she says when he opens the door.

"Jesus, Mary and Joseph," he mutters when he sees the full tub. "You don't put all the ingredients in and then put them in the mixer. That's what the mixer is for."

"You didn't tell me that," she snaps.

He taps his forehead. "You're a smart cookie. Try using that spongy stuff between your ears for something besides planning your next robbery."

Kelsey feels punched in the stomach. "I've never . . . I'm not—"

Dr. Hobbes has the bucket rope in one hand, waiting for her to take the other handle and help move it to the mixer. He straightens. "Look. I'm sorry. I shouldn't have said that."

"I'm not a robber."

"Well, Kelsey, you *were*. Shoplifting is stealing and stealing is robbing someone of what belongs to them. Still, I shouldn't have said that, and I'm sorry. Okay?"

She shrugs. "I guess." She takes the other side of the rope, and they drag the tub to the mixer. He makes a big show of checking that she powdered the peat before they take turns bailing it into the mixer a gallon pot at a time. When the bucket gets light enough, he helps her lift and pour the rest of it into the machine.

"You did a good job." He pats her shoulder.

"Thanks."

He shows her how to turn on the mixer and how to rotate the handle so that, once the mixing is done, it can be rolled upside down and emptied back into the tub. When that's done, he sets her to the truly boring task of filling the three-inch pots she washed and sterilized last week. By the time she's ready to leave for home, Kelsey has filled fifty little pots, but it feels like a thousand.

Even though she's dog-tired and covered in a soft powdery brown mix, she offers to take the mimosa for another ride.

"That would be great."

She rides to the end of the driveway, crossing back and forth, hitting every bump. The leaves stay open. He's waiting for her under the arbor. "How come they didn't close?"

"Touch one."

She does, and the leaves shut. "I don't get it."

Hobbes takes the plant, bounces his eyebrows at her, and walks away. "See you tomorrow," he says over his shoulder.

"Can't you just tell me?" she says to his back.

On the ride home, the impossible dawns on her. The mimosa no longer saw the bike ride as a threat.

CHAPTER 11

Thursday, it's raining. Kelsey decides Hobbes won't expect her to ride her bicycle all the way in the rain, so she doesn't go to the greenhouse. And since she doesn't have a phone number for him, she can't call to ask permission.

She considers not going on Friday, since she hadn't gotten into any trouble for not showing up the day before. Maybe he didn't notice she was missing and appreciated a day off from having to find jobs for her. But if she doesn't go, he might think she's quit. And she still has his change from buying the tomato. She'll go after school. Why not? It's there or home.

Rather than go to Rite Aid, she goes to the nursery near her house, only to discover they have two kinds of *Dracaena*. The one with skinny leaves looks like a scrawny palm tree. The other has wide flat leaves trimmed in yellow. She remembers he said he wanted one with broad leaves, so she buys that one.

"So where have you been?" He's holding a great gob of dripping moss, which he's packing against the sides of a wire basket. Boring, old-timey music plays through the greenhouse.

"No place." She holds the *Dracaena* behind her back.

"Punctuality is next to godliness."

Kelsey grins. That's so stupid, she thinks he's joking.

He glances at her. "Well?"

"I'm here now. What do you want me to do?"

"You could have helped me with an experiment if you'd remembered to buy the plant I asked you to get."

Kelsey pulls the *Dracaena* from behind her back, lifts a leaf and flaps it against his shoulder. "Boo."

"Good. Good." Hobbes takes it and carries it to his bunker, arms held out straight like it's a bomb. Once inside, he shouts for her to come quickly.

"I'm right here. You don't need to yell."

"Put your arms out straight."

She does and he loads her up with a one-burner propane stove, a sauce pan, and a box of matches. "Fill the pot with water and light the stove. Do you know how to light this stove?"

"Yes." She cooks on one of these every time PG & E cuts their power.

"Oh, this *is* exciting. Yes, yes." He shoos her, and closes the door, only to open it again. "Bring the water to a boil, then call me." He closes and opens the door again. "Clear a spot—" he points at the crowded benches. "Right there. Move all those plants."

"Where do you want me to put them?"

"I don't care. It's only for a short time. Phil won't mind."

Kelsey's still balancing the stove, a pot and the matches. Only Gen's in the greenhouse with them, stretched out in his favorite spot under a large fern. "Who's Phil?"

Hobbes steps out of the bunker, walks over and lifts the tendril of a vine. "You've forgotten. This is Phil. *Philodendron scandens.*"

"Have you named all your plants?"

"They all have binomials," he smiles. "I'll be happy to explain what those are and introduce you when we have more time."

"Instead of making fun of me, could you be the one to move those plants so I can put this stuff down?"

• • • • •

When the water in the pot is in a rolling boil, Kelsey knocks on the bunker door.

"Come in." Hobbes shouts.

The new *Dracaena* is wired up to the lie detector, with the discs attached to its broad leaves. Hobbes writes something on the polygraph paper, then flips a switch. The paper begins to roll.

"What are you—?"

"No time. Take this container and empty it into the pot."

"The earwigs?"

He gives her a look over the top of his reading glasses like she's a genius to recognize earwigs when she sees them. "Just do it."

"They're alive."

He flips his hand at her.

Kelsey goes out, turns her head so she doesn't have to see them die, and empties the earwigs into the pot of boiling water. Steam rises.

"Come back," he shouts.

She runs to the bunker.

"Do it again," he hands her another container. "Go. Quickly. Not all at once. Half now, half in twenty seconds."

Kelsey goes out and dumps in the few that had made it to the lid, then begins counting: one-one thousand, two-one thousand, three-one thousand. When she reaches twenty seconds, she upends the jar and pounds on the bottom until it's empty.

A whoop comes from the bunker. "I'll be dipped, Backster, you old buzzard, you may be right."

She's been invited in twice, so Kelsey feels braver going through the door. "Did it work?"

He turns from reading the polygraph's printout. "I was trying to recreate an experiment done decades ago. Look here." He holds the readout under her nose. "This is the *Dracaena*'s reaction to the death of the first container of earwigs." He jabs at the black scratches across the entire width of the paper. "This is where you put in the second batch, and right here—" he points to a calmer stretch of the readout "—is where you poured in the third container."

"It's not as jaggedy."

"That, my dear, is the point. It stopped reacting."

"The plant?"

"Absolutely." He pats the wired *Dracaena*'s top leaves as if it had a head. "I tried this experiment with Phil once, but didn't see anything conclusive. I thought a new plant —in other words, a stranger in strange surroundings— might test differently. In his experiments, Backster said the plants he experimented on habituated to the death of other organisms. It looks as if he might have been right."

"What's habituate mean?"

"Learn to ignore by repeated exposure."

Hobbes levels his gaze at her and holds her eyes. She looks away. "You do know you're talking about a plant, right?" She smiles and circles the side of her forehead with a finger.

Hobbes rubs an unwired leaf between his fingers. "We're only beginning to understand what plants are capable of. Certainly, we humans grow accustomed to all sorts of awful things."

"It's a plant!"

His face clouds. "Plants have different means of communication. Chemical, electrical—." He flips his hands at her. "Never mind. Go out and get to work."

"Doing what?"

"Just git. I'll be out in a minute to give you a job."

So much for trying to get along with him. She turns to go.

"Where's my change?"

Kelsey stops, digs into her jeans pocket, pulls out a dollar, a few coins, and the two crumpled receipts. "There's every penny."

"If that's all, keep it."

She slaps the money on the desk. "I don't want it." A lie. Every penny counts in her life.

Hobbes shrugs, shoos her, and shuts the door.

Figuring he'll come out and assign her some chore she'll hate, she attaches the long rod-like mister to the hose and begins watering near the tomato plant. While he's unhooking the *Dracaena,* she takes the chance to peek under the boxes covering the pots surrounding the tomato. Each dodder is a single, wire-thin orange sprout all of which are aimed toward either the slurry or the little tomato seedling, except the one under the glass dome.

She jumps when the bunker door opens, swings around, and hits one of his orchids. It crashes to the ground, shattering the pot.

Gen, curled under his fern, shoots straight up in the air.

"Now look what you've done." Hobbes steps back into his office and shuts the door.

"I'm sorry," Kelsey calls after him. She gathers the shards and puts them in the broken pottery bucket, pieces of which he uses to keep the holes in bottom of pots from getting plugged with soil.

The music stopped when she broke the orchid's pot. Now, it starts again with one long note before settling into that random, natural-sounding stuff her mother likes when she's in what Kelsey thinks of as the sweet spot, a short day or two, when her mother acts normal. Always short-lived before the roller-coaster ride continues and she lurches past a promising moment, headed either up to over-the-top elation, or down into the depths of depression.

Kelsey starts to repot the orchid. "That music is so boring," she mumbles to herself.

"It is not." Hobbes comes out trailing a printout from the polygraph. "That's the *Dracaena* singing."

"What?"

"I put one electrode into its roots and another on a leaf and plugged them into the music synthesizer. The music is caused by electrical impulses between the leaf and root." He hands her the sheet to hold and takes the orchid from her. "Orchids like their roots cramped. Use a smaller pot, and bark, not soil."

Kelsey glances at the readout and reaches to hand it back.

"Hold it for a second while I do this properly."

"What did you boil to death this time?" She points to the jagged bit.

"Nothing. That's where you broke the pot. It alarmed Phil. Look further up the sheet. See those jerky lines?" He taps the paper. "That's from last night when some hoodlum friends of yours came snooping around."

"What are you talking about?"

"I was in my office when Phil reacted to something. I turned off the light and watched two guys come into the greenhouse. They ran when I threw the bolt. Tell your cruddy little cronies I'll call the cops next time."

"I don't have any friends who'd come out here." There seems to be no escaping his low opinion of her. She turns her back so he doesn't see the tears spilling down her cheeks.

"Okay. Okay." His tone is softer. "Maybe they aren't friends of yours. One of them looked like that bum the courts sent me two years ago."

Will. Will had said, 'Been there, done that.'

"Here, finish this and wipe your nose." He put the orchid pot in her hand and pats her shoulder.

CHAPTER 12

Last night, Kelsey fixed spaghetti for dinner and had forgotten to put a lid on the bowl when she heated the sauce. Dried red globs now pock the inside of the microwave. Saturday morning finds her trying to clean it when her mother comes into the kitchen, hair combed, dressed in jeans, a clean T-shirt, wearing mascara and lipstick.

"Wow. You look nice." Kelsey's heart skips a beat. Not today of all days. "What's the occasion?"

"Does there need to be an occasion?" Lydia feigns surprise. "What are you doing?"

"Cleaning up the mess I made of last night's dinner."

"It was good."

"You didn't eat enough of it to tell." Her mother's appetite is another gauge of her slipping into depression. She eats less and less and sleeps more and more. Often fifteen hours a day.

"What I did eat tasted good."

The phone rings. Force of habit, Kelsey snatches it to prevent her mother from babbling drunkenly to some solicitor.

Lydia takes the sponge from her and attacks the microwave.

"Hey, Kels." It's Lauren. "Brie says we'll pick you up about four."

Kelsey glances at her mother measuring coffee into the filter basket. Wouldn't you know, this has all the earmarks of a sober day. Sober, her mother will never let her go to a party she has to be driven to by an underaged driver. "I don't think I can go. Mom's—" she walks into the living room and lowers her voice so her mother won't hear her lie to Lauren. "Mom's taking me to town to do some shopping."

"So, she's—" Lauren stops. "She's been sick, right?"

"She's better today."

"I'm glad, Kels, but I'll miss you." Lauren hesitates. "Maybe you'll get back in time. Want me to check right before we leave?"

Her mother has taken over cleaning the microwave. She looks over her shoulder and smiles at Kelsey. "Quite a mess."

Exactly what Kelsey was thinking about her own plans. And what if she's wrong? This won't be the first time she's been tricked into thinking her mother was taking a day off. It's early still. "That would be great," Kelsey says. "Thanks."

"Who was that, sweetheart?"

Kelsey carries the phone back into the kitchen. "Lauren. Want some eggs?"

"Which one is she?"

"She's just my best friend, Mom."

"Well, how would I know? You never bring any of your friends around."

"Are you kidding?"

"Of course, I'm not kidding. I'd like to meet your friends."

"Oh my God, Mom. Look at how we live."

"I can't help it if we're poor, Kelsey." Lydia rips off a paper towel, ready to dab her eyes if the need arises. "And true friends won't hold that fact against you. Lots of kids are being raised by single-mothers."

Kelsey swallows the urge to say, yeah, but how many mothers are being raised by single daughters. Her shoulders sag. She's been here, done this. "Drop it, okay."

Her mother's right about one thing. Lauren knows the truth, or enough of it without having seen it for herself, and is still her friend. But it wasn't lost on Kelsey that Lauren said, "I'll miss you," not "we'll miss you."

"Well, I'm glad you have nice friends." Lydia takes a glass from the drainboard. "Like that L'Oréal commercial says, "You're worth it.'"

Gag.

Managing low expectations with Lydia is easy. It's the moments of hope that break Kelsey's heart. Days like this are scary.

Lydia opens the fridge and takes out the orange juice. Kelsey waits for her to open the freezer for ice and the vodka. Instead, her mother holds up a second glass and raises her eyebrows. Kelsey shakes her head no. "You have lots of friends. Don't you?"

"Not many." Kelsey counts the eggs. Six left and five days before her next trip to the food bank. She takes out two.

"What did your friend—" She pauses, as she often does to search her alcohol fogged brain for a word or a name, "Lauren, right? –want?"

"There's a party out at Chelsea's."

"And you're invited. That's nice. When is it?" Lydia sits at the ugly red Formica table, hands wrapped around her glass of orange juice, staring up at the dead bugs in the ceiling light.

"This afternoon."

"Oh." Lydia picks at the chipped corner of the Formica. "Are you going?"

"Probably not. I don't care that much about going." Kelsey imagines the wire pens ripping from side to side on the lie detector. She'd love an evening away from her mother.

"Aren't you working today?"

"No."

Yesterday, in order to give herself time to dress and be ready to go to the party, she'd told Hobbes that she needed to leave at noon because her mother had a doctor's appointment. He'd cocked his head and squinted at her suspiciously. "What's that got to do with you?"

"I have to go with her—" She's creating this excuse on the fly and stops to consider what will work best. "I take notes so she won't forget the doctor's instructions." That would be the truth if her mother really had an appointment.

He took so long to react she was afraid he'd hook her to the lie detector again. Instead, he shrugged. "Don't bother coming at all then." And went back to snipping dead leaves.

"I'm glad," Lydia says. "You deserve a day off. Maybe we could watch some TV together."

"Sure. I guess." Kelsey cracks both eggs into a bowl, adds a dash of Tabasco and a little milk.

"How's work going?"

"Great."

"That's nice." Her mother gets up, rinses her orange juice glass, and opens the freezer.

Here she goes.

She takes out a tray of ice cubes, but not the vodka. "I think I'll have a Virgin Mary, would you like one?"

"No, thanks, I'm trying to quit."

Her mother looks at her, apparently trying to decide if Kelsey means to be funny or sarcastic.

"Joke, Mom."

It's impossible not to watch her mother's every move for clues as to what the day will be like. When Lydia's desperate for a drink, she goes straight for the canned Bloody Mary mix. This morning, her prep is more elaborate. She pours straight tomato juice over ice, adds a dash of Tabasco, and microwaves a rock-hard lime for ten seconds, then rolls it on the counter to try to get some juice out of it. More and more, it looks like it's going to be a rare sober day.

Kelsey beats the eggs.

Lydia adds a limp celery stick to her drink. "Why don't we do something fun today?"

"Like what?"

"I don't know. Take a walk. It's beautiful out."

"Okay." Kelsey wipes out the frying pan and puts it on a burner. "We could go to the Russian Gulch waterfall, or maybe to the lighthouse."

"They won't let you out to the lighthouse."

"Who won't?"

"The Coast Guard."

"It's a State Park now, Mom." Kelsey pours a little olive oil into the pan instead of using the nasty Food Bank margarine.

"Since when?"

"I don't know. Years. Don't you remember? It was in the paper. A bunch of volunteers fixed up the lighthouse and got the old lens working again. Now it's a state park."

"That's what happens when you don't have a local TV station. We never know what's going on in our own backyard." Lydia takes her drink to the dinette, sits, then gets up again and takes the frying pan off the burner. "Let's go out for breakfast."

"I don't think we can afford it."

"Maybe not, but we should do it anyway."

A familiar ache starts in Kelsey's chest. Every sober day makes her wish for another and wonder why they come so rarely, or at all. What throws the switch in her mother? How different life would be if her mother quit drinking for good.

Lydia's monthly disability check barely covers their expenses, much less the extravagance of going out to breakfast. Kelsey knows this because she's been signing and cashing those checks since she perfected cursive. She hides the money in her mother's recipe box, the last place Lydia would think to look. Every month she divides the cash from the check according to a budget she made up. She sets fifty aside to supplement their food stamps and her trips to the Food Bank under "F" for Food. She accumulates money for their property taxes under "T;" her mother's liquor under "B" for booze; "E" for electricity; "G" for gas for the car; and "W" for the water bill and wood.

They have baseboard heating, but it's too expensive to use, so they heat with a smokey old woodstove. When they can't afford to buy firewood, Kelsey drives her mother to construction sites and they scavenge scraps. Finding where a deck is being replaced is the best for aged, dry redwood. Kelsey uses a magnet to remove the nails from the ashes.

While Lydia looks for a jacket to wear, Kelsey covers the eggs with a chipped saucer and puts them back in the fridge. When she hears her mother brushing her teeth, she takes twenty dollars from behind the "G" in the recipe box, gas being their least likely expenditure since Lydia lost her license four months ago, and so, just this once, they can have a real breakfast of eggs, bacon, home fries, maybe even biscuits and gravy at the Home Style Café.

After breakfast, which only costs nine dollars because they shared a two-egg breakfast that came with four strips of bacon and a side of biscuits and gravy, they walk to the bus stop at Safeway and take it south toward Mendocino.

"I wish I could finish high school in Mendocino," Kelsey says, absently, as the bus makes the turn onto Point Cabrillo Drive.

"Why would you want to do that?"

"A fresh start." The bus goes around the twists in the road until the surfers in Caspar Cove come into view. They look silly trying to catch foot-high waves.

"Why do you think you need a fresh start?"

"'Cause I do."

Her mother turns and stares out the window, and says nothing more. A few minutes later, the bus stops outside the lighthouse parking lot, and they get off.

"It's my fault, isn't it?" They are standing in front of a huge boulder with a plastic plaque dedicated by the Daughters of the Golden West.

"What is?"

"You needing a fresh start because I haven't been a good mother."

Kelsey knows her mother hopes she'll say yes, you have, but she can't get that lie out, and her silence is probably just as hurtful. "It doesn't matter, Mom. Everything's okay."

"You deserve better than me. After your father left, I didn't know how to cope."

They never discuss her father or why he left. Kelsey has no memory of him, so he must have left when she was a baby. She's never seen a picture of him. If there had been pictures, her mother probably tossed them long ago. Kelsey would like to know more about him but is afraid asking would give her mother another excuse to binge. This is the first time Lydia's brought him up, so maybe today will be different. "You want to talk about him?"

"It's a nice day, let's not ruin it."

The walk to the lighthouse is a half-mile—downhill. Her mother smokes two cigarettes on the way and talks about the time, when Kelsey was a baby, she brought her to the Coast Guard wives' craft sale. "That's where I bought our reindeer head."

"I like that head."

The head is their one and only Christmas decoration. During the holidays, Kelsey relies on it—with its red felt nose and stuffed black fabric antlers. There was one Christmas Kelsey barely remembers. Lidia brought a plastic tree home from Rite Aid. They set it up together, wadded up an old bed sheet, and strung it with lights. Shortly afterwards, her mother got fired and the tree never accumulated gifts. At night, the walls of their house shown with colored-eggs of light until one by one they burned out.

Since then, no tree, no presents, except from her mother's sister in Nebraska, and some hand-me-down sweater or blouse her mother buys for her at the Paul Bunyan thrift store. Every year, Kelsey hangs the deer head on the front door so the neighbors will think they have the holiday spirit, and that her mother is together enough to know what month it is.

The restoration of three old lightkeeper houses is finished and one is open as a museum.

"Aren't they beautiful?" Lydia says. "I wish we had the money to fix up our house."

"Yeah, me, too."

Little chance of that ever happening. Lydia's total disability is based on 'Cognitive Impairment'—her mother's alcohol-induced inability to think, concentrate, formulate ideas, reason or remember anything important since Kelsey was about six or seven.

"Maybe, if you make a little extra money from this job of yours, we could at least paint it."

"I'm saving that money for college." Kelsey never expects to go to college, never mind that she isn't getting paid. She's not sure where that lie came from.

Her mother's head snaps around in surprise, but she recovers quickly. "I didn't know you were thinking about college."

"Well, I am." She looks her mother straight in the eye. What can it hurt to plant that seed? Let her mother start to worry about when Kelsey's not around to take care of her.

Kelsey has no memory of the Coast Guard wives' sale. The only visit to the lighthouse she remembers was a class trip in the fourth grade. Even though their house is less than a mile from the ocean, she'd never been that close to the water before, blocked as it was by the 400-hundred-acre Georgia-Pacific mill which owned and fenced-off Fort Bragg's oceanfront. Back then, she'd never even been to Glass Beach—the only coastal access within the city limits. All she remembers about that fourth-grade trip was how rough the ocean was. The water churned like a washing machine and large waves exploded against the cliffs. Today, it's sunny with a calm sea, though a fog bank, like a rolled-up gray blanket, lies just offshore.

The old blacksmith shop is their first stop. It holds a small marine science exhibit including a large saltwater tank full of local ocean critters. Kelsey and her mother use the flashcards hanging on a peg by the tank to identify the hermit crabs, abalone, red and purple sea urchins, nudibranchs—tiny, astonishingly colorful sea slugs—and four kinds of sea stars.

Back outside, they stare up at the giant, multi-faceted Fresnel lens turning in the glass room on top of the lighthouse. "It looks like a diamond, doesn't it?" Lydia says.

Kelsey feels oddly saddened by the sight of something so beautiful and perfect. It makes her life feel uglier.

Inside the lighthouse, there's a closed-circuit TV focused on the lens turning in its lantern room. A docent tells visitors about the 1850 wreck of the Clipper Brig, *Frolic*.

Kelsey feels ordinary standing there with the other visitors, listening, as if she and her mother are normal people like them.

Lydia must feel the same because she watches a tourist buy a memento from the gift shop, and says, "Let's find a little something for you."

"I don't need anything."

"I want to buy you a souvenir."

Kelsey looks for something inexpensive, starting with a dollar bookmark, then a refrigerator magnet.

Her mother shakes her head. "No, no. Something special."

The only piece of jewelry Kelsey owns is the thin silver chain she wears every day. It's the one that came with the cross she regifted to Lauren. At her mother's insistence, she picks a small, ten-dollar, jellyfish charm. It, too, is silver, and has dangly curlicue tentacles.

Kelsey unhooks the chain, threads it through the jellyfish eyelet, and bends her knees so her mother can refasten it behind her neck. She'll show it to Lauren and Brie and be able to say her mother bought it for her while they were shopping.

On the hike up the hill from the lighthouse, her mother takes her hand. Her fingers are soft and warm. Kelsey's a little embarrassed to be holding hands with her mother, but it also makes her feel like a little girl again, as though all the miserable years could be erased like a blackboard. About half-way up the hill, they stop to rest at a picnic table in the shade of an old Bull pine. While her mother smokes, Kelsey watches the flash of light from the lighthouse and fingers the tentacles of the jellyfish charm.

They get home a little after two. Lydia says she wants to fix Kelsey a special dinner to celebrate their day together, but first she's going to rest her feet and have a small glass of wine.

"Wait a little longer, Mom. Please." Kelsey puts her arms over Lydia's shoulders and her forehead against her mother's. She closes her eyes. Against her cheek, she feels the tips of her mother's fingers brushing back and forth, like the wings of a butterfly. The tenderness of the touch makes Kelsey think they'll be okay.

Her mother straightens and turns to the fridge. "Just a little wine, dear. That isn't like a real drink."

Lauren calls at three-thirty. "You're home. Did you have a nice day?"

"We did." Kelsey stands in front of her mother, who's asleep, her chin on her chest.

"No getting out of it now." Lauren laughs. "We'll pick you up at four."

Kelsey makes grilled cheese sandwiches, quartering her mother's sandwich so there's less chance she'll choke. While Kelsey eats hers, she replays the day in her head, and remembers the cliché: "Today is the first day of the rest of your life." After watching her mother slide into her nightly oblivion, she thinks if today is the first day of the rest of her life, she is not sure she wants to stick around for the rest of it.

She shakes her mother's shoulder. "Dinner's ready, Mom."

Lydia stirs and opens her eyes. "Looks good. Maybe later." She reaches for her glass, which is empty. "Oopsie daisy. Look who needs a drink."

"Mom. Eat, please."

Her mother's heavy-lidded eyes blaze for a moment, then she swings her legs off the side of her Barcalounger without putting the footrest down. "I'll get it myself." She scoots forward, which tips the recliner. Lydia slides to the floor.

Kelsey doesn't move to help her up.

Lydia rolls to the side and onto her hands and knees, then uses the hassock to help her stand. She steadies herself with her hand on the recliner's headrest, near the oily stain in the center.

Emotions churn in Kelsey's mind: hatred, love, disgust, then pity as she watches Lydia lurch toward the kitchen.

CHAPTER 13

It's four. The sun is still warm on Kelsey's left shoulder. She's waiting on the stoop for Brie and Lauren, picking leaves off the dead fuchsia in a pot by the front door. She's thinking it would be nice to get something new, and this time keep it watered.

She hears the BMW tires squeal as Brie pulls away from the stop sign at the bottom of the hill. Kelsey jumps up and hurries to meet them at the curb of the better-looking house next door. Lauren gets out and hugs her. "I'm so glad you could come. This is going to be fun." She holds the seat forward for Kelsey to get in the back. Once seated, she meets Brie's unfriendly eyes in the rearview mirror. "Hey."

"Hey, yourself. How's your mother?" Brie's tone is snarky.

"Fine. Mom got me this when we were shopping." She holds up the jellyfish charm.

"That is *so* cute," Lauren says. "Love the little tentacles."

Kelsey settles back and relaxes. She left her mother sound asleep. As an added precaution, she'd emptied the ashtray and hidden Lydia's pack of cigarettes along with the car keys, in the fridge's vegetable bin. There's no place nearby for her to buy more.

Once residential Oak Street turns into narrow, densely tree-lined Sherwood Road, Brie steps on it, screeching around bends and making Kelsey glad she's in the backseat and had discreetly fastened her seatbelt.

The road comes out of the redwoods to rolling, golden hills dotted with oak trees. It dips past horses grazing, then up and around a bend. Dozens of cars are parked along a driveway that leads up a hill to Chelsea's house. Even with their car windows rolled up and the A.C. on because it's thirty degrees warmer this far inland, the music makes Kelsey's chest vibrate.

"Wow," Lauren says. "Word sure got out."

Brie laughs. "Boy did it."

Brie parks the BMW near the bottom of the hill. There's a ditch on Kelsey's side, a clump of poison oak in front of the car, and Sherwood Road behind them. Brie cuts the engine and turns to them. "Don't drink anything anybody gives you, okay. Get your own drink, open it and don't put it down anywhere. And don't eat anything."

"Why?" Kelsey says, then, "Oh." Brie's matter-of-fact warning makes the back of her knees tingle the way they do when she sees someone get a shot on TV.

"How come?" Lauren asks.

"To keep someone from slipping you something," Brie says. "You ever heard of the date-rape drug?"

"Oh." Lauren looks over her shoulder at Kelsey, smiles, and rolls her eyes.

Once out of the car, they stand at the bottom of the driveway looking up at the crowd of kids.

"What if we get separated?" Lauren says.

"I'll meet you all back here—" Brie looks at her watch. "—at nine-thirty." She puts the car key on the front tire. "In case one of you gets here first."

The shouting and laughing male voices are deeper than the boys their age. "Sounds like Chelsea's going have some explaining to do when her parents get home." Brie laughs.

"Those guys don't sound like high school boys," Lauren says.

"So? That's why I told you not to drink anything anybody gives you." Brie hooks her arm through Lauren's. "Come on, chicken," she says to Kelsey.

As they walk up the hill, Kelsey scans the faces and sees only one she recognizes. Will. He's at the railing on a second story deck, watching them climb the driveway. At least there's someone here she knows. Oddly, her stomach suddenly fills with butterflies.

When Brie spots Will. She waves. "Isn't he the best-looking thing!"

Just as well, Kelsey thinks. Something about Will always reminds her of a dog that's growling and wagging his tail at the same time. She never knows which end to trust. She stops. "I think I'll wait here for a while."

Brie turns. "You're being a baby, Kelsey. If you do what I told you, nothing can happen."

Kelsey's tempted to say if she wanted to be around drunks she could have stayed home.

"We won't stay long if it's awful." Lauren puts her arm around Kelsey's waist. "Come on. You and I will stick together."

Will disappears from the railing into the dense crowd. Kelsey watches Brie weave and dodge through the group of boys outside the front door. One says, "Hey, sweet thing," and grabs her butt. Brie laughs and knocks away his hand. A moment later, Will appears. Seeing him, the boys part and let Lauren and Kelsey through unmolested.

When they're inside, Will puts an arm around Brie, but winks at Kelsey over the top of Brie's head. One of the boys latches onto Lauren and leads her to where kids are dancing. Kelsey's left alone. At school, she doesn't attract much attention from boys, but drunk boys might not be put off by her head-down, humped shoulders, and mousy looks. She finds an empty chair in the corner by the kitchen. She's not there long before Will's buddy Ryan, breath reeking like her mother's, drags her to her feet. "Come on, Kels, let's dance." He pulls her close.

"I don't want to." Kelsey jerks free and turns. She hears him laughing as she runs the gauntlet of guys at the front door, slapping away hands that reach for her. She retreats down the driveway, and crosses the yard to a huge oak tree where a swing hangs from a thick, sturdy limb. She sits on the swing and wraps her arms around the ropes. It's going to be a long night.

The music thunders, and the voices inside grow slurred and louder. Someone has built a bonfire in the side yard. From a safe distance, she watches sparks lift and swirl. An ember pops, igniting a small grass fire. One of the boys notices, shakes a bottle of beer, and uses it to extinguish the flames.

Kelsey soon tires of repeatedly walking the swing back, lifting her feet, and whooshing forward. After darkness falls, she tires of looking at the stars and trying to remember the constellations. She's half mad at Lauren for not trying to find her, and worried that she might be in some kind of trouble. They both thought Brie's warnings were over the top. Kelsey crosses the yard and retrieves the key from the front tire. She turns on the ignition to see what time it is. 9:05. She reclines the soft, leather seat, puts her head back, and closes her eyes. The music from the party is muted to a thudding rhythm.

Shrill laughter from the house wakes her. She turns the key in the ignition to check the clock again. 9:52. She puts the seat upright, climbs out, locks the car, puts the key back on the front tire, and starts up the driveway. Pairs of kids sit like dark boulders around the dying embers of the fire. The boys are gone from the front door. Inside acrid-smelling smoke hangs in the air. Everywhere couples lie on the furniture and the floor, tangled together, making out.

In the darkness, Kelsey can't tell who's who. She weaves her way through the crowded room. "Brie? Lauren?" she whispers.

"Brie. Lauren," someone mimics.

"Brie?" She shouts this time.

In the dim light, she sees a guy sitting by himself, watching her. It's too dark to see his features clearly, but it chills her. She looks away.

She steps over couples sprawled on the staircase. At the top, she calls Brie's name again.

"What?" Comes the muffled reply.

"Where are you?"

A bedroom door opens a crack. Brie's face, lipstick smeared, hair tangled, appears in the gap. "What do you want, Kelsey?"

"We have to go."

"Soon," she says.

"Now, Brie. It's ten." Kelsey pushes the door open and takes Brie's arm.

"Come join us, Kelsey." It's Will's voice.

Brie pulls free, loses her balance, and falls on top of the couple on the floor.

"Watch out," a voice says. Not Lauren's.

Kelsey opens the door wider. The hall light exposes four or five couples in varying degrees of exposed body parts. Kelsey reaches in and pulls Brie to her feet. "Where's Lauren?"

"Did you say ten?" Brie's voice is slurs. "Jesus, my parents will be home soon." She pulls her blouse closed, staggers, and nearly falls again trying to button it.

"Lauren?" Kelsey shouts when they reach the bottom of the stairs

"Lauren," two male voices answer.

"Maybe she's waiting in the car." Brie giggles

"I just came from the car," Kelsey snaps.

To their left, a bathroom door opens, and Lauren comes out helping Chelsea walk. "You'll be okay now." She deposits Chelsea in a chair. The smell of vomit lingers. The front of Chelsea's shirt is wet where someone tried to wash it out.

"Thanks, Lauren." Chelsea starts to cry. "My parents are gonna kill me."

"Probably," Lauren says, and turns to Kelsey. "I tried to find you."

"Some turd hit on me and I cut out. Are you okay?"

"You're always adding new flavors of weird to the mix, Kelsey," Brie says. "You need to chill."

"Ignore her," Lauren says. "She's drunk."

"You're supposed to be kind to weirdos," says a voice from the darkness.

"I'm not a social worker," Brie says, which elicits laughter.

"Stop it, Brie." Lauren pulls off her purple scrunchie, shake her dark hair loose, and puts the scrunchie on her wrist. "Go." She pushes Brie out the door.

At the car, Lauren takes the keys from the front tire, unlocks the door, and gets behind the wheel.

"What do you think you're doing?" Brie says.

"You're drunk. I'm driving."

"I am not drunk, and it's my car."

"It's your mother's car."

Brie walks to the middle of the road, holds her arms out, and walks the faded center strip singing 'Mi Casa, Su Casa.' "See. Sober as a judge." She giggles. "Sorry, Kelsey."

"About what?"

"Mentioning judges."

"Drop dead, Brie." Kelsey pushes the passenger seat forward and climbs into the back.

"Move over." Brie tries to shove Lauren out of the driver's seat.

"All right. All right." Lauren lifts herself across the console to the passenger seat. She reaches behind her head for the seatbelt, then twists trying to find it.

"Forget it," Brie says. "It's broken."

Since someone managed to park behind them, Brie drives forward over the poison oak, then reverses and drops the right rear tire into the ditch.

"Brie, you are drunk. Let me drive."

"Am not." Brie pulls forward spitting gravel and mud onto the grill of the car behind them. Lauren and Kelsey scream when Brie fishtails onto Sherwood Road and stomps on the gas.

Kelsey buckles her seatbelt.

CHAPTER 14

The right side of Kelsey's head throbs. She touches where it hurts. Her fingers come away warm and sticky. She opens her eyes to flashing lights bouncing off the trees. The last thing she remembers was Lauren screaming at Brie to slow down, followed by a weightless sensation as the car went airborne.

Someone shines a flashlight through a dark red smear on her window, blinding her.

"Are you okay?" A man asks.

"I think so." Kelsey releases her seatbelt and scoots forward. The windshield on Lauren's side is gone and her seat is filled with beads of glass, in alternating colors of red and blue.

Brie's seat is empty, too.

The beam from the flashlight shifts from the front seat to Kelsey in the back. It's held by a man in a beige highway patrol uniform.

"Where's Lauren?"

He pushes Brie's seat forward, leans in, and lifts Kelsey from the car.

"Where are my friends?"

"One's in my car."

"Which one?"

"Can't say, Miss."

From down the road comes music booming from a car radio, followed by the squeal of brakes, and boys laughing.

Two policemen walk past. "As if one mangled kid ain't enough," one mutters.

Fear rises from deep inside Kelsey's chest. "Who's mangled?"

"What happened off-cer?" she hears one of the boys say. "Anybody hurt?"

"How about you boys step out of the car."

The highway patrol officer puts Kelsey on one of the stretchers. She lifts her head as she's pushed toward one of the ambulances, and sees the BMW is folded around the redwood tree like a crushed soda can.

A paramedic comes up the steep incline from the woods carrying Lauren. The long wavy dark hair Kelsey has always envied cascades over the medic's arm in dark clumps. Lauren's arm, with the purple scrunchie, dangles limply. As they near, Kelsey sees Lauren's kind face is bloody and gruesome in the flashing lights.

Kelsey rolls on her side, leans over the side of the stretcher, and vomits.

The paramedic lays Lauren on the stretcher. "This one's critical but still breathing."

Tears turn the lights into blinding blue and red stars. Kelsey trembles.

As they wheel Kelsey past a CHP car. Brie's in the backseat. "I'm sorry," she sobs. There's a little bump above the left side of her forehead and her nose is bleeding. Her eyes are wide and desperate, like someone whose mouth and nose are sinking into quicksand. "I'm sorry." She turns palms up as if begging for someone, now or ever, to forgive her.

•   •   •   •   •

Kelsey wakes. A curtain hanging on a series of thin chains from a track attached to the ceiling, encircles her bed. *Her bed?* Not *her* bed.

"I'm so sorry," says someone on the other side. "We tried."

A woman begins to wail. Her body convulses, causing the curtain to sway. Someone tries to comfort her, but she swats and bats at them, breaks free, and sags against the railing—*railing?*—of Kelsey's bed, pulling the curtain taut.

There's a smell Kelsey remembers. Clorox and something antiseptic. Her mother with a cast on her arm. This is their local hospital's emergency room.

Kelsey's head throbs. She reaches to touch where it hurts the most and feels a bandage. "Oh God," Kelsey moans. "Lauren."

A hand grabs the edge of the curtain and rips it back along the track. Mrs. Wells. Her anguished expression turns to hatred, before she recognizes

Kelsey. Mr. Wells takes Lauren's mother in his arms and presses her head to his chest. "We're glad you're safe, Kelsey." He guides Lauren's mom away from the bed next to hers. The sheet draped body looks small, as if all that was wonderful about Lauren in life has vanished, leaving only her shell behind.

From somewhere in the room, Brie complains that it hurts to breathe.

"You've got a cracked rib and a broken nose. You'll live." Kelsey hears the nurse's icy disapproval.

CHAPTER 15

A nurse comes to the foot of Kelsey's ER bed. "Are your folks out of town? We haven't been able to reach anyone."

"No." It's hard to imagine her mother's still too drunk to even answer the phone. Then again.

"Well, there's a CHP officer here to take you home. Can you stand?" He lowers the railing on the bed.

Kelsey sits upright, swings her legs over the side, and closes her eyes against the stabbing pain in her temple.

The nurse places his hand on her shoulder. "You're lucky you were wearing your seatbelt. Hit your head a little harder and a little higher and you might have fractured your skull."

She wonders how much worse that would be than living with the pain she knows will never go away.

•   •   •   •   •

At her house, Officer Smith, the CHP cop she recognizes from the accident, picks up the key she drops trying to fit it into the lock, unlocks the door, and holds it open for her.

"I better come in and talk to your parents." he says, then spots her mother slouched in the recliner, exactly where Kelsey left her seven hours earlier. She hopes, but doubts, that he'll mistake this scene as a parent dozing off while waiting up for her kid to come home.

"Thanks, but I'll be all right."

He steps inside anyway and crinkles his nose at the smell of alcohol and the stink of a dirty ashtray. "I've got a daughter your age," he says. "What happened to you kids tonight is a parent's worst nightmare. He takes a card from his pocket. "Take this. If you ever want to talk, call me." He glances again at her mother.

Almost nothing hurts worse than pity. Tears roll down Kelsey's cheeks. "She was my best friend."

"I'm sorry. There's nothing I can say except that it will get easier in time."

No, it won't. But Kelsey nods.

·   ·   ·   ·   ·

The next morning, Kelsey stands in the kitchen doorway and watches her mother trying to steady her hand enough to sip her coffee. Lydia looks up and smiles, then sees the bandage on Kelsey's forehead. "What did you do?"

One part of Kelsey wants to pour out the whole story, have her mother take her in her arms and hug her, say how grateful she is Kelsey survived, and how awful for her daughter that someone she loved died. Her more realistic self is terrified that if her mother knows what happened, she wouldn't do any of those things. She'll somehow make it worse—maybe even say the girls brought this on themselves, which is, of course, true.

Kelsey shrugs, which hurts the shoulder the seatbelt bruised. "I hit my head on an open cupboard door."

Lydia tsk, tsks. "You should be more careful."

·   ·   ·   ·   ·

Kelsey stays in bed all Sunday and Monday, and most of Tuesday, with the exception of an occasional trip to the kitchen to grab something to eat when she hears her mother in the bathroom. She lies in bed with her knees drawn up to her chest to ease the knot in her stomach. She hears the phone ring a few times, and assumes at least one call is from Hobbes. When it rings again, her mother comes to find her. Kelsey rolls off the far side of her bed, onto the floor, and hides out of sight. Her mother shuffles back to the kitchen and says something to the caller that Kelsey can't hear.

She has nightmares. In one, she enters her Language Arts class and there's Lauren in her usual seat. Kelsey is thrilled to see her alive, and squeals in delight. Lauren moves her backpack off the chair she's saved for Kelsey, but when she turns, she has no face. Kelsey wakes crying.

In another nightmare, Kelsey's in the seat behind Brie, who's taking the curve too fast. They all scream as the car starts a long, slow-motion slide toward a redwood tree. Lauren looks back at her and says, "This is going to break my mother's heart."

On Tuesday, when she hears her mother in the shower, Kelsey slips into the kitchen and listens to the messages. There are three solicitations, a call from the school checking on her, and a garbled message from a sobbing Josh. "Brie's gone. Her parents sent her away. Good thing, the whole school wants to kill her."

Another is from Dr. Hobbes: "Kelsey?" Then nothing for so long she thinks he's hung up. "You need to let me know what's going on, why you've stopped coming." There's another long pause. "Call and tell me. I won't call JJD for another day or so, but I'll have to let them know eventually." She flips him off, then jumps when the message continues, as if he's seen her: "Okay, then." Long pause. "This is Hobbes, over to you."

"Kelsey," her mother calls. "Is that you? Are you home?

Kelsey quietly opens the fridge, takes out the second half of the bologna sandwich she couldn't finish two days ago, and slips out the back door. The fog is so heavy their old lichen-encrusted apple tree drips as if it's raining. She sits on the back step, shoulders hunched, and nibbles at the sandwich. After the third bite, she gags, spits it into her hand and throws it and the rest of the sandwich into the yard for the ravens to find.

She wishes she knew what to do. Where to go. She considers running away, but to where, to what? Wouldn't her aunt in Nebraska be thrilled to have a thirteen-year-old juvenile delinquent show up on her doorstep?

Kelsey goes inside, tiptoes down the hall, past her mother's room to the bathroom. There must to be something in the medicine cabinet that can help her sleep again.

She finds Vick's vapor rub, her mother's thyroid medication, her Lithium, and a bottle of Valium with an expiration date of March 2012. Seven years old. She holds the bottle in her hand and tries to imagine being dead. She sees Lauren, cold and blue-lipped, but can't picture herself the same way. She pours the twenty or so tablets into her hand. They're yellow with vee-shaped holes in the center. How sweet of the drug manufacturer to produce pills you can kill yourself with that look like tiny little valentines. At least her mother isn't hooked on prescription drugs, too.

·   ·   ·   ·   ·

Josh calls Tuesday afternoon. "They're cremating her today. The funeral is tomorrow at four."

Kelsey listens to the message a second time, then deletes it. She runs down the hall and closes her door just as her mother comes out of the bathroom.

Lydia crosses the hall and taps on her door. "Kelsey?"

Kelsey backs into her closet and holds her breath until she hears her mother move away. She throws on jeans and a sweatshirt, opens her window, and crawls out.

At the far end of the Rose Memorial Cemetery, a lone man works with a post-hole digger, pulling dirt from a small, round hole.

"Excuse me," Kelsey says. "Do you know where they cremate—?"

"Right there." He jerks his head toward a small building behind the cemetery's office. Heat waves and dark smoke rise from its chimney. "I'm sick of digging graves for young people," he says. "What's with you kids? You all seem to have a death wish. Drugs, booze, driving fast like you have some place important to be." He shakes his head, raises his arms, and brings the post-hole digger down with all his strength.

The man's truck is parked on the path. In the bed is a roll of fake green grass, a pile of folding chairs, and the yet-to-be assembled parts of a canopy. This is to be Lauren's grave, small and round, the size of an urn.

For a long time, Kelsey sits at the base of a eucalyptus tree and watches the smoke rise. At first, she feels sickened, especially when the unmistakable smell of hair and flesh burning reaches her. For two more hours, she keeps Lauren company through this part of her journey, plucking blades of grass, and releasing them. The smoke eventually turns white and a breeze molds and shapes it into a graceful line, like a genie escaping a bottle. There's a certain freedom, she thinks, in being smoke, at the beck and call of the wind.

She watches until the last wisps disappear and only the smell of eucalyptus remains before getting to her feet. She walks her bike onto the path, takes a deep breath of the air Lauren is now part of, and starts for home.

CHAPTER 16

Kelsey gets up late Wednesday morning, showers for the first time in three days, and dresses. She hears Lydia in the kitchen, then her footsteps coming down the hall. There's only the sound of her mother breathing on the other side of the door for a full minute before she knocks. "I'm fixing French toast. Do you have time to eat before you go to school?"

Kelsey stands with her forehead pressed to the door's cool wood. Tears run down her cheeks. "Momma," she whispers. "Lauren's dead."

Her mother knocks again. "Are you in there?" She jiggles the knob. Kelsey keeps it from turning by pressing down on it with her full weight.

"What's going on? Why don't you answer me?"

Kelsey flings open the door. Her mother pitches in and lands sprawled at the foot of Kelsey's bed.

"When I need you, you're drunk, that's what's going on."

Lydia pushes herself upright. "How dare you talk to me like that. I'm your mother."

"Which only makes it worse." Kelsey runs from the room and out of the house. She wheels her bike out of the garage and jumps on. The funeral is an hour away so she rides aimlessly, twice passing Lauren's house on Alder Street without consciously seeking it out.

At 3:30, students begin to arrive at the cemetery in small clumps. At first, no one pays any attention to Kelsey, slouched under the same Bishop pine from which she watched the gravedigger. A couple of girls glance at her over their shoulders and whisper, but most seem stunned, quietly lost in their own grief. Chairs begin to fill, except the front ones reserved for family. A yellow ribbon curls around the tops of each back rest.

Josh spots her and comes at her like something to cling to in a flash flood. He throws his arms around her and weeps against her shoulder, which makes Kelsey uncomfortable. "Everyone's staring, Josh."

"I don't care."

"Shush." Kelsey pats his back and whispers against his ear. "Don't let them see you doing this. Lauren wouldn't want you to cry."

"She accepted me, Kelsey. I was an okay person to her."

"I know." Kelsey can't break his grip. "Let go, Josh."

He steps back. "Sorry."

"Don't be. I locked myself in my room for three days and cried so much there are no tears left. She accepted me, too."

"Are you gay?"

"No!" Kelsey says it sharply and regrets the way it comes out. "I steal and lie."

"At least you can change."

"And you can accept yourself."

"My father disowned me, and my mother takes me to a shrink."

"Well, my father left us and my mother's a drunk." The contest to prove who's more miserable makes her smile.

"Could we stay friends?" Josh says.

"Sure, we can."

She notices people whispering, heads tilted toward one another. By the glances, Kelsey thinks they are passing along the information that she, too, was in the car. She can easily imagine they probably think she is the one who should have died instead of Lauren. She agrees. The right to life should be granted on merit. Kelsey will never live up to the promising one Lauren lost.

Silence falls and heads turn. Mr. and Mrs. Wells, with Lauren's brother, Harrison, between them, have stepped out of a black SUV. Other relatives—probably aunts and uncles, nieces, and nephews—exit cars parked behind the limousine and follow them toward the front row of chairs.

Kelsey's stomach begins to roil. "I can't do this," she says to Josh.

"Can't do what?"

"Stay. Listen to some feel-good bull crap about Lauren being with God." Kelsey pulls her hand free of Josh's, slips around to the back side of the tree, and starts to run. Two blocks past the Food Bank, she's stopped by a chain link fence and a row of giant eucalyptus trees so dense she can only glimpse Pudding Creek. Kelsey grips the wire and presses her forehead to the backs of her hands. She is oddly comforted knowing Gen is over there, on the other side of the creek, waiting for her.

•   •   •   •   •

Kelsey returns to school on Thursday. In the hallway announcement case is a big picture of Lauren, framed with swags of black crepe paper. The table beneath it holds a vase of Calli lilies, a picture of Jesus, a hand-colored printout of the 23rd Psalm, and a guest book with pages and pages of tributes: *You were the sister I never had; Math isn't the same with you gone; This is so wrong;* Beneath that someone wrote, but didn't sign, *I hope Brie rots in hell. The wrong person died,* appears over and over. Kelsey suspects they could be referring to her as well as to Brie.

She feels the same. If one of them had to die, it shouldn't have been Lauren. But wishing, hoping, praying for a different outcome will change nothing. Brie's father will probably fix this, but nothing he does can ever fix Brie. She'll have to live her life knowing she killed her best friend. Kelsey can't imagine a hell worse than that.

In her classes, just like at the funeral, kids look at her and whisper. She sees one point out the butterfly bandage over the stitches on Kelsey's forehead to the girl seated next to her, but Kelsey doesn't hear what she says, about it or about her. She imagines it's snarky. No one does what Lauren would have done: hug her and say she's sorry.

•   •   •   •   •

After school on Thursday, Kelsey rides her bike to the greenhouse. She hasn't cried for days, but when Gen waddles out to meet her, she drops her bike and kneels. Just as he'd done that first day, he hops onto her lap, puts his front paws around her neck, and squeezes. This hug does her in. Tears erupt. She buries her face in his fur and holds tight. When she opens her eyes, Dr.

Hobbes stands in the greenhouse doorway. She puts Gen down, wipes her eyes with the heels of her hands, and gets up. "Did you turn me in?"

"I did not." He turns and enters the greenhouse.

She follows. "How come? You could have gotten this over with for both of us." She really doesn't mean that. This place feels more like a refuge than ever.

He stops and looks at her. "Is that how you feel?"

"Don't you?" Rather than meet his eyes, she examines the tomato-plant experiments on the table next to where they are standing. An orange dodder tendril has wormed its way through the pinhole in the side of the box and its creepy tip is wrapped around the cotton ball Hobbes soaked in the slurry of tomato leaves. The seed under the glass dome has grown straight and is pressed against the glass like a trapped animal. Even creepier, the third seedling sprouted inside a dark box. A single orange tendril had found its way down the length of the straw and into the plastic milk jug, where it has driven an orange spike into the tomato's stem.

She feels Hobbes watching her, and he hasn't answered her question. Out of the corner of her eye, she sees him smile.

"Well?" she says.

"No, I don't feel that way." He looks at Gen instead of Kelsey. "I read in today's paper there was an accident last Saturday. Did you know the girls?"

"I was in the car." Her voice cracks. "The one who died was my best friend."

"Was she the drunk kid driving, or the other one?"

Kelsey's fists knot. "The other one. She was thirteen."

"What would your friend say to see you moping around?"

"I don't know what she'd say. That's what dead means. I'll never get to talk to her again."

He's picking at the electrical tape around his broken fingers. His voice softens. "I'm sorry for your loss."

She feels the sting of tears, but refuses to let him see that even his lame expression of sympathy gets to her. "Put it in a card and mail it to me." She spins and heads for the door.

"I logged your hours as if you'd been here," Hobbes calls after her.

"Thanks for nothing." She reaches the outside and starts to run. She blindly runs past where she dropped her bike and has to go back for it. She glances over her shoulder as she rides away and sees him watching from under the rose arbor. Tears stream into her ears, but she's too proud to turn around.

CHAPTER 17

Kelsey quits going to the greenhouse. She can't stand to be around that sneering, smelly old man. All she wants to do is crawl under the covers and sleep the pain away.

Every day she expects the witch from Juvenile Justice to knock on the door, but no one comes. She wonders why Hobbes hasn't turned in, but by week two, she quits worrying about it. If she comes, she comes. How different could Juvie be from the prison she's locked into every night? At least there she won't be responsible for her mother. She might even make friends with kids more like her. Look what being a good person got Lauren.

•   •   •   •   •

Brie never returns to school. It's rumored she's been sent to live with an aunt in Pleasanton.

Josh is like gum on Kelsey's shoe. He meets her for lunch every day, saves her a seat in the three classes they have together, and calls her every night. Kelsey tries to be like Lauren for him, but he wants to talk about every single wonderful moment of his and Lauren's friendship while Kelsey wants to forget. She begins to resent his neediness the way she does her mother's.

Lydia apparently forgot the fight they had the morning of Lauren's funeral. She never mentions it and Kelsey doesn't either. Why bother? Her mother never met Lauren. Worse, Lydia read the story of the accident in same newspaper Hobbes did—even asked Kelsey if she knew who the girls were, since it only mentioned their ages, not her name or Brie's. Lydia didn't even remember that Lauren Wells—the only one named—was her daughter's best friend.

•   •   •   •   •

During the fourth week in October, two weeks after Lauren died, Fort Bragg has its first serious rain. The San Francisco weather people keep on and on about how it might mean the seasonal "storm door" has opened early.

On Sunday morning, two days after the storm, Kelsey rides her bike to Rose Memorial Cemetery to sit with Lauren. The grass around her grave has been worn down to hard ground, and the grave itself is littered with fading, water-logged, stuffed animals, and grief-stricken notes from Lauren's friends sealed in Ziplocs to keep the ink from running. Her Hispanic friends have brought religious candles and prayers written in Spanish.

Kelsey's Ziploc is there, too. Every time she comes to visit, she reads the new notes aloud to Lauren, and adds a few lame words to her own plastic bag . . . *here to say hi. Miss you, Kels,* and the date.

This morning, Kelsey finds a new note. It must have been left yesterday because the bag is dry and the ink fresh: *Hi Lauren, It's me, Brie. I don't live in Fort Bragg anymore. Everyone here hates me. I suppose you hate me, too. That's okay; I hate myself. I just came to say I'm sorry. My parents are getting a divorce. Mom wants to move to Pleasanton, where I live with my nightmare aunt, and Dad can't 'cause of work, so they're breaking up. I've ruined their lives, too. I'd crawl in there with you, if I could. Someone left a ton of roses. They're pink. No note, but I guess you know stuff like that now.*

Kelsey wants to tear it to shreds, but she doesn't. The roses Brie mentioned have bowed their heads and are turning brown. There are fourteen of them, probably from Lauren's parents, for what would have been her fourteenth birthday on October 19th.

Josh calls that night as usual, and Kelsey tells him about Brie's note.

"I'm glad she's miserable," he says. "I've wished a thousand times that she was buried in there instead of Lauren."

Kelsey doesn't answer. Wishing Brie dead won't change anything, and Brie's life might as well be over. She'll probably end up like Lydia. That thought makes Kelsey wonder *why* her mother drinks. Her drinking has been a part of Kelsey's life for as long as she can remember, but it never occurred to her to question the reason. Maybe she killed someone.

"Kelsey?"

"I'm here. Hey, Josh, remember that elephant Lauren was trying to win at Denny's?"

"Yeah."

"Let's go tomorrow and play that game until we get it for her, okay?"

"Don't you have to work?"

"Time off for good behavior."

"Then sure. What time?"

Josh waits for her in the alcove. "It's not there anymore," he says when she comes in.

"Damn." Kelsey looks for herself. "Safeway has one of these Toy House machines. Let's go there. I need change anyway."

Kelsey gets two dollars in quarters from a surly Safeway checker and Josh, in line behind her, gets another two dollars' worth.

"Next time you have to be a customer," the checker says.

"I am a customer," Kelsey says. "I'm just not buying anything today."

There's no elephant in the Safeway Toy House machine either.

"The bunny is cute," Josh says.

"No, it has to be an elephant. Besides, she's got a bunny." Kelsey kicks the machine. "Let's try the one in the Company Store."

At the Company Store, there's a really ugly purple elephant, but it's in the right rear corner of the glass case, under a blue bear.

The timed operation gives them fifteen seconds for fifty cents. When the joystick moves the claw over the blue bear, Kelsey pushes the red button. She completely misses the bear and only bumps it into a more secure position on top of the elephant on the second try.

"This is a big, fat rip-off," she says.

"Let me try," Josh says.

He snags the bear on the first try, but time runs out as he tries to move it to the chute for the win.

"What are you doing? You're not trying to win the stupid bear, are you?"

"Why not? We've spent $2.50 trying to get it."

"Geez. Let me do it." She knocks him aside with her hip.

Kelsey whoops when she gets the elephant by the trunk, but swings the claw too fast toward the chute. "Dammit. How much money do we have left?"

Josh opens his palm. "Fifty cents."

"Go to the Cookie Company and get some quarters."

"I don't have any more money."

"Look in my wallet." She turns so he could unzip her backpack.

"You look and let me try. I'm better at this than you are."

"What makes you think so?" Kelsey says.

"I just am."

While Kelsey fishes around in the bottom of her backpack, Josh wiggles his fingers and pops his knuckles.

Kelsey smacks him. "Just do it." She opens her palm. Two quarters and a dime."

"That's it?"

"That's it."

"Okay," Josh says, "you put the money in, that way I won't waste seconds getting hold of the joystick."

"Okay. Say when."

Josh bends his knees and grabs the joystick. "Now."

Kelsey drops the quarters into the slot. Josh swings the claw into the elephant's corner and pushes the red button. The claw closes over the elephant's head.

Kelsey hops from foot to foot.

The elephant dangles from the claw as Josh maneuvers it toward the chute. The closer he gets, the faster he tries to move it. The elephant swings wildly and slips out.

Kelsey hits his arm. "Why'd you drop it?"

"I didn't mean to." Tears swim. "I was trying as hard as I could."

Kelsey hugs him. "I'm sorry. I know you were. I'll get some more money, and we'll try again tomorrow."

·   ·   ·   ·   ·

Josh lives two miles away in a house on Todd's Point that probably has a view of the ocean from nearly every window. Kelsey lives in the shabby side of town. They ride off in opposite directions, turning once to wave goodbye.

Kelsey told Josh she'd get money and try again tomorrow, but there's no money left to get. She already blew her self-established allowance behind the letter "A" in the recipe box trying to win one ugly elephant.

Once Josh is out of sight, she turns north on Franklin, and rides straight to the Coast-to-Coast hardware store, where she locks her bike to the railing near the rear entrance. She cuts through the hardware store and out onto Main Street. The Spunky Skunk toy store is midway up the block. She's going to get Lauren the one thing she wanted most in the world, and she's going to get it today. With no schoolbooks in her backpack, there's plenty of room for a nice elephant, instead of the crappy one in that thieving Toy House machine. Kelsey takes off her backpack before entering the store, and carries it low.

"May I help you?" The clerk's a short woman encased by counters on three sides, all of which are piled high with displays of stickers and keychains. Kelsey has to find a gap to see who asked the question.

"I'm just looking," she says. "My little sister's birthday is next week and I'm trying to get an idea of what I can afford."

The clerk nods and smiles, but eyes Kelsey with suspicion. "Let me know if you have questions."

"I will, thank you."

Kelsey wanders the store, picking up and looking at dolls, a few wooden puzzles, a finger-paint set, all the time drifting toward the back room which is filled floor to ceiling with stuffed animals. She enters, wondering how they keep from being robbed blind, buried as that woman is behind card racks and display units. As nonchalantly as possible, she locates the camera above the door.

Take your time, she cautions herself.

She figures there's a blind spot directly beneath the camera, so she leaves her backpack, unzipped, near the door. She circles the room looking at and handling a dozen animals. When she spots the smoky gray elephant with a wrinkled brow and sad, worried eyes, she avoids touching it. Instead, she reaches for a giraffe on the shelf above it and knocks the elephant and a couple of its shelf-mates off with her elbow. She overcomes the strong temptation to look at the camera as she carefully replaces all but the elephant, which she kicks closer to her pack. From this room, she can't see the clerk. She goes to the doorway. "Do you gift wrap?" she calls.

The clerk moves into view. She's out from behind the counter and in the aisle with another customer. "Yes," she says. "Any purchase over ten dollars."

"Thanks."

The clerk pauses then turns back to the customer.

Kelsey snatches the elephant and jams it into her backpack. Her heart romps around inside her rib cage, making her feel giddy enough to laugh out loud. Carrying the backpack low, she goes down the aisle on the far side a series of card display racks—mostly out of view of the clerk. She stops and pretends to look at a couple of cards. "I found a couple of cute things in there, but she's also into being a princess, so I can't decide."

"We have wands," the clerk says, but she isn't looking at Kelsey. She's looking up.

Kelsey follows her gaze. She hadn't noticed there was a second floor. A giant, stuffed black bear is attached to the railing as if midway into a suicide attempt. A woman stands behind it with a phone to her ear.

Kelsey feels her throat close. "I'll be back." She says as calmly as she can. "I still have a week." She walks slowly toward the front door and resists glancing up at the woman. She knows they have her. The elephant's zipped inside her pack; too late to put it back. They'll have her cold whether she's still in the store or walks through the doorway. The clerk goes into the stuffed animal room. Kelsey's sure she's only pretending to straighten up, and is really looking for what's missing. Kelsey examines a model train near the front door, crosses her fingers, and steps outside. No bells, whistles or buzzers go off. She looks both ways. No cops. She walks casually for a few yards, then takes off running. She slows at the hardware store's front entrance, goes in, and walks slowly through to the back door.

She sees Jerry Curtis' patrol car when she steps outside. It's parked, with its lights flashing, on the far-left side of the parking lot. He's leaning against the hood with his arms crossed over his chest.

"Hey there, Kelsey." He smiles. "I thought this was your bike."

CHAPTER 18

"Hi Jerry. Whatcha ya doing—?"

He drops his arms and comes toward her. "Got you on video this time, kiddo."

For once in her life, Kelsey thinks she might faint. "It's. . .it's a present for Lauren's grave."

"Well, it's commendable that you never steal anything for yourself. Turn around."

"What for?"

"Turn around."

When she does, Jerry lifts off her backpack and unzips it. "Nice elephant." His radio squawks. He pushes the button on the microphone attached to a strap on his shoulder. "Tell the owner I've got her."

"Hold your hands out, Kelsey."

"You're going to handcuff me?"

People coming out of the hardware store stop to watch.

"Yep. I'm giving you the full treatment today." He slaps a cold metal cuff on each wrist.

Kelsey's nose is running. She tries to wipe it on her shoulder.

Jerry's eyes soften a little. He takes out his handkerchief and holds it to her nose. "Blow."

She's sobbing as Jerry puts his hand on the top of her head and guides her into the squad car. The fiberglass seat is hard and cold against her back.

"I'm coming in with a 488 with priors," Jerry says into his radio. "Juvenile. Kelsey McCully. M-C-C-U-L-L-Y."

"Jerry, please let me go. I promise on a stack of Bibles, I'll never steal another thing. We tried to win her an elephant from that machine at the Company Store but we ran out of money."

Jerry's eyes are framed by the rearview mirror. "Kelsey. There's no talking your way out of this one. The judge warned you. I warned you."

"Where are you taking me?"

"I'm going to have to book you, Kelsey."

"Oh my God, Jerry. Please don't do that. I promise. One more chance. Please."

There are four stop signs between the hardware store and the police station at the south end of Franklin Street. At every one of them, Jerry waves the other cars through, as if giving everyone plenty of time to stare at her in the backseat, sobbing in big, disgusting gulps.

At the station, Jerry pulls around back into a large parking lot filled with police cars. He backs in next to a windowless white van. He waits to open his door while another officer loads a man with cuffed hands and shackled ankles into the cramped forward section of the partitioned van. Once inside and seated on the narrow, gray padded bench, the man's knees touch the floor to ceiling metal divider that separates him from the driver.

Jerry turns to look at Kelsey through the steel mesh between his seat and hers. "That'll be your transport to Juvenile Hall."

She starts to tremble and though she's only been to church once—a Sunday after Lauren died—she silently prays he's only trying to scare her.

Without removing the handcuffs, Jerry leads her toward a building at the rear of the station. Before going inside, he locks his gun and holster in one of a half dozen compartments, like post office boxes, attached to the wall next to the door.

As if this is a class field trip, Jerry explains, "We don't carry our weapons into the interrogation room." He unlocks the steel door and guides her inside, then takes her elbow and marches her the length of the short hallway to the computer where he makes her stand to one side while he types in her name and address.

After he fills out the form on the screen, he removes the handcuffs and places her hands one at a time on the thing that looks like a Xerox machine to scan her palm-prints. He then moves her hands to a smaller pane of glass and rolls each finger individually. "Only the latest technology for you, Miss McCully—ink-free fingerprints."

She tries to pull away, but his grip is iron. "Jerry, please let me go." She squeezes her legs together to keep from peeing.

Jerry ignores her struggles, finishes the fingerprints and, with a painful grip on her upper arm, leads her back down the hall to a small room. Inside is a desk, a computer, and two chairs, one of which is bolted to the floor. Next to it, on the wall at hip level, is a thick metal railing. Jerry makes her sit and lifts her right wrist.

Kelsey starts to cry again. "I won't move, I promise."

"Sorry, kiddo. No exceptions." He unlocks the cuff on her right hand, snaps it to the railing, and gives it a sharp tug.

"Jerry, please. I swear on my grandmother's grave, I'll never take another thing."

"Look at the camera." He points to the far upper corner.

She glances up and is blinded by a flash of light.

"Wait here." Jerry grins at his little joke. He walks back to where he fingerprinted her. From where she sits, Kelsey watches him take the wrinkled-brow, sad-eyed, elephant from her backpack. He glances over his shoulder and holds it up. "The evidence." He pulls a length off a roll of plastic bags like the ones in the grocery store for fruit and vegetables, only thicker, puts the elephant inside, heat-seals both ends, then places the elephant inside a door in a line of small wooden doors.

He comes back carrying a stack of folders.

Kelsey's gone numb, but tears keep coming, as if she's sprung a leak. Jerry hands her his still damp handkerchief and rifles through the folders on the table between them. She uses her uncuffed hand to wipe her eyes and blow her nose. He makes a neat pile of the papers he's taken from each file, creating a bouquet of colors: pink, pale blue, yellow, light green. Then he waits, watching her.

"Do what you're going to do," Kelsey says. "What are you waiting for?"

He nods and takes a card from his shirt pocket. "I'm going to Mirandize you, so listen up." He smiles. "You have the right to remain silent. You have the right to an attorney . . ."

When he finishes and asks if she understands. Kelsey nods. "It was just an elephant," she croaks, her voice hoarse from crying.

"It's not the value of the item taken, Kelsey, it's the number of offenses. If you were an adult, you'd have three strikes. A felon with two priors can shoplift a loaf of bread and be sent away for twenty-five years. That's the law." He puts the Miranda card back in his pocket. "So, you're clear on your rights, is that correct?"

She nods, then hiccups.

The top form is pink. "I have a Mendocino County Juvenile Referral questionnaire here. There are fifteen questions. Are you ready?" He starts without waiting for an answer.

The first four are questions he already knows the answer to: "What is your full name? How old are you? Where do you go to school? What grade are you in?"

Kelsey mumbles answers.

"Do you know the difference between doing something that is right and doing something that is wrong?"

"Of course, I do," she says.

He writes that down and goes on without comment.

"Tell me something you know is wrong to do."

"Stealing is wrong."

"Tell me something you know is right to do."

"Paying for stuff."

It goes on like that for a few more questions, then he asks: "Do your parents punish you for doing something they have told you is wrong?"

"I don't *have* parents."

Jerry records her answer and reads on. "Have your parents told you it is wrong to steal?"

"You're not listening to me. I don't have parents. I don't have anyone who cares what I do." Kelsey struggles to pull her hand free of the handcuff. "Don't you get it," she screams. "There's no one."

Jerry watches. When she gives up, he continues with the questions.

"Have your parents told you it is wrong to steal? Do you think it is wrong to steal? Why is it wrong to steal? Do you want to do what you know is right? Do you avoid doing what you know is wrong?"

Kelsey continues to hiccup and mumble answers: "Yes. Yes. Because it is. Yes. Yes."

Jerry signs the form, shuffles it to the bottom and goes on to the next: Fort Bragg Police, Department Juvenile Detention Record. "This is the last one. I'm required to advise you that you will be detained in this facility no more than six hours."

Kelsey leans forward and puts her forehead on the table. *Six hours, six months. Whatever.* Then jumps when Jerry pushes back in his chair. He comes around the desk and unlocks the handcuff. "Come with me."

They cross the hall to another steel door. Near the top is a small window of double-paned glass with a wire mesh core. When he opens it, Kelsey gasps, "Oh, no." She grabs the doorframe.

"I'm sorry. I really am. You're better than this, Kelsey, I don't see why you think you have to steal things for people." He pulls her fingers loose, puts his hand on her back, and presses her forward into the concrete room.

"Please let me wait in the office. Handcuffed even. I don't mind."

"No can do, kiddo." He gives her a gentle shove.

She turns, pleadingly.

Jerry's eyes soften. "It's your future you're throwing away, Kelsey." He shuts the door and turns the key.

Kelsey batters the door with her fists, gives up, and sobs with her forehead against the cold steel. When she turns, she keeps her back pressed to the door. A long stone bench runs the length of the concrete cell. There's a small, barred window that she could only see out of if she stood on the bench. On the right, a shoulder-high wall blocks her view of the rest of the room, which reeks of urine.

A forgotten prisoner could be hiding there. She begins to tremble. "Hello?" Her voice bounces off the walls. At least her hiccups are gone.

She stays backed against the door listening for any sound but her own breathing. Her heart pounds as she edges along the bench to where she can see what's on the other side of the wall: a stainless sink and toilet. In the center of the floor is a drain hole. She's desperate to pee, and eyes the toilet. The floor around the drain is stained and still looks wet. *That man in the van.* She stays close to the wall and circles to the sink. The floor around the toilet is so sticky her flipflops snap and slap her heels. Kelsey rolls her pant legs up to keep the hems from touching the floor, takes her pants down, and squats over the seat-less, lidless, steel bowl.

She sits on the bench with her back pressed into the corner where two walls meet, draws up her legs to her chest, and wraps her arms around her knees. In spite of being cold and hungry, and exhausted from crying, she dozes off with her cheek on her knees.

It's nearly dark when she hears keys jangle. She looks up and sees a policewoman's face at the window in the door. The woman opens it and steps inside. Her nose crinkles at the smell. "I can release you into an adult custody, but I only get a busy signal at your house. The operator says there's no conversation. Do you have someone else we can call to come get you?"

Kelsey shakes her head.

"Who shall I call then?"

Kelsey shrugs. Her mother's either taken the phone off the hook to stop the spam calls, or answered the phone, or hasn't hung up properly. She's done both before. By now, Lydia must be passed out in her chair. "There's no one else."

The woman turns to leave.

"No, wait." Kelsey launches herself off the bench. "Dr. Hobbes. Jonathan Hobbes. I don't know his number, but he lives on Pudding Creek."

After the policewoman leaves, Kelsey's left to wonder why, of all people, she thinks he might help her.

It's dark when the policewoman returns and unlocks the door again. "You've been signed out. Come with me."

As Kelsey follows her across the parking lot, she inhales the cool, clean evening air. Nothing has ever smelled more wonderful. Inside the station, the woman points down the hall toward the door to the street. "He said he'd meet you out front."

"Did he have to pay anything to get me out?"

"No. He only had to guarantee your appearance in court."

Dr. Hobbes is parked in front of the station in his rusting, old pick-up truck with the engine running. "Sorry," he says when she finally gets the passenger door unstuck and climbs in. "I had trouble getting the engine to turn over. Once I got it started, I was afraid to turn it off."

"Thanks for coming to get me."

"Sure."

"I would have shown back up eventually."

He acts like he hasn't heard her. "Where do you live?" Gears grind as he tries to find first gear.

"On Maplewood."

In front of her house, he catches her hand as she starts to get out. "I'm the only chance you have left, Kelsey. I've put an hour a day down on your form for every day you missed, so you owe me. I'll see you tomorrow, won't I?"

"Yes, sir."

"Promise?"

She nods.

"Kelsey."

"Uh huh?"

"It's not going to stop until you wise up."

"What's not gonna to stop?"

"The problems you're having."

"Not all of them are my fault."

"Then stop compounding things by making bad decisions." He looks past her at the house. "Isn't it hard enough living with what you're living with without making matters worse. Can't you see that?"

She shrugs. "I guess." Does he really know what her life is like?

"Feed the good, Kelsey, starve the bad."

Like a head cold, she thinks.

She's nearly to the door when he finds first gear. As his truck bucks away, backfiring every few yards, she wonders why he didn't ask what she'd done this time.

CHAPTER 19

It never occurs to Kelsey to wake her mother and tell her about the arrest. Why would she? Lydia will make it about herself—God punishing her for being a bad mother. Lydia's solution: make a stronger drink and beg Kelsey to tickle her feet.

The next day, to Kelsey's surprise, she can't wait to get to the greenhouse and hates the feeling. So he bailed her out. A thank you should be enough, not this urge to ride there as fast as her old bike will allow. When she turns down the driveway and sees Gen coming at her like a black and white bowling ball, she bursts into tears. He's what she needs. She drops her bike, scoops him up, and buries her nose in the soft fur of his neck. He rubs his chin against hers and rumbles.

"Come say hello to Phil, too." Dr. Hobbes stands in the greenhouse doorway as Kelsey crosses under the arbor with Gen in her arms. "He's as excited to see you as Gen is."

Kelsey rolls her eyes.

"Think I'm crazy, huh? What time do you have?"

She looks at her mother's old Timex. "3:45."

"Come here." He crooks a finger for her to follow him into the bunker. He picks up the running strip of paper. "See this."

The lines are the usual relaxed pinking-shear shape up to a point where they become jerky. In pencil, Hobbes had written *3:39*, opposite the raggedy part. "That's when Gen ran out to meet you."

"Why did that make the lie detector react?"

"It didn't. It recorded Phil's being 'startled'"—he makes air quotes— "by Gen's reaction to your arrival." He nods toward the tangle of wires attached to the philodendron's leaves.

"You're certifiable, you know that?" Kelsey smiles, so he'll know she's kidding.

"A lot of people would tend to agree," he says, with a hint of a smile himself. "However, you're mistaken, and so are they."

"How can you expect me to believe Gen startled a plant?"

"Remember the mimosa?"

"Yeah. It got over being scared of—" She looks at him. "Okay, but how?"

"Plants produce electrical or chemical signals. In order to register on the polygraph, the signal has to be electrical. Beyond that, I'm not sure."

He's obviously been working on repotting a fuchsia on the potting table where the tomato experiments had been. He's packing dripping-wet sphagnum moss around the inside of a new basket.

"What happened with the tomatoes?"

"Dodder is parasitic, remember? It 'smelled'"—air quotes again "out the tomato, attached itself, and sucked it dry. I burned the lot of them."

Gen lifts his chin to encourage Kelsey to keep stroking it. "Is that what you were expecting?"

"It was."

"Well, you'll never convince me a potted plant reacted to Gen." She kisses the cat's cheek and puts him down.

"Doubt is good." Hobbes scoops potting soil into a new fuchsia basket, then glances at her. Kelsey sees either sadness or pity in his watery, blue eyes, she isn't sure which. "Gen loves you, and you love Gen. Human emotions create an energy field and emit a chemical odor. Have you ever heard that dogs can smell fear on people?"

"Yes. But I don't believe any of this other woo-woo stuff." Kelsey absently plucks yellow leaves and dead flowers from the fuchsia.

"If our emotions are detectable, we can assume the emotions of other animals are, too. Gen may have known you were here because you sent out an emotionally charged signal. Just because we don't understand the mechanism, doesn't mean other living organisms can't also detect these chemical signals. Plants respond to external hormones called pheromones. They emit them, too. Maybe Phil picked up on Gen's response to seeing you, or, maybe—" he smiles, "he has his own crush on you. Who can say?"

Hobbes runs a knife around the edge of the fuchsia to loosen it from the sides of its old pot. He lifts it out, exposing a tight mass of roots, and uses the knife to make four deep slits into the fuchsia's root ball.

"Why are you doing that?" She drops the dead leaves on the ground.

He mock-slaps her hand away. "The dead bits go in the compost. And I'm breaking up the root to expose them to fresh soil. If I don't, the roots will stay bound together." Then, without looking at her, he says, "Have you ever stolen a book?"

"Are you gonna start being mean to me again?"

"No. I'm being nosy. You might not believe this, but I think you are a pretty smart cookie and I wonder if you ever stole anything educational?"

"The answer is no."

He shrugs, puts the knife down, and steps into his bunker. He opens a drawer beneath his computer, and returns carrying a box from Amazon. "I ordered these for you."

She shakes the box. "What's in it?"

"Books." He settles the fuchsia into its new basket and begins to fill in around the root ball with some of the potting soil Kelsey mixed.

"What are they about?"

"I'm going to let you find that out when you get curious enough to open the box."

"I don't know why you'd buy me a present."

"It's not really a present."

"What do you call it then?"

He hesitates. "One is a copy of the book that re-energized my life. Maybe it will make a difference in yours. The other may answer some of your questions."

Oh brother. "One's not a Bible, is it? We have a Bible."

"Nope. Not a Bible." Hobbes presses down lightly on the soil, then adds more.

"Okay, then." Kelsey puts the Amazon box in her backpack and zips it. "What do you want me to do today?"

He looks disappointed. "Start watering in the orchid house." He shoos her in that direction.

On the back wall of the second greenhouse, above where the hose is coiled over a cleat, is a huge spider web. Spiders give Kelsey the heebie-jeebies. She goes to the storage closet for a broom, and swings at the web, but still can't reach it. She looks around, spots a concrete block, and carries it over to stand on.

"Stop!" Hobbes shouts from next door. "Whatever it is you're about to do, stop." He rushes in, panting. "What were you doing?"

She points at the web. "I hate spiders. I was going to knock it down."

"Where do you get off thinking because you don't like something, you have the right to destroy it? That's where she chose to build her web. That's where she stays."

"Spiders creep me out."

"Apparently, you creeped her out, too." He points.

She looks up. The spider is at the very edge of its web. Kelsey leans back and has to swing her arms to keep from falling off the block.

The spider dashes up the web and into a crack between the roof braces.

"See. She doesn't like you either."

Dr. Hobbes brushes past her and lifts an upside-down clay pot on the bench below the web. Beneath it is a white cardboard container with tiny air holes punched in the lid. "Carlotta, darling," he coos. "Are you hungry?"

Kelsey stands behind him. "You named a spider?"

"Sure, and back off. She's afraid of you."

As Kelsey moves away, a few of the spider's legs appear from beneath the roof brace, then her head, topped by two stalks with dark tips Kelsey guesses are her eyes.

Hobbes roots in the container with two fingers and fishes out a small worm from the flaky red bran. Kelsey recognizes it as the same stuff Lydia, during one of her manic-turn-my-life-around periods, used to sprinkle on her toast in the mornings as a source of roughage. Now she relies on olives and the occasional stalk of celery.

She peers at the bran. "Is that a dried-up slice of potato?"

"It is. The bran is food and the potato is food and moisture." Hobbes flicks the writhing worm into the web like someone discarding a cigarette butt.

The spider runs to the bottom edge of the web, arriving an instant after the worm lands. She grabs it and begins to roll and wrap it in silk. Within seconds, the worm looks like the cotton end of a Q-tip. The spider moves back up the web, turns and watches the worm twitch.

Kelsey edges closer. She looks at Hobbes and grins. "That is so cool."

"It is, isn't it. She's so fast I've never been able to tell if she injects a neurotoxin to paralyze the worm, and then wraps it in silk to keep it from escaping, or if she wraps in silk, and then injects the neurotoxin. Either way, when she's hungry, she'll inject a substance that liquefies its insides, and she'll drink it."

"Yuck."

"No more yucky than a jar of soupy meat baby food."

"If she's poisonous, aren't you afraid she'll show up in a plant or something and bite you?"

"She's not poisonous, she's venomous, but not to humans. She'd only bite to protect herself. It would hurt and itch for a while, that's all."

"How'd you know I was about to knock that web down?"

He smiles. "Phil tattled on you."

Kelsey blinks. "What? I don't believe that."

"Frankly, I don't care whether you believe it or not. I'm telling you he registered alarm and I figured you were up to something destructive."

Hobbes takes the broom away from her and leans it against the potting table. "Come with me." Outside, he points up. "Look how blue the sky is, and the way tree branches move in the breeze."

"So?"

"See the bees on the *Grevillea* and that drop of water on the tip of this hydrangea leaf."

"Okay."

He leans in like he was going to whisper a secret. "This is life, Kelsey, and all of life is our biological kin." Hobbes studies her face. "At least while you are here, consider every living thing family."

CHAPTER 20

Two weeks have passed since her arrest. Maybe it was all to scare her straight and they'll let it go. She begins to relax, then Monday's mail contains the notice of her court date. Next Wednesday, 8:30. That night, Kelsey dreams her hands are cuffed and her ankles shackled. Jerry makes her climb into the van and sit on the narrow, gray padded bench while he attaches her ankle chains to the metal tie-down rings. She cries and pleads. Jerry smiles, sadly, and takes the wilted brown gardenia from behind his badge and hands it to her. The sad-faced elephant, still sealed in the plastic bag, sits on the dashboard, staring at her through the divider. "It can't breathe, Jerry," she sobs. "Please, it can't breathe."

She asks permission to leave the greenhouse early on the Saturday. She's a little surprised Hobbes doesn't ask why. She rides her bike to the Paul Bunyan Thrift store to buy something to wear to court. The last time she went in jeans and a T-shirt. This time she wants to show how seriously she's taking this appearance. The only dress she owns is a years-old church dress from one her mother's upbeat, turning-over-a-new-leaf periods. She stands in the doorway, surveying the racks of clothes and tries to remember how long it has been since she bought anything new for herself. Of course, nothing here is new, only new to her.

The woman behind the counter looks up. "What are you looking for?"

"Something to wear to . . . something like you'd wear to church."

"Try that rack in the far corner."

"Thanks."

Kelsey finds a denim skirt that fits, except it hangs two inches below her knees.

"That's too long on you." The woman comes up behind her. She tilts her head and studies the skirt on Kelsey, then walks to a rack of shirts. She finds a blue and white striped flannel shirt, brings it over and holds it under Kelsey's chin. "What do you think?"

The long skirt and the baggy shirt make her look anorexic. "It's nice," Kelsey says to be polite.

The woman lays the shirt on top of a pile of used shoes. "Lift your arms."

Kelsey holds her arms up, and the woman rolls the waistband of the skirt over twice, which brings the hem up to the middle of Kelsey's knees. "One problem solved. Do you have a T-shirt you could wear untucked?"

She does. It's old, but it's blue. "Yes, ma'am."

"Good." The lady picks up the striped shirt. "You can wear this as a jacket and nobody will be the wiser."

Kelsey feels sure she'll look ridiculous, but the woman's been so kind, she pays the eight dollars for the skirt and shirt, thanks her, and leaves.

On Wednesday, Kelsey rolls the skirt. The Paul Bunyan lady was right. Her blue t-shirt covers the waistband, and the flannel shirt looks nice as a jacket.

"Where are you going all dressed up?" her mother asks when Kelsey wakes her at seven.

There's no way to trick Lydia this time. "You need to get dressed. We have to go to court again."

Her mother's hand goes to her heart. "Why?"

Kelsey places a cup of coffee on her mother's nightstand. "I got arrested for shoplifting."

"Oh my God." Lydia bites her fist. "When?"

"It doesn't matter. Go get dressed. We have to be there in an hour."

"You need to explain yourself, young lady."

Kelsey chooses the nicest, least worn dress from Lydia's closet, and lays it on the foot of her mother's bed. "I'll wait for you in the car."

"You come back here," her mother shouts.

•   •   •   •   •

The smell of liquor and cigarette smoke trail Lydia into the car. And she must have had herself a good cry. She's still sniffling and dabbing her eyes beneath her sunglasses.

Kelsey risks driving them to the courthouse on Franklin Street, since not only is Lydia already too drunk to drive, but still months away from getting her license back. Kelsey occasionally glances at her mother, who stares straight ahead and gnaws the cuticle on her left thumb. Twice she bites off a bit of skin and chews it, jaws flexing. By the time they park on a side street where someone like Jerry is unlikely to see her driving, the cuticle is ragged and bleeding.

Kelsey feels sad and angry at the same time. Her heart's like a rubber band, stretching and expanding with love for the person next to her, then snapping back in disgust. After she parks, she watches her mother's hand shake nervously as she tries to open the car door. *What will happen to you if I go to jail?* Kelsey's heart fills with pity. Then snaps back. *Why do I care?*

•　•　•　•　•

Jerry Curtis testifies first, adding that Kelsey seemed remorseful. The clerk from Spunky Skunk starts her testimony with, "I smelled trouble the minute she walked in." Kelsey goes last and gives the judge the whole story about trying to win a stuffed elephant for Lauren's grave.

When everyone has said their piece, the judge looks down at Kelsey. "According to your JJD report you've been conscientious about doing your community service hours."

Kelsey looks at her feet so her lying eyes don't meet his. "Yes, your Honor."

"But you promised you were never going to appear before me again, didn't you?"

"Yes, your Honor. And I wouldn't have, if—."

"There are no ifs, Miss McCully. You broke that promise. I'm going to keep mine. I hereby sentence you—"

"Your Honor."

Kelsey turns. Dr. Hobbes steps across someone's legs into the center aisle and walks to the railing.

"Who are you, sir?" the judge asks.

"Dr. Jonathon Hobbes, your Honor. I'm the recipient of many of our local delinquents."

"Of course, Dr. Hobbes," the judge says. "It's been a long time."

"May I have a moment, your Honor?"

"Certainly."

"Over the years, I've accepted some good and some not so good kids— mostly the latter. They all have excuses for what they did and rarely, if ever, take responsibility for their crimes. Kelsey here is no better and no worse than most of them."

Out of the corner of her eye Kelsey sees her mother smile and nod as if her daughter has been complimented.

"There's no excuse for what Kelsey did. However, this is the first time I've ever thought one of these kids deserved another chance."

"Why is that?" Judge Lehan says.

"She's different. I don't think for a second she would have shoplifted if she'd had the money to buy her friend the stuffed animal." He glances at Kelsey's mother, who smiles up at him. He looks back at the judge and an exchange takes place only in their eyes. Hobbes continues, "Kelsey needs one person who cares what happens to her—"

There's a barely audible intake of breath from Lydia. Out of the corner of her eye, Kelsey sees her mother bow her head.

"I'm willing to be that person." Hobbes says. "I will take full responsibility for her behavior. If she makes a single misstep, I will deliver her to you myself."

No matter what the judge decides, Hobbes cares what happens to her. Tears erupt, roll down Kelsey's cheeks, and drip onto her hands that have a white-knuckled grip on the back of the seat in front of her. She straightens her shoulders but makes no attempt to stop the tears. Her mother isn't capable, her father's gone, Lauren dead, and Josh is as messed up she is. Maybe Hobbes sees in her whatever Lauren saw. Something worthwhile.

The judge stares at Kelsey for an uncomfortably long time, then down at his own hands. When he looks up again, he levels his gaze at Kelsey over the top of his reading glasses.

Dr. Hobbes stands close enough for Kelsey to take his hand. She wants to, but she remains stick straight as she meets the judge's eyes.

"Miss McCully, you are a lucky young woman. I'm tempted to respect Dr. Hobbes' assessment of your character. He's had more time to know you than the rest of us, but I want to hear what the owner of the Spunky Skunk has to say. She's the one you robbed."

The owner sits directly behind Kelsey. She stands.

Kelsey raises her hand.

"What is it, Miss McCully?" Judge Lehan says.

"Can I say something, your Honor?"

"You may."

Kelsey turns to face the owner of Spunky Skunk. "I want you to know, no matter what, I'm really sorry. You have every right to say no. I won't blame you." She looks at the floor. "I just want you to know I'm sorry." Her heartbeat whooshing in her ears as she turns to face the judge. She closes her eyes.

For a long moment, there's no sound in the courtroom, then her mother begins to softly snore. Everyone turns to look at Lydia, who's fallen asleep with her chin on her chest. Kelsey feels the room fill with disgust—and sympathy. It's becoming hard to tell the difference.

"The toy she stole," the owner says, loudly enough that her mother starts and lifts her head, "was worth less than twenty dollars. If Dr. Hobbes thinks this girl can be saved, I won't argue against giving her another chance."

Kelsey covers her face with her hands.

Her mother looks up at her. "Why are you crying?" Lydia tries to stand.

"Sit," Kelsey says, then hears someone whisper, "Poor kid."

"Miss McCully," Judge Lehan says, "your case is dismissed. JJD will give you the paperwork. There will be no more chances—none—not even if the Governor of California shows up to vouch for you. Is that clear?"

"I promise, your Honor."

"You are free to go."

Kelsey looks for Dr. Hobbes, but he's gone. From outside, she hears his truck backfire.

She turns to the Spunky Skunk owner. "Thank you."

The woman nods. "It wasn't just for you. I did it for myself—a small deposit in my karma bank."

"I don't understand."

She glances at Kelsey's mother. "Your life, my life, everyone's life is tough. If Dr. Hobbes is right about you, and I hope he is, it would have been wrong for me to insist on prosecution. If he's wrong, it will only be worse for you. I have done the right thing for the moment." She squeezes Kelsey's hand. "Good luck. Let me know how you fare, will you?"

Even the clerk pats her hand before she follows the owner into the aisle. "Good luck."

Kelsey nods, and puts her hand on her mother's shoulder. "Time to go, Mom."

CHAPTER 21

Her mother is silent for the first few minutes of the five-minute ride from court back to their house. Kelsey sees Lydia watching her, but still she jumps when her mother speaks. "That went well. And the guy you work for seems nice."

Kelsey guesses by 'went well' her mother means they are headed home instead of to the slammer. "I'm glad you noticed."

"What does that mean?"

"You fell asleep, Mom."

"Maybe I did, maybe I didn't."

Kelsey looks at her mother and nearly runs a stop sign. "You started snoring."

Lydia smiles. "Let's go to lunch to celebrate."

"I don't think our food stamps will cover lunch."

Her mother doesn't flinch. "Well, let's take a drive. You could show me where you're working."

"Some other time. It's a school day, remember?"

"Oh, of course. Okay."

Kelsey pulls into their weed-choked driveway and parks in the garage.

Her mother opens the car door. "I'll fix us something special for dinner. How's that?"

Believe it when I see it. "Fine."

•   •   •   •   •

Riding to school on her bike, Kelsey thinks back to when Lauren was alive. It always embarrassed her to have Lauren find out about the trouble she was in. Kelsey worried that eventually Lauren would move on, and choose friends with whom she had more in common. Now, Kelsey thinks of Lauren as someone who existed on a level she will never achieve. But she's determined to try to be the kind of person she thinks Lauren would have moved toward, not away from.

At school, Josh sits at their same old table in the back of the room. He waves and takes his backpack off the chair he's saved for her. He'd called the day after she stole the elephant to say he'd robbed his mother's change jar and had a fistful of quarters; did she want meet and try again? Kelsey said, "No. Forget it. That elephant was too ugly, anyway." She never told him about stealing one. It's still possible he doesn't know she'd been arrested. The weekly paper doesn't publish the names of juvenile arrests the way they do adults.

Before today, she thought her friendship with Josh had developed out of his need, not hers. Now she isn't so sure. She wants to share with him how scared she'd been in court, and about that disgusting holding cell, but she changes her mind. Starting today, she'll break the routine—establish a new pattern. Instead of focusing on the depressing parts of her day-to-day life, she'll spend more time looking forward to the good bits. She'll try to do better in school, and show more interest in what Hobbes is doing. She might even admit to him that going to the greenhouse *is* the best part of her day. Gen always waits for her by the driveway, and she likes the work, the mindless watering or readying pots for the seeds she pokes into the starter mix, and the anticipation of the first green sprout. Once there, she spends the time dreading going home. Her life circles her mother's needs endlessly, like leaves caught in a whirlpool.

Starting today, she vows to be different. The road she's headed down is no longer a dead end.

That's her mood when she arrives at the greenhouse Wednesday afternoon. Gen meets her in the driveway. Hobbes is in his bunker rewrapping his splayed fingers with electrical tape. Before she can thank him for saving her, he says, "Did you start the book I gave you?"

She'd taken the box out of her backpack and put it someplace but can't remember where. "Not yet. You know, with everything going on. It looks awesome though."

"I'm glad," he says. "I wasn't sure you would be interested in astronomy."

Astronomy? "Well, I might be after I've read your book."

Hobbes snorts. "You haven't even opened the package."

"How do you know?" Then she realizes how he knows. "I figured it was a Bible or something."

"I told you it wasn't a Bible, but if you're not interested enough to open the box—." He goes back to wrapping his fingers.

She's already disappointed him, and he's implying he's pegged her wrong. Yesterday's Kelsey rears up. "I've had a few—" She stops and looks at Gen spread out on Hobbes' desk. His tail flicks. "A few other things on my mind."

If Hobbes notices the change in her tone, he doesn't show it. "You have to move on." He is trying to hold the spool of electrical tape with his teeth, and cut it with the scissors on his Swiss army knife.

Kelsey takes the knife away from him and cuts the tape. "How?"

"You're only thirteen, for God's sake. You've got nothing under your belt. In a few years, you'll be on your own, maybe get married, have a kid or two, or go to college and make something of yourself."

Gen stands and bumps Hobbes' arm. He picks him up and rubs his ear.

She wants to hear something nice out of him. What he hopes lies ahead for her, but she doesn't know how to get more out of him, and if she did, she's not sure what she'd do with a compliment. "I'll never be anything."

"Not if you think like that, you won't."

"How am I supposed to be upbeat and happy with a drunk for a mother, no father, and no friends?"

Hobbes rocks Gen, who's lying on his back like a baby in his arms. "You've got friends."

Some friends: a cat, a wacky old man, and a potted plant. "Lauren was my only real friend. She liked me in spite of what I am."

"What do you think you are?"

"You know."

"No, I don't."

"I'm a liar and a thief."

"That's only if you decide not to change. If you let lying and stealing define your life, then that *will* be who you are."

Kelsey blinks back tears, realizing that she wants him to keep going, to keep talking to her like a father would. "What does being good get you? Lauren was nice. She never stole anything or lied."

"The accident was a random act, Kelsey. The wrong place at the wrong time. She didn't deserve to die. She made a single bad decision. She got into the car with a drunk friend instead of calling her folks to come get her."

"Her parents were at a Giants' game and should one mistake kill you?"

"Sometimes. It's like dodging bullets. It only takes not ducking one of them."

"If it's random, then what's the use?"

"It's about living as well as you can under the circumstances. You're not a hot-house orchid, Kelsey." He gestures at the greenhouse's glass ceiling. "You're being forced—" he hesitates "by circumstances, to nourish yourself, and that's what you have to do—feed yourself, make as many right choices as you can, and your life will improve. Even Lauren's death gives you another opportunity."

"Oh my god. Her dying is supposed to be a learning opportunity?" Kelsey's fists knot and she suddenly wants to break something.

"Relax. She was a kind person and valued you as a friend. You have a chance to prove she was right. Muster your moxie."

"What's moxie?"

"Courage. Perseverance. I know you have that." He smiles, but not in a mean way.

She stares down at her beat-up Nikes, the ones she and Brie stole over a year ago. "Do you believe in karma?"

He shrugs. "I just told you what I believe."

"The Spunky Skunk lady said she let me go because of her karma bank."

"You're a good kid, Kelsey, in spite of what you think. The toy store owner took a chance that I'm right about you."

Gen jumps from Hobbes's arms to the desk, skirts the computer's keyboard, and butts Kelsey with his head. She lifts him and presses her nose into his neck. "Why do you take in kids like me?"

Hobbes picks up a pencil on his desk and puts it the coffee mug with about two dozen others pens and pencils. "Once a teacher, always a teacher, I suppose."

The fact he doesn't look at her makes her think there's more to it than that. "Why did you take a chance on me? That's what I'm trying to understand. Maybe if I understand it, I'll believe it."

"I told you the first day you were here. Gen likes you and his judgment is good enough for me. I always accept his assessment."

"That's not a good enough reason. He's a cat."

"Animals are capable of knowing the human heart. They can perceive threats. Plants can also perceive threats and can warn their neighbors. If Phil and Gen are good with you, so am I.

"Geez." She smacks her forehead. "Quit telling me that plant likes me. I'm asking a serious question."

"Well, then, damn it, read the book I gave you."

•　　•　　•　　•　　•

Before Lauren died, Kelsey asked Hobbes if she could try and root a fuchsia for the pot on their front stoop. He'd seemed pleased that she asked and said sure but, with fall coming, it wasn't likely to take. She'd chosen a white one with purple center. He'd cut off a couple branches and shown her how to remove most of the leaves, leaving a few to photosynthesize. She buried them deep enough in the rich, damp potting soil to cover the nodes left exposed by the leaf removal. Since then, she hadn't given the fuchsia another thought.

The next day, when she arrives, she spots her fuchsia under the glass dome Hobbes used to test the dodder's sense of smell. He's kept it watered and warm. There are new leaves and a single bloom. She blinks back tears.

He smiles when she recognizes it. "It's ready to be repotted, but you should probably wait until it's more established to take it home."

"Thank you," Kelsey says because it is a stronger expression of her gratitude than just thanks.

Later, while she's misting the ferns, Hobbes comes out of his bunker. Her back is to him, so when he says, "Forgive me, Buddy," she turns and sees him snip a leaf off Phil, and go back inside. That tuneless, bing-bongy music is playing on the stereo, but stopped when he clipped Phil's leaf.

"Is that racket my fuchsia singing again?" She grins at her own joke.

He comes to the door. "It's not racket. Remember? The plant is creating electrical impulses between the leaves and its roots. When hooked to the synthesizer, it makes music."

"When it can write the lyrics, I'll be impressed. Right now, it's just racket."

"Umph."

She remembers her vow to act more interested in what Hobbes is doing. She turns off the hose. "So, why'd you apologize to Phil. . . geez, now you've got me acting like that plant's got a brain."

"Because plants can feel. Not feel like an emotional awareness, which would take a brain, but they do perceive physical sensations. I can prove it to you." Hobbes crooks a finger for her to follow him. On the way out of the greenhouse, he opens a drawer under one of the potting tables and takes out a magnifying glass, a long pair of tweezers, and a stopwatch.

In the second greenhouse Kelsey now thinks of as Carlotta's, Hobbes takes the lid off a large aquarium filled with Venus flytraps. "Do you know what these are?"

"Carnivorous plants."

"Well, well." He smiles.

"Why do they eat insects?"

"Because they live in bogs where the soil is notoriously poor, wet, and highly acidic. They meet their nutritional needs by consuming protein in the form of bugs, even small frogs."

Kelsey glances up at Carlotta's web. She's out of hiding and watching them.

"Plants not only feel, they have a form of memory. Look at this." Holding the magnifying glass over one of the flytraps, he uses the tweezers to point to the inside. "See those hairs?"

The aquarium is almost directly under Carlotta's web, so Kelsey moves behind Hobbes and peers over his shoulder. "Yeah."

"An insect that wanders into a Venus flytrap must touch two of them in less than 20 seconds for the trap to close."

"How come?"

"Because it takes a lot of energy to close and if there's not a worthy meal as a reward, it takes a lot of energy to reopen." He touches one of the hairs with the tweezers. Nothing happens.

"Get a couple mealworms out of that container, will you?"

Ick. But she lifts the pot and takes out the cardboard container. Carlotta moves to the very bottom of her web. With one finger, Kelsey stirs the bran until she uncovers a writhing mass of worms.

"Get out a big one for Carlotta and a small one for me. I want to show you something."

She holds out a big fat one in the palm of her hand. "You give it to her."

"Don't be a chicken."

Kelsey tosses it at the web and misses. She finds it behind an orchid pot and tries again. This time it lands nearly dead center, and Carlotta's up her web in a flash.

"Yikes. That's creepy."

"Is not."

Kelsey gives a small worm to Hobbes. He pinches it gently with the tweezers and hands her the stopwatch. "When I touch one of the hairs, you start the timer. Stop it after 20 seconds. Ready?"

She nods. He brushes the little worm against one of the flytrap's two hairs. Heads practically touching, she and Hobbes lean and peer into the aquarium. There's no other sound except the quiet ticking of the stopwatch. "Done," she says.

Hobbes touches the second hair with the worm. Nothing happens.

"I'm beginning to feel sorry for that worm," Kelsey says.

"Some lessons are worth a sacrifice."

"Where's the lesson?"

"Keep your britches on. This time, let's wait 15 seconds. Ready?" He touches a hair. She starts the timer.

"Five. Ten. Done."

Hobbes brushes the worm against the second of the two hairs. The flytrap's two sides snap shut just slowly enough for Hobbes to leave the worm and jerk the tweezers out of the way. "You see?"

Kelsey grins. "It's under-20-second, short-term memory is pretty good. After that it needs Prevagen."

Hobbes actually laughs. "You watch too much TV."

"Don't I know it."

· · · · ·

A little after five, Kelsey pokes her head into the bunker. "I'm about done here. What else do you need me to do?"

He thinks for moment. "Do you have time to wash my truck?"

"Yeah, sure. If you want me to." She grins. "Aren't you worried that the dirt's all that's holding it together?"

He smiles. "I'll risk it. There's soap, a sponge, and a bucket in the little shed with the rakes and shovels."

She finds a dried-up bar of deodorant soap that has cracked open like a walnut, and a stiff, rock-hard sponge. The bucket is in reasonably good repair, but has a broken handle. She puts the soap and sponge in little water to soak until they soften, and entertains herself watching two hummingbirds battle over the rights to a fuchsia full of flowers.

After she finishes washing his truck, she knocks on the bunker door. "I'm done," she says when he opens it.

"Good. Thanks. It's been a while. Maybe its engine will start now that it's clean." "What's that fish with feet named Darwin mean?"

He looks mystified.

"You've got a little plastic fish on the back of your truck. It has feet and Darwin spelled out in the middle."

"Oh that. One of my Berkeley students gave it to me years ago. It's a poke at the Creationist Theory."

"Are they the people who don't believe in evolution?" Maybe to get a rise out of him, or as an excuse to stay and talk, she adds, "I don't believe in evolution either. It's just a theory that we're related to apes."

He gazes at her over the top of his reading glasses. "We're not only related to apes, we're related to zucchini. And as for it being only a theory, so is gravity, my dear, but things still fall down not up."

There's a row of books on the shelf above Hobbes' desk. "It wouldn't kill you to read this either." He takes down a copy of Charles Darwin's *Origin of the Species* and hands it to her. "When Darwin wrote this in 1859, evolution *was* a theory, and long before there was any real understanding of genetics. It's no longer a theory. Evolution means change and over time everything changes. Only a few of the mechanisms of change remain hypothetical."

"Like what?" She holds the book in her lap, picks up her feet, and spins his desk chair.

"Natural selection, for one. You've seen the different rhododendrons I have?"

She nods.

"Most are hybrids. I created them by crossing different colors flowers with one another. That's artificial selection. Pretty much everyone who is in the business of growing things, plants or animals, uses artificial selection. Is it so hard to believe that Mother Nature does the same thing—weeds out the weak, and lets the strongest, or at least the most well adapted survive? Over time, through generations, species become better suited to their environment because the most adapted individuals survive to pass on their improved genetic traits. Adapt or die and disappear."

"Like dinosaurs?"

"Dinosaurs were very successful. Their extinction was more likely cataclysmic. Some scientists think it was caused by an asteroid hitting earth. Others believe their decline was gradual and due to climate change. They lived for millions of years then, poof—in a blip of time—a few million years—they were gone."

Kelsey looks at him. "You're really smart, aren't you?"

"Smart is only potential; I'm well-educated."

"I'd like to go to college." When she said it to her mother at the lighthouse that day, it was a lie. Now, to her surprise, she means it.

"I hope you will."

Kelsey shrugs. "I'd better get going." She puts the book on his desk and gets up but stands for a moment with her hands in her pockets, staring at her feet. "Dr. Hobbes, thanks . . . for . . . you know. I promise I won't let you down."

"I know you won't. And, it's about time you call me Hobby. All my good friends do."

CHAPTER 22

Kelsey arrives home to find her mother in the kitchen where the counter looks like a bomb went off. There's a package of ground beef defrosting, two slices of bread that look a bit moldy, ketchup, an onion that has sprouted, a few fuzzy-looking carrots, and an egg. The pans, usually stored in the rarely used oven, are on the counter, along with a couple of mixing bowls.

"Whatcha doing?"

"Fixing dinner." Lydia turns and smiles.

"What are we having?" She barely hides her surprise, or her worry that Lydia is headed for one of her over-the-top periods of euphoria, followed by the inevitable crash.

"Meatloaf, mashed potatoes—" she holds up a box of instant mashed potatoes. "And roasted carrots."

"That's like my favorite meal." Something's up. It's the *what* that's chill-inducing.

"I know."

"What's the occasion?"

"I've turned over a new leaf. I'm going to cut back on the drinking and start having supper ready when you get home from that job of yours."

Kelsey can't keep the skepticism out of her voice. "Really?" Then, remembering her own new-leaf pledge, "That would be great, Mom." And she means it. Maybe getting arrested, yet again, was a wake-up call for her mother, too.

Lydia removes the moldy bits as she tears the bread into small pieces. "You've only got one parent and she hasn't been doing a very good job lately. It's about time I took better care of you."

The new Kelsey refrains from saying aloud: *I'll believe it when I see it.* Instead, she turns to the silverware drawer to get knives and forks. She takes two real—not paper—plates from the cupboard, and heads toward the living room. At the door, she looks at the overflowing ashtray on her mother's TV tray, turns, and goes to the dinette under the back window. She put the plates and silverware down and stares out. Their beautiful old lichen-covered apple tree fills her view like a framed photograph. Kelsey clears away the catalogs littering the table, sets their places, and folds two paper towels to make triangles which look more like real napkins.

Lydia puts a hand on Kelsey's shoulder. "That looks nice."

Kelsey tilts her head so her cheek rests against her mother's hand, then straightens and crosses to the fridge. She gets out a quart of milk and takes two water glasses from the drainboard.

"Not for me, Honey. I'm going to have wine."

Kelsey gives her a sharp look.

"Red wine is good for me. It's not vodka."

"I didn't say anything."

"You rolled your eyes?" Her mother opens and closes two cupboard doors. "Do you know where the meatloaf pan is?"

"In the drawer under the oven."

"Thanks." Lydia gets it out, adds it to the debris on the counter and picks up the onion, sniffs it and wrinkles her nose. "Do we have Lipton Onion Soup mix?"

"If we do, it will be in the one above the microwave." Kelsey exchanges her mother's water glass for a wine glass.

"Brown sugar for the carrots?"

"On the top shelf."

When she looks out at the apple tree again, she sees that the window framing is actually filthy. Raindrops have pocked the dirt, and there are cobwebs in the top corners and dried insect-parts in the bottom corners. Dead center is a banana slug slime trail which ends in a zigzag line of poop. She's going to play along with her mother's most recent resolution because she is starving, both for dinner and for real change.

While the meatloaf bakes, they watch the news. True to her word, Lydia makes her glass of wine last through the local news and the national news, only pouring a second glass when they sit down to eat. Kelsey's about to pick up her fork when Lydia reaches across the table and takes her free hand. "Shall we say Grace?"

For a moment, Kelsey thinks her mother's joking, but Lydia's expression is 100% serious. "I guess." Kelsey bows her head and waits.

Silence.

She looks up.

Lydia shrugs. "I can't remember what Gram used to say."

"Well, I don't know any graces."

"Oh well." Lydia raises her wine glass. "Thanks God."

As they eat, Kelsey feels her mother watching her.

"You're not talking much," Lydia says.

"I love this dinner too much to talk." Kelsey continues chewing but adds a few appreciative sounds around each mouthful.

At times like this, when her mother isn't drinking too much and seems open to conversation, Kelsey is tempted to ask about her father, but if this turns out to be a sober night, she doesn't want to ruin it.

Lydia pokes at her food with her fork. "In court yesterday—."

Kelsey's head comes up, a bite poised at her mouth. "What about it?"

"I figured it would go easier if they felt sorry for you, so I pretended to fall asleep. That's a hell of thing to have to rely on your mother for—to draw out the pity of strangers." She blinks like she might be about to cry.

Kelsey stares in disbelief. Lydia has just exposed a devious side of herself Kelsey doesn't recognize. Until this moment, couldn't have imagined. "You...you didn't really fall asleep?"

Lydia shakes her head without looking up from her plate.

Chill bumps rise on Kelsey's arms. How much of what her mother does is an act?

"That Lauren person is obviously a bad influence on you. Why did you steal that bear for her? Why didn't she get it herself if she wanted it so badly?"

"You're kidding, right?"

Her mother looks indignant. "No, I'm not kidding. I don't want you seeing her anymore."

"Not much chance of that, Mom. She's dead. And it was an elephant." Kelsey scrapes her chair back and stands.

"What? When?"

"A month ago."

"Why didn't you tell me? I'm sure you never told me. How did she die?"

"The car we were in hit a tree, remember?" Kelsey sweeps her bangs to one side and leans for her mother to see the scar on her forehead. "It happened the day we went to the lighthouse—you remember, the last time you turned over a new leaf."

Lydia blinks and deflates. Tears swim in her eyes. "Kelsey, give me a chance. I mean it this time. I'm going to start being a real mother to you."

Kelsey sets her jaw. "It's getting pretty late, Mom. I'm nearly fourteen."

"Was she older?"

"What do you mean, was she older?"

"Your friend? Was she old enough to drive?"

"Lauren was my age. Not old enough to do anything."

"Why did her parents let her drive?"

She wants to say, not for the same reason you let me drive. "They were out of town. And Lauren wasn't driving. Brie was."

"Did Brie die, too?"

"No."

"Too bad." Her mother takes a sip of wine.

Her mother's "too bad" makes Kelsey furious. Lydia hasn't earned the right to judge. To hell with tiptoeing around, burying her needs trying to keep her mother sober. Kelsey sits back down. "I want to know about my father."

Lydia doesn't bat an eye. "Not much to tell." She tilts her head back and drains her glass. "He's dead."

The air leaves Kelsey's lungs. "You never told me that. How did it happen? When?"

"You never seemed interested."

"I've asked about him a hundred times. You always said you didn't want to talk about it. I thought you drank because he left us."

"He did leave us. He died later. In the Iraq War."

In some tiny corner of her mind a door shuts; the one Kelsey had kept open believing her father would show up one day and bail her out of this life. She feels a tightness in her chest, as if the oxygen has been sucked from the room. The windows are shut, the doors locked, and here they are, just the two of them. "Then why'd you burn all his pictures? You could have saved one so I'd know what he looked like."

"I never wanted to see his face again."

"If he's dead, not much chance of that," Kelsey says and immediately regrets it. "I'm sorry, Mom." She tries to imagine being left alone with a child and an addiction.

Lydia waves away her apology. "I didn't want to be reminded. Do you understand?" She gets up and goes to the freezer.

Kelsey jumps up and places her hand against the door. "Please, don't, Mom. Just this once, tell me about him and I'll never ask again."

"You don't want to know."

"Yes, I do. It's worse imagining."

"Let me fix a drink first. Just one."

"Then you'll tell me?"

"Yes." Lydia's desperate-for-a-drink expression is all too familiar.

Kelsey twists the plastic ice tray to pop the cubes loose. She puts as many chunks of ice in her mother's glass as she can fit.

Lydia measures a shot glass full of vodka and pours it over the ice, then adds another splash.

"Go easy, Mom." She turns from refilling the ice cube tray. "Please."

"You don't know what it's been like for me all these years."

"I want to understand."

Kelsey carefully carries the topped-off tray to the freezer, then clears their plates and puts them in the sink to soak. When she turns, her mother's gone. Kelsey rushes from the kitchen and runs into Lydia in the hallway, coming out of her bedroom. She's carrying a book.

"What's that?"

"My senior yearbook."

Kelsey takes it. *Breath of Ocean, 1995*. Fort Bragg High School.

"I thought you grew up in Willits."

"I did. Mostly. My parents sent me to live here with Gram when I was your age."

"Why?"

Lydia shrugs. "I was crazy about a boy they didn't like."

"What's this got to do with my father?"

"Your dad and I went to high school together. We're both in here."

Clutching the yearbook to her chest, Kelsey follows her mother into the living room. Lydia goes to the kitchen to get her drink; Kelsey waits on the sofa, her index finger tracing the foamy white wave on the tooled-leather cover.

Her mother settles into her recliner and reaches for the remote.

"Mom," Kelsey says. "Don't turn that on yet. Dad, remember?"

"Sorry."

Kelsey opens the book in the center. "What was your name before you married Dad?"

"Kelsey."

"What?"

"My maiden name was Kelsey."

Once again, that odd feeling creeps in, like she got when Lydia said she only pretended to fall asleep in court. She can't explain why. Or how she could live nearly fourteen years and not know her first name was her mother's maiden name?

Kelsey shakes off her unease as she flips through the pictures of young people looking oddly foreign, as if they came from a different country instead of a different time. Girls with perms, or straight hair purposely messy. She reaches the names beginning with J, and with her heart fluttering in her chest, flips on to the Ks. *Lydia Marie Kelsey* is in the top row center. Unlike the girls pictured on either side of her mother, with bangs long enough to tuck behind their ears, making them look like water-buffalos, her mother's blonde hair cascades over her shoulders. She smiles in the picture—a smile that almost touches her pale eyes and makes her look on the verge of laughing out loud.

Beneath each picture is a quote. Her mother's reads: *She will live all the days of her life,* which sounds like a dark prediction or even a curse, as if this pitiful existence was in her mother's stars.

"Where did the quote come from? Did you choose it?"

"Yes, but I don't remember where I saw it." Lydia takes a drag off her cigarette and blows the smoke toward the ceiling.

Kelsey looks up. She's never noticed before that the ceiling above the Barcalounger is stained yellow.

Beneath the quote is a list of her extracurricular activities: *Pep Club 10, 11, 12; Folk Dance Frolic 11, 12; Red Cross 10; FHA 10, 11, 12.* "What's FHA?"

Lydia snorts. "Future Homemakers of America."

Kelsey suppresses her own urge to laugh. "You were really beautiful, Mom."

"*Were* is the operative word." She flips her hand at Kelsey, dismissively. "You wanted to see your father. What are you waiting for?"

"I don't know. I kind of expect him to have two heads or something." She turns the pages slowly, until she reaches the Ms. Her father's piercing eyes stare glumly at her from the center of the page. Blond bangs cover one eyebrow. *Jonathon James McCully, My road calls me, lures me: West, South, East and North. Most roads lead men homeward, my road leads me forth. Football 10, 12; Track 10, 11, 12; Jamboree 10, 12; Student Council 12; FFA 11, 12.* If the FHA club was for girls, Kelsey wonders if FFA was a club for future fathers of America. She doesn't ask. "He's so handsome," she says, softly.

"That he was. Handsome and he knew it."

Kelsey resents her being mean about this boy—man—her father, who's dead. She soaks him up, his features, examining his hairline, the shape of his nose, his ears, his eyes looking into hers. *My father—right here in this book all along.* "What color eyes did he have?"

"Black. Like his heart."

"Stop it! Just stop it."

Her mother gets up, marches into the kitchen, and jerks open the freezer door.

Kelsey no longer cares whether she stays sober. *Go ahead.* She'll have him all to herself when her mother passes out.

"Was he your high school sweetheart?"

"Off and on."

Ice cubes clink, followed by the glug, glug, glug of vodka pouring. Lydia carries a brimming glass back into the living room with her hand held beneath it to catch drips. "We met up again at our tenth high school reunion. Lucky me. You were born—nine months later."

"If you loved him enough to marry him and have me, what was so bad about him?"

Lydia stands over Kelsey looking down at the yearbook. "We never married. I took his name to protect you."

Kelsey looks up. "Protect me from what?"

"Illegitimacy carries a stigma. At least it used to."

Before Kelsey can react to this news, Lydia says, "When he found out I was pregnant, he split. I never saw him again." There's gloating in her mother's tone. She's proven her point.

Kelsey stares at his picture, trying to see sleaziness in his eyes, but he looks nice. Other boys on the page look sullen and pissed off. Not her father. He just looks uncomfortable with having his picture taken.

"How do you know he's dead?"

"Dead?"

"Yeah, you said he died in the Iraq War. How'd you know?"

"I don't remember. Someone told me he'd been killed." Lydia gazes at Kelsey. "You look just like him, except his hair was blonder."

My fault he left and I'm here every day to remind her. "Sorry," she says.

"Don't be."

Kelsey waits, hoping her mother will say something more, but she picks up the remote, pushes off first one slipper then the other, flexes her toes, slides one crusty bare foot closer to Kelsey, and shakes it. "Be a sweetie and scratch my feet for a while, will you? I feel tense."

Kelsey can't say which sickens her most, the sweaty, rubber-soled smell of her mother's feet or the image of herself sitting on the floor, close to those yellowing, overgrown toenails, fingers scraping the dry skin. She's always hated it, but tonight it makes her want to gag. "I've got homework." She wraps her arms around the yearbook and goes to her room. She's going find a place to hide it so her mother can never take him away again.

CHAPTER 23

Kelsey rides to the greenhouse the next day excited to tell Hobby about finding a picture of her father. On the way, she thinks about the last two months, how she would never have believed that the best part of her cruddy life starts every day when school lets out and she's free to go to her court-ordered job in a greenhouse.

As usual, she struggles to get her bike up the hill. In the cold air, her breath comes out in fog-like puffs. Today, the sky and the water are the same color gray, like it might or might not rain. At the top of the hill, she stops and turns to look at the ocean. She keeps meaning to ask Hobby why the horizon stays eye-level, looking capable of sweeping her away, no matter how high above sea-level she stands.

Kelsey steers her bike down Hobby's driveway expecting Gen to be waiting for her under his favorite rhododendron. He isn't there.

She leans her bike against the rear bumper of Hobby's truck and tosses her coat over the handlebars. Compared to the cool, crisp breeze off the Pacific, the greenhouse's warm, humid air feels unusually thick and heavy enough to make taking a deep breath hard.

"Gen? Hobby? Anybody here?" Kelsey walks the left aisle to the back of the greenhouse and knocks on the steel door to Hobby's office. No answer. She steps to her right and waves her hands over her head in front of the office's one-way glass window. "Hey, old man. I'm here. Check me in."

When he still doesn't answer, she shrugs, and reaches to take her gloves off the hook beside the door. They're gone. She knows she hung them there yesterday. Hobby's a stickler for putting things back where they belong. To her right, pieces of Phil, his beloved philodendron, litter the ground, and the bark chips that line the path are scraped away in places, exposing bare earth.

Alarm causes her stomach flutter. "Hobby?" She raps on the one-way glass, then moves to her left and pounds on the steel door. "Hobby," she shouts. "Answer me. Are you okay in there?"

There a few shiny scratches on the door. She bends for a closer look. The black paint along the frame is dented and chipped as if someone tried to pry it open. The padlock has a nick in it. *The padlock? He can't be inside if the padlock's in place.*

From somewhere behind her, Gen meows. She whirls. He's sitting halfway down the greenhouse's right aisle beside a pile of dirty clothes. Hobby would never leave a mess like that. "Hey, buddy." She steps toward Gen. "Where's— Oh my God!" Kelsey covers her mouth. The crumpled pile of clothes is Hobby. His wild hair stands out in all directions around a bloody hole in the side of his head. She sinks to her knees beside him. "Hobby?" She touches his arm. Even in this heat, his skin feels cool and clammy. She presses her fingers to his neck like they do on TV. She doesn't feel anything, but she really doesn't know where on a person's neck to find a pulse. A foot away lies a crowbar with blood and white hair stuck to the curved end. Blood soaks through the knees of her jeans.

Ride to the recycle center for help. She scrambles to her feet. Coagulated blood sticks to her jeans making it hard to bend her knees as she runs from the greenhouse. She immediately realizes there's a better option, races back inside, and down the row opposite where Hobby lies. At the bunker door, her hands tremble as she lines up the four zeros at the bottom of the padlock. Inside, surrounded by the quiet hum of his machinery, she finds the phone and dials 9-1-1.

Town is only two miles away. The 9-1-1 operator is still asking her questions when Kelsey hears the first siren. She waits sitting beside Hobby, stroking his arm. "You'll be okay," she whispers. "You have to be okay." Tears stream down her face. She can't be left behind again, left without Hobby in her corner.

Gen meows once, climbs into her lap, stands on his hind legs, and puts his front legs around her neck. He presses his face in the curve of her neck the way he did on her first day here.

A sob catches in her throat. "He'll be okay." *Please God.*

Kelsey hears the ambulance miss the driveway and continue up Pudding Creek. She moves Gen off her lap, jumps up, runs out of the greenhouse, and down the long driveway to the road where she waits for it to return. When it comes into view, she waves her arms over her head until the driver sees her, then runs back down the driveway to the greenhouse.

She's beside Hobby again when she hears tires on the gravel and sees dust billow over the rose arbor as the ambulance skids to a stop.

"In here," she screams.

Paramedics rush through the arbor with a stretcher. The first one through kneels and feels Hobby's neck for a pulse. "Pulse weak and thready," she says to the other paramedic, who's a cute guy and looks young enough to be a middle school classmate.

"He's not dead?" Kelsey chokes back tears.

"Nearly. How long have you been here?"

"About ten minutes." She begins to tremble. He isn't dead, but he might still die.

The wail of a police sirens grows closer, followed by the crunch of gravel, and another cloud of dust.

Police begin to fill the greenhouse, but stand aside as paramedics lift Hobby onto the stretcher, hook up an IV, and place an oxygen mask over his nose and mouth.

"Someone cracked his skull open," a paramedic tells one of the cops. "He's alive, but just barely. We've got to move quickly."

"Are you a relative?" one of the cops asks Kelsey.

"I'm a—" She starts to say a court-referral, but changes her mind, not because he might think she did this, but because she wants him to understand how much Hobby means to her. "I'm his friend. I help him here."

"Did you touch anything?" The cop glances at her blood-stained knees.

"I don't think so, except the padlock. It was locked and the phone's in there."

"So, you knew the combination?" He examines the scratches on the doorframe.

She nods. "Those marks weren't there yesterday. Someone tried to break in."

"Looks like it. What's all that stuff?"

"Equipment for his—" Her voice catches in her throat. He's going to die—like Lauren, like her dad. "He does experiments with plants." She covers her face with her hands.

There are more sirens, then the crowd parts for an imposing man. "Sheriff." One of policeman shakes his hand.

"This is a damned shame." He stands aside as the paramedics wheel Hobby out and slide the stretcher into the ambulance. "I've known Hobby for decades. He's a top-notch man." He looks at Kelsey. "You'd be his latest court referral, right?"

"Yes, sir."

"She didn't tell me she was a CR." Suspicion clouds the young cop's face. "She said she was a friend."

"I *am* his friend."

A man and a woman in suits, carrying large metal cases, file into the greenhouse wearing Latex gloves and blue booties over their shoes.

"What are you doing time for?" the sheriff asks.

Kelsey looks down at the bloodstains on her knees. "Shoplifting."

"Was that room open when you got here?"

"No," Kelsey says.

"Yes," the cop says.

"So, you opened the door?" the sheriff says to Kelsey.

"Yes."

"Before you found him or after?"

"After. That's where the phone is."

The sheriff studies her face. "How'd you know the combination?"

She skips telling him she once peeked at the opened lock. "He's the same as me. He never made up a new combination, just left it with the one it came with—four zeros."

"These marks look as if someone tried to break in," he says to no one in particular.

"I know. I told him." Kelsey nods toward the young cop. "They weren't there yesterday."

The people in suits begin to take pictures. One of them puts the crowbar into a plastic bag. Another dusts the door and the lock for fingerprints. "Is *she* our suspect?" the man asks.

"Not if that crowbar has black paint on it and it matches the paint chips from that door," the sheriff says. "She knew the combination."

When the guy dusting for prints finishes, he crooks a finger at Kelsey. "I need to print you."

Jerry pressing her hand to the scanner flashes in her mind. "You have my prints," she whispers.

"Fort Bragg police do. I'm County." He takes her right thumb and rolls it on the ink pad, presses, and rolls it in the box on the card marked *1. R. Thumb*

He continues with all ten fingers as tears seep down her cheeks.

"Here, here. Don't cry," he says. "This is so we can eliminate your prints and Dr. Hobbes'. Any other prints we find will become suspects."

"Are you the only CR?" The Sheriff asks.

"I think so." Kelsey sniffles. "I never saw anyone else here."

The suit-wearing woman comes over and introduces herself as Detective Johanna Moran. She asks to take Kelsey's statement: What time did she get here? Did she see anyone leaving? Has she disturbed anything? Has Dr. Hobbes been concerned about anything in particular lately?

Kelsey responds to each question the same way she did when asked the first time. To the last one, she says she doesn't think so.

"That about does it." Detective Moran closes her pad. "Can you think of anything else that might be relevant?"

When Kelsey says she can't, Detective Moran rechecks her name, address and telephone number, and tells her she's free to go. "And I'm sorry," she adds. "I can see you cared about him."

Cared. He is going to *die*. "He was a friend to me first," she sobs, "before I knew I liked him. You know what I mean?"

Detective Moran puts her arm around Kelsey's shoulders. "I do."

"What about this cat?" the fingerprint guy says.

Gen disappeared when the paramedics arrived. Now that everyone but the sheriff, detective Moran and the fingerprint guy are left, Gen has come out of hiding and is on the bench, beneath the cascade of Phil's leaves.

"That's Genera. Hobby's cat." Kelsey walks over and picks him up. He presses a paw to her cheek and stares into her eyes.

"Can you take him?" the Sheriff says. "Or we can call Animal Control to come get him."

"Please don't," Kelsey says.

"This is a crime scene. It won't do to have a cat running around in here," he says.

"I can't take him." Kelsey feels the sting of tears again. "My mother's allergic." She cradles Gen's head. "I'll come every day to feed him, if you'll let him stay."

Detective Moran speaks up, "We can shut him out of here. It will be fine as long as you feed him outside."

"Thank you," Kelsey says.

"He clearly thinks he's your cat now, doesn't he?" Detective Moran says.

"He's not though." Kelsey hugs him.

She, Gen, and Detective Moran walk outside.

"You need to prepare yourself for the worst," the detective says. "A blow to the head like that—" She squeezes Kelsey's shoulder.

•   •   •   •   •

Kelsey crosses under the rose arbor, picks up her bike, and turns to go. One of her gloves is stuck on the handle of a rusty shovel that's leaning against the side of the house. It looks as if it's been placed there casually, like a hand waving. The second glove lies on top of a *Ceanothus* shrub. Her first thought is to carry them back inside to show Detective Moran, but she decides she probably shouldn't touch them. She walks to the greenhouse, Gen at her heels. Before opening the door, she picks him up. "Detective Moran." She cracks the door and calls. "Someone moved my gloves. I always leave them on the hook, but they're outside now."

Detective Moran comes out. "Show me."

"Hey," the fingerprint guy says. "Let's see the bottom of your shoes."

Kelsey turns and holds a foot up.

"Too bad. These are yours." He points to the marks on the exposed ground under Phil. "I thought we had something."

Kelsey shows Detective Moran the shovel. "Seeing these makes me remember something. A few weeks ago, Hobby said a couple kids had been here snooping around. He was real mad and thought they might be—" Kelsey shifts her gaze away from the detective's piercing stare. She doesn't want to tell her that Hobby thought they were friends of hers. "—court referrals from a couple years ago."

"That's important information. Did he tell you their names?"

"No ma'am." Kelsey kisses the side of Gen's head and hugs him close. "Hobby didn't deserve this."

CHAPTER 24

Kelsey pumps her bike pedals with all her strength down Franklin Street. Through the blur of tears, she sees Hobby crumpled on the greenhouse floor. And the blood. She's in the middle of the road when a horn blasts behind her. She swerves out of the way, hating the driver.

"Please be sober," she prays, as she rolls into their yard, drops her bike, and runs up the front steps. "Mom?"

No answer.

Lauren, her father, now Hobby. Her heart pounds in her chest. She screams, "Mom?"

She runs down the hall, checks both bedrooms, the bathroom, then back to the kitchen. She looks out the window. The garage door is up but the car is still there. She turns away, then looks again. A clear heat, shimmers from the tailpipe.

Lydia's passed out, head back, mouth agape. Kelsey opens the driver's door and places her hand against her mother's shoulder to keep her from falling onto the ground.

"Huh?" Lydia groans. Her eyes open and she blinks to focus. "Hi, Honey." She looks around. "Why am I in the car?"

"I don't know. Come on, let me help you back to the house."

"No. No." She bats Kelsey's hand away and reaches to close the door. "I have a little slopping to do."

"You're too drunk to drive, and you no longer have a license, remember?"

"Don't tell me what I am or am not s-able to do. I'm your mother."

"Aren't I the lucky one," Kelsey says.

Tears well in her mother's eyes. "What did I do to deserve this treatment?"

Kelsey wonders that herself. Hobby told her most people are the main ingredient in their own misery, that even tiny decisions can affect a person's existence from that day on. Kelsey believes this. Like Lauren's decision to let Brie drive. She's made plenty of mistakes, but right now, she needs her mother.

"Come on, Mom, let's go back in the house. I'll fix you some lunch."

Her mother lets Kelsey guide her. "Maybe afterwards, you could tickle my feet?"

"Maybe," Kelsey says.

"What happened to your knees?" Her mother points to the bloodstains on Kelsey's jeans. "Did you fall off your bike?"

"Something like that."

Her mother is snoring when Kelsey comes back with two bowls of *Top Ramen* noodle soup. Kelsey stands with the steam rising. She feels numb, unable to decide whether to stand or sit, eat or not eat. Minutes pass before she moves. Long enough that steam no longer rises as she carries the bowls back to the kitchen. She covers her mother's with a saucer and eats most of hers at the dinette table, staring out at the apple tree.

The books.

She stands, nearly tipping over her chair. Where are the books Hobby gave her?

She hadn't bothered to open the box and never thanked him. She'd put them somewhere but can't remember where. She leaves her soup unfinished and begins looking. The more places she looks, the more panicky she gets. If she's lost them, and he dies, she'll never find out what he wanted her to know.

When she's searched everywhere she can think of in her room, she starts in her mother's. Maybe Lydia found the box and thought it was something she ordered. It wouldn't be the first time. Before Kelsey took control of their finances and starting hiding cash in the recipe box, she was forever sending back things her mother ordered from the mountain of catalogs that arrive almost daily in the mail. She feels like she's cancelled a thousand catalogs only, to have new ones show up.

Kelsey starts in her mother's closet, then moves to the chest of drawers, her nightstand, the cupboard under the bathroom sink, and finally under her bed where she finds lots of dust and a shoebox. She assumes it contains shoes and pulls it from beneath the bed to take to the closet. It's so light, it feels empty. When she shakes it, the contents shuffle from side to side.

On top is an expired passport dated a year before Kelsey was born. In it her mother looks much the same as she did in her high school yearbook. Now, thirteen years later, Lydia looks old and worn out. Did having her do this to her mother? Or was it having to raise her alone?

There are no travel stamps in the passport. Had her mother once planned a trip somewhere foreign and never made it? Beneath the passport are a few photographs. Kelsey goes through them, looking for a more recent picture of her father, one her mother might have forgotten to burn. The boy in the high school yearbook was so young looking, it's hard for Kelsey to imagine him as a father, especially *her* father.

One picture is of an old couple standing next to a logging truck. She guesses the man is her grandfather and the woman, who is the image of her mother, must be Kelsey's grandmother. Lydia is the tow-headed six- or seven-year-old standing between them. The man has his hand on the top of her head, as if holding her in place. The woman holds a younger child—three maybe—her aunt, no doubt. Kelsey looks more closely. She surprised to see how much her mother and grandmother look alike.

As a baby Kelsey, too, was blonde. Now her hair is brown and frizzy, as is Lydia's, though her mother's grays daily. There are two other pictures of her mother as a young woman with her hair bleached to a youthful blonde. In one, she waves to the camera from a Mustang convertible. In the other, she's in a canoe and trying to splash the photographer. Pictures of her mother happy make Kelsey sad. She tries to imagine the moments before and after the photo was taken. Did the person taking the picture give chase. Did Lydia run screaming and laughing? It doesn't work. Kelsey's mind hops to her mother now, splayed in her Barcalounger.

She looks on the back. *June 2005.* A shock runs through her. These pictures may have been taken by her father when they met again at their tenth reunion. She counts the months off on her fingers. Nine months would be March 2006. Kelsey's birthday is February 22. Close enough. She closes the box and slides it back beneath the bed.

She hears the toilet flush, gets up, and tiptoes out of her mother's room. "I made you lunch," she says to the bathroom door. "Want me to reheat it?"

"No, thanks. I'm not hungry." Comes the muffled response.

"Have you seen an Amazon box? I can't find it."

Lydia opens the door and steadies herself with a hand on the doorframe. "I don't know what you are talking about."

"Dr. Hobbes ordered a couple books for me and now I can't find the box."

Lydia heads for the kitchen holding the backs of furniture for balance.

"Well, have you?"

"Have I what?"

"Damn it, do you listen to me at all? Ever?"

Lydia stops in the kitchen doorway. "I'm a sick woman. Don't talk to me like that."

"I know. I know. You're my mother." Kelsey brushes past and runs from the house. She picks her bike up off the step where she dropped it and rides to the end of the driveway. Where does she think she's going? She rolls her bike back along the driveway to the garage and leans it against the wall. There on the shelf, above where she always parks, is the Amazon box. She rips off the black electrical tape Hobby used to reseal it. Inside is a note:

Dear Kelsey,

All living things are connected: you, me, Gen, Phil, even Carlotta. As alone as you feel, you are not. When the first book was written, there was no scientific evidence that any of it was true. Most of the anecdotes were unproven and controversial. For me, it excited my interest. Now, all these years later, we know plants can change their chemistry to ward off predators and alert their neighbors of impending attack. I hope you will read this and see possibilities for yourself.

The second one is more up to date, and based on scientifically provable, peer-reviewed studies.

Your friend, Hobby.

Kelsey touches his signature and blinks back tears.

The first book is *The Secret Life of Plants* by Peter Tompkins and Christopher Bird. The second is entitled, *What a Plant Knows: a Field Guide to the Senses* by Daniel Chamovitz.

Kelsey takes the books to her room and props herself up on her pillows. It's strange what a difference a day can make, even a few hours. The cover of *The Secret Life of Plants* is a flower with a sweet, Gerber-baby face emerging as a blossom. It claims to be "A fascinating account of the physical, emotional and spiritual relations between plants and man." If she'd opened this before Hobby was attacked, she might have laughed out loud and pitched it off in some corner. She's sure wouldn't have tiptoed to her room to be alone and read. She hopes to discover something between the covers that will keep him in her life. Whatever it is Hobby believes, she wants to believe.

The inside flap promises the latest discoveries about *"plants and their relationship to mankind."* She flips to the Library of Congress page to see when it was first published. 1972—forty-seven years ago. She's disappointed. When he said this was an old book, she didn't know it was *that* old. She feels herself lose interest until two words on the inside flap catch her eye: *". . . includes remarkable information about plants as* lie detectors *and plants as ecological sentinels; it describes their ability to adapt to human wishes, their response to music, their curative powers, and their ability to communicate with man."*

Hobby's been testing these theories, or whatever they are. Boiling earwigs to get a rise out of a plant, acting like Phil cares about spiders and what time she arrives for work. She still thinks that's a lot of bunk, but if he wanted her to read these, she will. .

CHAPTER 25

First thing Sunday morning, Kelsey rides her bike to Purity to buy a can of cat food with a dollar she took from behind "B" in the recipe box. If she can't find where Hobby keeps his cat food, she'll have to get more from the pet rescue people at the Food Bank on Monday.

She'd lain awake most of the night worrying about Hobbes and dreading what she'll hear when she goes to the hospital today. She finds herself crying as she pushes her bike up the long hill to Hobby's. When she turns onto his driveway, Gen runs to meet her. Kelsey drops her bike and scoops him up. "It's okay, buddy. I'll take care of you."

He buries his face against her shoulder, purrs, and drools.

•   •   •   •   •

After she feeds Gen and waters the plants in the greenhouse that's not a crime scene, Kelsey rides to the hospital and chains her bike to the newspaper machines outside the entrance.

Everything about the place reminds her of trips here with her mother. A year ago, Lydia took too many aspirin for a headache, chased them with vodka, and stopped breathing. Racing behind the ambulance on her bike, Kelsey remembers thinking—this time—she might come home alone. What she feared more than having to move in with her aunt in Nebraska is foster care. While waiting in emergency, sure someone would come and tell her the ambulance got there too late, she planned ways to ward off Child Protective Service's attempts to put her into a house full of strangers, with other kids from homes as bad as hers.

Inside, at the front desk, she asks for Hobby's room number.

"He's in ICU," the white-haired volunteer tells her.

"What's ICU?"

"Intensive Care Unit. Are you a relative?"

"Why?"

"Only family members are allowed in ICU."

"Yes. I'm his niece. Does that count?"

"It does." The woman comes out from behind the desk, takes Kelsey's arm and leads her out of reception and into the hallway. "Go down there and take a right. You'll see it. Knock before you go in."

No one answers when she knocks, so Kelsey opens the door a crack. Hobby's lying in a small room within a larger room full of machines that blink and whoosh. There's a big window so visitors and nurses can see him. On the far side of the little room, a picture window looks out on a carpet of yellow dandelions. The barred sides of his bed are up and his head is bandaged. A bag of clear liquid dangles from a pole, the tubing ends at a needle stuck into the thin, splotchy skin on the back of his right hand.

His left hand rests on his stomach. The black electrical tape is missing and his last two fingers stick out at odd angles, one pointing up, the other east. Kelsey dashes from the room. In the hall, she runs smack into a nurse.

"Are you all right?" The nurse's voice is soothing and manicured.

"Someone took the tape off his fingers."

"Excuse me?"

"The electrical tape. He wouldn't want to be lying there with his fingers pointing every which way."

"Are you a relative?"

"I'm his niece. You have to put the tape back on."

"We could bandage his fingers, I suppose."

"Not white tape. Black tape. Electrical tape is his favorite."

"Well, I'm not sure. Perhaps when his sister comes to see him—"

"What? Oh—she lives far away." If she is going to lie, she needs to remember what she's said. "In Nebraska."

"I thought you were his niece."

"I am. I'm his . . . his brother's daughter, but . . . but my dad is dead. Dr. . . . . Uncle Hobby is my last living relative, and he'd want his fingers taped."

"When I get a minute, I'll see if we have any, but I'll have to check with his doctor first."

"Thank you." Kelsey follows her back into ICU. "How's he doing?"

"Holding his own. He's in a coma and there's swelling in the part of his brain where the injury is, but when that goes down, we'll be able to tell better what kind of damage was done."

"How long do comas last?"

"Days, weeks, years. It all depends."

Years! Kelsey puts her hand against the cool glass. "Do you let relatives go in the room with him?"

"Not yet. Maybe in a day or two."

"Can I bring him a plant?"

"Oh, no. Nothing with foreign microbes."

Kelsey nods. She remembers Hobby mentioning the importance of certain microbes in the soil, but there are bad microbes, too, like viruses. At least the look and smell of the whole set-up make her hopeful. Machines track how he's doing, the nurse's desk faces Hobby's glass room so he isn't out of her sight, and there's a medicine-y odor, like mercurochrome and Clorox.

"When you're in a coma, can you hear?"

"No one knows for sure. It's best to suppose he can."

Kelsey leans with her hands on the windowsill and her forehead against the glass. If Phil and Gen know when she's nearby, maybe Hobby can hear her thoughts. She's heard of mental telepathy where people bend spoons with their minds. She closes her eyes and concentrates her thoughts. *I'm taking care of everything.*

She opens her eyes to watch for any sign he heard her.

"It's good to pray," the nurse says.

"Huh?"

"Prayer. It's a good thing."

"Yeah." She turns back to the window. Outside, a guy goes by on a lawn mower, mowing off the dandelion flower heads. Kelsey glances at the nurse. "Can you make him stop?"

"Stop what?"

"Mowing."

"I don't know. Why?" Her brow creases like Kelsey is a mystery.

"Uncle Hobby loves flowers. It would be nice if they were there when he wakes up."

The nurse picks up the phone. When someone answers, she asks about having the mowing stop. She smiles at Kelsey while she waits. "Thanks anyway." She hangs up. "Sorry. Today's mowing day." As if that's a good enough reason. "What kind of work does your uncle do?"

"He's a famous scientist."

"Really? What field?"

"He studies plants."

"He's a botanist." The nurse gathers some charts off her desk and goes to the door. "I'll be right back. Stay as long as you like."

"Hobby," Kelsey whispers after the door closes behind the nurse. "I've been lying to that lady, but I don't think it matters. I just want you to know I'll take care of your plants and Gen. Don't you worry, okay?" Kelsey crosses her fingers behind her back. "I'm reading the book you gave me." It will be the truth by tonight.

Kelsey goes outside to retrieve her bike and hears the mower. She unlocks her bike from the newspaper rack and rides around to the back side of the hospital. The guy on the mower is making a turn at the far end of the half-mown field. Kelsey lays her bike down and walks to meet him. She finds Hobby's room and waits. When the yardman to spots her, he turns off his motor.

"May I help you?"

"My uncle is in this room."

The guy rises from the mower's seat and looks where she's pointing.

"He's in a coma—"

"I'm sorry to hear that."

"He like flowers."

"Okay?"

"I was wondering if you could not mow the one's outside his window so when he wakes up—" she swallows the lump forming in the throat. "If he wakes up, he'll be able to see them blooming."

"I'm supposed to—" he stops.

"Please."

He shrugs. "Sure. If the boss askes, can I tell him which room?"

Kelsey can see the machines blinking on the other side of the glass. "I don't think it has a number, but it's called ICU."

"That'll do. And Miss, I'll pray for your uncle."

Kelsey's throat constricts and she nods.

CHAPTER 26

On Thursday, the story of the attack on Hobbes is in the weekly paper. The article went on to say he was found by his young volunteer, Kelsey McCully. The next day at school, Josh rushes to hug her, which brings tears to her eyes. She's had no one to share her worry with. Then Josh does what she hoped he wouldn't. He goes into over-supportive mode. He always saves a seat for her the two classes they have in common, but after she tells him about Hobby, he's waiting outside her other classes to walk with her to the next one then runs off to keep from being late to his own.

At school on Friday, Josh asks if she wants to go someplace for lunch and to a movie on Saturday. His treat. Kelsey turns him down, which, of course, hurts his feelings. Between her mother, her responsibilities at the greenhouse, and checking on Hobby every day, she doesn't have the energy to deal with Josh on weekends, too.

But Saturday, she changes her mind and calls him.

"Good," Josh says, "Let's go to the Headlands. I'm dying for those spicy vegetable samosas."

She really wants Chinese but doesn't say so since he's buying.

When they come around the corner onto Laurel Street, Will and Ryan are sprawled on the sidewalk. She should have guessed they'd be there.

Will gets up and grins like they've made his day. "Hey Kels."

She hasn't seen him since Chelsea's party. All that heartbreak floods back.

Ryan scrambles to his feet. "I didn't know you was a lesbo."

"Bite me." Kelsey steers her bike around him.

"Did you know she was a lesbo?" Ryan says to Will. "I hear queers hang together, so she must be."

"So do assholes," Kelsey says.

"Chill," Will snaps at Ryan, who looks at him, surprised, then at his feet.

"Kidding, buddy." Will punches Ryan's shoulder. Then to Kelsey. "What's happening, good-looking?"

"Nothing." She remembers him winking at her over Brie's shoulder and can't help wishing he was a nicer person.

Ryan walks toward Josh, who tries to back his bike away, but is blocked by the newspaper vending box. Ryan grabs the handlebars.

"What did you do to your hand, Ryan?" Kelsey says.

Ryan glances at the Band-Aid across his right knuckles. "Knocked a fag's teeth out."

Kelsey puts her hand in her sweater pocket and feels for her house key. If she has to punch Ryan, she wants it to hurt. Instead, she finds the roll of electrical tape she's brought from home in case the hospital will let her in to fix Hobby's fingers. "Hey Ryan, catch," she shouts and throws the roll of tape.

Ryan lets go of Josh's handlebars and catches the tape.

Josh is down the alley in a flash.

"See ya." Kelsey follows him.

They don't slow down until they get to the old Figueiredo's video store two blocks away.

"Thanks, Kelsey."

"They're not worth spit, either of them," she says.

"I'm glad you're my friend."

Kelsey feels a rush of guilt for thinking of Josh as baggage leftover from her lost friendship with Lauren.

They ride to the south end of Franklin Street, passing up the Asian Buffet. They make a big circle in the Harbor Lite Lodge parking lot, high above Noyo Harbor. "Let's go down there to eat," Josh says.

"Where?"

"I don't care. Mexican, Fish and Chips at Sea Pal, maybe Silver's."

"It means we have to come back up that hill," Kelsey says. She's lived here all her life and has never been down to the harbor.

"Don't be a sissy," Josh says.

"Come on then. I'll race you."

"I don't want to race," Josh says. "The road's too narrow."

She almost says, now who's the big sissy, then remembers what Hobby said about making bad decisions. Maybe he popped into her head to remind her to be careful.

They come down the long, steep hill with their brakes squealing and stop at the bottom to let their hearts quit pounding. A load of tourists, bundled up like they've been in a blizzard, are getting off a charter boat. A boy about ten sees them watching and proudly holds up the salmon he caught. Kelsey smiles and gives him a thumbs-up.

"I used to live over there." Josh points across the river.

"In the Coast Guard building?"

"No, the red one next to it. It was a bar when I was little."

"Was there an apartment upstairs?"

"Nope. I lived in the parking lot."

Kelsey looks at him. This is a painful memory he's sharing. He glances at her and tries to smile. "My mother was a mechanic at the mill. Dad used to drop her off every morning and go to that bar to drink."

Kelsey's insides chill. "Every day? For how long?"

"How many hours or how many years?"

"Start with the hours."

Josh shrugs. "All day on weekdays. Mom worked nine to five, Dad drank 9:30 to 4:30."

"How old were you?"

"It started when I was about four and ended when I started first grade."

"What did you do all day?"

Josh shrugs again. "I'm not really sure. Just sat there, I think."

"All day?"

"All day, every day."

"What about food and going to the bathroom?"

"I don't remember. I only remember sitting there. Our dog was with me. I guess I talked to him."

Kelsey watches the gulls swooping back and forth above the fish-cleaning stand. "My mother—" *is a drunk*, she thinks, "Drinks," she says.

"I know. That's why I told you about my dad. All I really remember is how lonely it was. At night, when Mom was home, they'd both drink and fight. My father picked on me. Said I was a fag and used to try to beat it out of me. It finally stopped when Mom quit drinking and left him." He glances at her. "So, I do know what it's like."

"Your mother quit drinking?" That sounded miraculous.

Josh nods. "She went to AA."

"Alcoholics Anonymous?"

"Yeah. They have meetings and help each other quit drinking."

Kelsey looks across the river. "My mother would never go to meetings, but thanks." She leans over and hugs him.

·   ·   ·   ·   ·

After a to-die-for lunch of fish and chips at Sea Pal, Josh and Kelsey push their bikes up the steep incline that makes the Pudding Creek hill look like a molehill. At the top, she waves goodbye to Josh and rides her bike back to the hospital.

She goes to ICU and checks in to see that Hobby is still alive. His fingers are still every which way, but there is a half a field of dandelions beyond his window.

She leaves with no real destination in mind except she isn't ready to go home.

On Laurel Street, she rides past where Will and Ryan had been earlier. On the sidewalk, written in short strips of her electrical tape, they've written: PEPOLE SUCK.

CHAPTER 27

Kelsey rides out to Hobby's every day to feed Gen and water the plants that need it in the east greenhouse. A yellow X of crime scene tape still blocks access to the west one.

A week after Hobby was attacked, Kelsey arrives to find a few torn bits of yellow plastic caught in the staples in the wooden door frame. Did the police remove it, or have the thieves come back? She walks in slowly, nothing else seems disturbed.

Traces of Hobby's blood remain on the wood-chip floor, though most of where he'd lain has been trampled. Kelsey feels bad about that. There should be more to mark where a person's life nearly ended than footprints and bloodstains. She's heard that the tree Brie hit on Sherwood Road has become a memorial, with a white cross and plastic flowers beneath the gouge in the tree's bark.

She waters, starting with Phil. Gen shadows her, rubbing against her legs, or walking the rim of the potting tables, purring at her elbow. He's lost weight in the last week, which makes Kelsey feel guilty. She's sure Hobby fed him twice a day but she can only come in the afternoons. She'd added canned cat food to her weekly trip to the Food Bank, but if she can find Hobby's stash of dry food, she can leave it out for him to eat in mornings, and hope the raccoons and skunks don't find it first.

The padlock is in place on the bunker door. She assumes the police created a new combination, but just in case, she dials in the four zeros. It falls open.

As many times as she's been inside the bunker, she's never really looked closely at its contents. Gen follows her in, goes straight to a floor to ceiling cupboard, and meows.

"Let me guess," Kelsey says. "Your food's in there." Sure enough, the bottom shelf contains a bag of dry cat food and three stacks of canned food.

Gen nudges the bag with his nose and purrs. He weaves in and out and around Kelsey's ankles until she nearly trips trying to fill his bowl.

On the shelves above the cat food are office supplies—pens, yellow legal pads, markers, Post-it notepads, extra printer paper, ink cartridges, and a cardboard box full of rolls and rolls of polygraph paper. Hobby's desk is an old door. Two narrow shelves, made from plywood planks supported by concrete blocks, rest against the back wall. Centered on the top plank is a TV monitor. It's attached to a video camera set up to record through the window into the greenhouse. Kelsey pushes the eject button, but there's no cartridge in the recorder. Either there hadn't been one or the police took it. On the same shelf with the TV is the stereo. The speakers are attached to the outside wall of the bunker. The rest of the space is taken up with dozens of books. In the corner by the polygraph is a terrarium and next to it a microscope under a dust cover. Another machine, a Hewlett Packard gas chromatograph, sits in a corner.

She turns on the stereo and finds KOZT, a soft rock station—a compromise between hard rock, which Hobby says his plants hate, and the classical music they supposedly love, but Kelsey hates.

The police turned off the polygraph but haven't removed the wires that feed through the wooden frame of the one-way glass window. She goes to the door, parts Phil's leaves, and finds where the wires are attached to disks clipped to Hobby's beloved philodendron.

"Told any whoppers, lately, Phil?" she says and goes back into the bunker. There's a huge pile of paper on the floor beneath the lie detector. Kelsey takes a pencil and marks a line across the place where the tracings ended, writes today's date and time, and turns on the polygraph. The office hums as if Hobby has just stepped out for a moment. The wire tracing pens begin to move in a jerky, nervous line like her mother's handwriting in the morning before she downs the first of the drinks she needs to quiet her nerves.

Kelsey leans out the door. "Hi Phil. It's me." She looks over her shoulder at the printout. The tracings stay the same.

Gen finishes his dry food and jumps up on the desk. "Feel better?" Kelsey rubs his ears and hears the pen scratch across the paper. She turns in time to see them settle back to the rippling tracking, but they had jerked right then left at the exact moment she petted Gen. "Come here, Gen," Kelsey picks him up, kisses him, and gives his ears another rub. The cat purrs, but Phil's readout stays the same. Nothing. Not a twitch. Just her imagination.

In a bone-dry fruit jar on Hobby's bookcase is the branch she remembers Hobby apologizing to Phil for cutting off the day before he was attacked. The leaves have wilted. She carries it out to the hose, refills the jar, and puts it back on the bookshelf. For a moment, she stands in the doorway watching the needles' gentle motion before reaching over and snapping off one of Phil's leaves. The needles swing so violently, Kelsey jumps. "Yikes!" She drops the leaf. "I'm sorry."

The whole place looks messy and reminds Kelsey of Hobby. She begins to tidy up, starting with the bookcase. She stacks the magazines, lines up the books with the tallest in the center, shorter volumes on each end. She collects all the pens and pencils and adds them to the ones in a *Smell the Grass* coffee mug. She finds a rag and dusts the machines. When she gets to the polygraph, she sees another series of sharp jerks. She looks out. Gen's right under Phil, licking his paws. Kelsey turns off the polygraph, the stereo, the lights, and leaves, padlocking the door behind her.

•　　•　　•　　•　　•

At home, a liquor delivery from Redwood Liquors, still in the bag, sits on the counter by the refrigerator. Kelsey puts two of the fresh bottles—one gin, one vodka—in the freezer.

Lydia sits at the dinette and watches her as she stores the other two bottles in the pantry. "Don't ever drink, Kelsey."

"I won't." This is not the first time her mother's warned her.

"No. I mean it. Don't take the first sip. Don't smoke either. And no drugs. You'll get hooked if you do. Addiction is in our blood."

Kelsey turns from the sink. Her mother isn't looking at her. She's staring at the refrigerator door. "I won't, Mom. I promise."

"I promised, too." Tears well in Lydia's eyes. "My mother tried to tell me, and I promised. Even after years of watching my parents drink their lives away, and now look at me. I've been sitting here since that bag arrived an hour ago, trying not to get up and fix a drink, trying to will myself to stop."

Kelsey watches her mother's face, thoughtful, remembering some point in the past. Then right before her eyes, she sees her mother's resolve crumble and fall away. Kelsey takes a deep breath. There would be no better time. "Mom, Josh's mother stopped drinking with the help of AA."

Lydia pushes her chair back and gets up. "I'm not going to sit in a room full of Bible-bangers." She goes to the freezer, pulls out the bottle of vodka, and carries it to the sink. Seconds tick by before she breaks the seal, unscrews the lid, and holds it, poised to pour it down the drain.

Do it, Mom.

A dead fly lies on the windowsill. Lydia brushes it off into the sink, pulls a glass from the drain board, and pours it half full of vodka.

Kelsey bites her bottom lip and sighs. "Why did you start drinking after you promised you wouldn't?"

Her mother stirs a little water into her drink with a knife from the drain cup. "I didn't believe for a minute I'd end up like my parents. Everybody else drank. I didn't want to be the lone holdout, and when everyone else gets drunk, it's unbearable unless you're drunk, too." Lydia lifts the glass in both hands and takes a sip like someone taking communion.

"Did Dad drink?"

"I can't remember. I suppose he did. We all did back then."

A little later, Kelsey carries out a grilled cheese sandwich and a cup of tomato soup to her mother who's watching an interview with Donald Trump. "That's a bad man," Lydia says.

"Why do you say that?"

"Look at his mouth, and the meanness in his eyes."

Kelsey studies Donald Trump's face while he talks. His eyes are squinty and angry-looking, but it's his voice she can't stand. "I thought you liked him. You never used to miss *The Apprentice.*"

"Not because I like him. I watched because I don't like him."

"That doesn't make sense. Why would you watch a show you don't like?"

"For the same reason people watch those real housewives. Disgusting behavior is interesting."

Kelsey guesses that's true. She wonders if she and her mother might make a reality show worth watching. Are their lives disgusting enough? Probably not. Too routinely disgusting. Tonight, though, they'll have an okay evening, the kind where Kelsey feels more sorry for her mother than resentful.

By the time *Wheel of Fortune* ends, Lydia's fighting to stay awake. She doesn't look up when Kelsey stands.

"I've got homework. I guess I'd better get started."

Her mother gives a long slow blink. "You're a good girl, Kelsey. Smart."

"Thanks, Mom."

Lydia closes her eyes and smiles.

Kelsey goes straight to her mother's room and pulls the shoebox from beneath the bed. She roots through the pictures looking for more of the blonde girl who had once been her mother, The two she'd seen before are the only ones. Kelsey studies her mother's face. What changed that happy, smiling young woman of twenty-seven into the woman passed out in the living room? Had her father taken this picture? Had his leaving caused her to turn into an alcoholic? If so, Kelsey's glad he's dead. He deserves it if he did this to her mother.

CHAPTER 28

Later that night, Kelsey props herself up in bed and starts to read *The Secret Life of Plants.* By page five she's hooked. What's immediately clear is that Hobby was trying to duplicate the experiments Cleve Backster did in the late 1960s.

Backster was an instructor in the use of the polygraph for the CIA, when his secretary gave him a plant to add a little green to his office. One day, for the heck of it, he hooked the plant up to the lie detector to see what would happen when he watered it. It was a *Dracaena fragrans,* sometimes called a corn plant since its leaves grow like the ones on a stalk of corn.

Kelsey doesn't quite understand the author's explanation of how the polygraph actually works—galvanometers and Wheatstone bridges—but she gets that it has to do with electrical impulses. By attaching the Galvanic Skin Resistance disks to the *Dracaena*'s leaves, Backster expected the electrical impulses to increase as the water traveled up the stem, and that he'd be able to tell exactly when the water reached the leaves. That made sense. Even Kelsey knows water conducts electricity really well. When Hobby tested her, he was looking for sweat—a sign of stress.

Instead of a "trending" upward as the electrical impulses increased, the tracing moved downward, as if the plant was having an emotional response to being watered—like a sigh of relief. What Backster did next changed his life. He decided to light a match and burn a leaf, but all he did was think the thought and the plant reacted, causing a long, upward sweep of the pen.

That's impossible! Then again, Kelsey wasn't looking at the printout when it occurred to her to yank one of Phil's leaves off, so she doesn't know if he knew what was coming or not. He certainly reacted when she did it. She remembers Hobby showing her Phil's reaction to her arrival after Lauren died. He said it was probably because Gen heard her coming, and Phil reacted to Gen's emotional bump.

To read her mind, Phil would have to be able to visualize her mental image of tearing off a leaf? That was too crazy. But the more she thinks about it, the more she remembers from her new favorite class—biology. Ms. Sholars, her teacher, says plants, when attacked by plant-eating insects or disease, send out chemical signals, probably to their own leaves. But it travels through the air, warnings other plants nearby to build their defenses by becoming toxic, or at least no longer as tasty. She remembers Ms. Sholars talking about pollinators and how the flowers of some plants create smells that mimic the scent of a female moth attracting the male to the flower. He'll be covered with pollen and carry it to the next flower. And some carnivorous plants lure insects with sweet smells so they can trap and eat them. And what about dogs and other animals being able to smell fear on a person? Maybe Mr. Backster didn't know all that stuff over fifty years ago when he was doing his experiments. Maybe Phil detected her intention from an electrical impulse she sent.

It's after ten when she closes the book and turns out the light, but she lies awake thinking. The possibility of plants and animals knowing—by whatever means—what humans think, even feel, blows her mind.

•   •   •   •   •

On the next Saturday, Kelsey leaves home early, stops by the hospital, and finds Hobby unchanged. He's been in a coma now for nearly two weeks. She's seen pictures on the news of people in comas and how, after a while, their muscles shrivel, twisting their hands and feet into pitiful shapes. She worries this will happen to Hobby if he doesn't wake soon.

At the greenhouse, Gen waits for her at the end of the driveway. She picks him up and snuggles him. "Yum, you've been sleeping in pine needles, haven't you?"

"How you trending, Phil?" she asks, opening the padlock. Before going to the cupboard to fix Gen's breakfast, she turns on the polygraph for its comforting hum and the sound of the pens scratching. She mixes a little wet food into a scoop of dry. "Losing a few pounds hasn't hurt you any, Butterball." She takes Gen's food out to the spigot where the hose is attached and adds a little water.

"Want a drink, Phil?" She gives him a little squirt and darts into the bunker to see his reaction. There is none.

Too late, she remembers she didn't put Gen's bowl on the ground. Gen has jumped on the potting table and is eating as if he hasn't been fed in a week. He drives the bowl toward the edge and, before Kelsey can catch it, it falls off and lands upside-down. Gen looks at her and meows.

"I'll fix more. Don't worry."

Kelsey remakes his breakfast, then gets a spade and a dustpan to clean up the first meal. She'll pitch it outside for the jays. As she gets up, she spots the drawer under this section of the potting table. She'd forgotten about it. She pulls it open and rummages through it. Besides the magnifying glass, the tweezers, and the stopwatch they used to test the Venus flytrap's memory, it contains clippers, a paperclip with a single small key, a few metal plant stakes, and a collection of stiff white, plastic labels with pointy ends for writing a species' name and sticking into newly potted plants. At the back of the drawer, she finds a yellow canister of pepper spray. Hobby must have been trying to get to it when he was hit with the crowbar. She found him just a few feet away. The fact the pepper spray is still here, and that the drawer isn't obvious, may mean the police didn't find it.

Kelsey follows her regular routine by watering the begonias in the lath house, then starts on Carlotta's greenhouse. Carlotta's mealworms are under a clay pot on a shelf next to a box of Miracle Gro. Each day, Kelsey has mined the container of the red bran for a worm for Carlotta. It's still a surprise to come into the greenhouse and have a spider run from her hiding place, down her quivering web to meet her.

Kelsey gets the worm container and works a finger through the bran. Carlotta waits, watching. "I'm looking. I'm looking," she says. There are plenty of beetles, but Carlotta doesn't like them. She prefers the worms. Kelsey has discovered the mealworms are beetle larvae, changing from worm to pupa to beetle. She wishes she could do that—transform. Change from what she is into a better person.

"You're out of worms, Carlotta. I'll ride to town and get you more, okay? Wait here."

There's a jar full of loose change in the back corner of Hobby's desk. She remembers he told her he buys the worms at the feed store, but she's not sure how much they cost. She counts out five dollars in quarters, writes the amount on a Post-it note, adds *for worms*, and puts it in the jar.

Fort Bragg Feed and Pet is on the south side of the Pudding Creek bridge, less than two miles away. Kelsey gets her bike and starts down the driveway. She's nearly to the road when she remembers the bunker door is open. She'd never forgive herself if Hobby's stuff got stolen on her watch. She goes back to lock it.

The feed store is practically across the street from Denny's. Every time she passes the restaurant, she thinks about Lauren. She feels older since Lauren died, and can't imagine ever again being silly and giggly the way they'd been that day at lunch.

It takes Kelsey thirty minutes to get to the feed store and back with the mealworms. When she wheels into Hobby's driveway, the hair on the back of her neck tingles. She slows dismounts and walks up the path. When Gen doesn't run to meet her, she knows something's wrong. She looks over her shoulder at the souped-up car parked on the opposite side of the road. Was it there when she left?

CHAPTER 29

Kelsey halts her bike beneath the rose arbor and watches two shadows move around inside the west greenhouse. Her pulse skyrockets, but before she can back away, Will throws open the door. Ryan's right behind him. "Hey, Kels."

A laugh escapes. "Oh my God, you guys scared me. What are you doing here?"

"In the neighborhood," Will says. "Came by to see if you was still doing time."

"As you can see." Kelsey dismounts and leans her bike against the rose arbor, but her heart continues to pound. She imagines Will can see the pulse in her neck. He's looking at her like he did the first time she saw him, hooded black eyes, then a long slow blink. He must see his affect on her, but his smile seems like he's genuinely happy to see her.

Ryan breaks the spell. "Looking good, Kels." He picks at the loose end of the filthy Band-aid coming loose from right knuckles.

"That's so sweet of you." Her voice drips with sarcasm. She lifts the small plastic bag from her basket.

"Whatcha got there?" Ryan says.

Kelsey holds up the writhing mass in a see-through plastic bag. "Mealworms."

"Lunch?" Will says.

Kelsey grins. "Full of protein. Want some?"

"You first," Ryan says.

"What are you still doing here, anyway?" Will says. "I saw in the paper the old man is in the hospital. You're kinda off the hook, ain't you?" He snaps a branch off the rosemary bush near his right hip and crushes it in his fist. "Smell this." He shoves it in Ryan's face, then tosses it aside, and laughs.

"I still gotta do the hours. Feed the cat. Water the plants."

"We came by to see if you wanted to go for a ride," Ryan says. If he had a tail, it would be wagging. Kelsey sees him glance at Will, and realizes Ryan has proudly made up an excuse for them being here. Kelsey walks past them, oddly chilled.

The boys follow.

The air inside the greenhouse feels electric, causing her skin to tingle. *Silly.* As tough as Will acts, she's never been afraid of him. Far from it. And Ryan is nothing but a pitifully sad joke on his parents.

Kelsey remembers the first time she saw Will. She, Lauren and Josh were eating lunch at one of the picnic tables on the school patio. "Don't look now but that cute boy's staring at you," Lauren said. Of course, Kelsey turned. Will leaned against one of the breezeway posts, watching them—her, actually, which was weird since Lauren was the pretty one. He didn't do anything, just looked at her with no expression. She glanced away, embarrassed, then looked again. He smiled. She smiled back. She's never forgotten the lazy way his eyes took her in. She'd been both attracted to him and a little frightened.

"Where you headed?" Kelsey says.

"No place in particular," Will says.

"You need a plan, don't you?" She smiles.

For a moment, Will's face is a blank slate, then he laughs. "Guess we do. Let's get some beer and go to Glass Beach."

"Let me finish here and I'll meet you," Kelsey says. "At the trestle end, right?" She has no intention of meeting them, and Will knows it.

"Why don't you ride with us?" Ryan says.

Kelsey holds up the bag of roiling worms. "Gotta feed the carnivores."

Will leans against the door jamb. "I like those bug-eating plants. They're cool to watch."

Kelsey's insides feel full of worms, too. The staring at her that first day, the wink behind Brie's back at the party, and the way he's looking at her now. Does he like her *that* way? Does she hope he does?

"You ever seen inside the old man's vault back there?" Will jerks his head toward the bunker.

"Sure. A few times."

"Gotta lot of good crap in there."

Even though the air's warm and she's wearing her windbreaker, she feels gooseflesh on her arms. "You think so?"

Will has the focus of a cat stalking a bird. He looks at her with no expression.

"I guess maybe." She hesitates. "He is—was—pretty secretive about it. I never really paid much attention. The cops took his laptop. The TV's old. I doubt there's much left."

Will shrugs and glances up. Tendrils of fuchsia hang above his head. "Too bad this ain't mistletoe." In one sudden move, he catches her neck in the crook of his arm.

A short cry lodges in Kelsey's throat as he pulls her head down and gives it a noogie with his knuckle, hard enough to hurt. He lets her go and jerks his thumb for Ryan to follow. "See ya around, Kels."

"Yeah. See ya."

She stands there until she hears their car start and the sound of tires peeling rubber. Now she gets why the air in the greenhouse is so charged. She runs to the bunker and dials in the combination with trembling fingers. Gen comes out from under the potting table. Kelsey holds the door for him before slamming it behind her and sliding the inside bolt.

She sits in Hobby's chair, her heart thundering in her chest. She knows as well as if she'd seen them do it that Will and his doormat, Ryan, with that Band-aid on his knuckles, are the ones who put Hobby in a coma. Every living thing in the greenhouse recognized the threat and electrified the air with a warning. She'd felt the hair on her arms stand up, and is sure that Will felt it, too. Like any successful predator, he can smell fear.

CHAPTER 30

When her heart slows, Kelsey gets up and goes to the window. She'd locked the bunker before going to the feed store, but she hadn't turned off the polygraph. At her feet is the growing pile of paper. The tracings are calm on the sections she can see. Kelsey sees her image reflected in the glass. Hobby's desk lamp shines above her head so she looks like a person in a cartoon when the light bulb of an idea comes on. Kelsey drops to her knees and begins lifting sheet after sheet of the printout. There are three places where the tracing runs wildly from side-to-side. She can't be totally sure, but the last one is probably when Will grabbed her. A few folds further down, the sheet is blackened with lines. Was this when she rode up on her bicycle? Kelsey lifts another section of the printout, maybe five minutes' worth, and finds the wildest tracing of all. She's positive this is when Will and Ryan first entered the greenhouse.

She sits on the floor with the paper spilling and folding across her knees. She looks out at Phil. *How is this possible? No eyes, no ears, no brain.* Yet she knows Will or Ryan attacked Hobby, and so does that potted plant. She gets up and turns off the polygraph. She puts a classical CD on for the plants, and, on her way to feed Carlotta, she opens the secret drawer and takes out the pepper spray. If Phil knows what happened that night, all the plants know. Her mind zigs and zags between thinking the possibility is ridiculous and being dead sure she's right. Maybe the heat and humidity in the greenhouse has made her brain spongy, but she feels an odd kinship, as if she's acquired a batch of new friends. What did Hobby say? All the living beings are our kin—our family.

It's getting late and Gen shadows her to remind her he's hungry. Outside Carlotta's greenhouse, the air has chilled. It will be a cold ride home. "Come on, Tubby, let me feed you so I can get home and watch my mother drink the night away."

Feeling enough time has passed since Will and Ryan left, Kelsey puts the pepper spray back in the drawer, closes it, then opens it again, and takes out the small key she noticed earlier. In the bunker, she looks for keyholes. There aren't any. She gets on her hands and knees and looks under the desk for another secret drawer. Gen rubs his chin on the side of the pantry and meows, so Kelsey puts the key in her pocket, opens the cupboard, and takes out his food. When she puts the sack of dry food back, she spots a small metal box on the top shelf. She hadn't noticed it before because it's stored on end as part of a row of books.

The key opens it. Inside is a journal. Though she knows she shouldn't, she takes it out. *Dr. Jonathan Hobbes, Berkeley, California* is scrawled on the inside of the front cover. Her skin tingles and she automatically glances over her shoulder out of guilt for snooping through Hobby's possessions. She gets up, closes the bunker door, slides the bolt into place, and opens his journal near the middle:

August 19, 2019: The new kid arrived today; a pretty little thing with a chip on her shoulder the size of a redwood burl. Even if I can interest her in the plant studies, she may skew the data. She's a mighty angry young lady. On the other hand, it may work perfectly—if she doesn't scare the chlorophyll out of them every time she's here.

She closes her eyes against the sting of tears. "I'm sorry, Hobby," she says aloud, unzips her backpack, and puts the journal inside. She wonders, sadly, if the plants had sensed her attitude and electrified the air the day she arrived—sending out a warning to Hobby.

·   ·   ·   ·   ·

Back home in her bed, Kelsey props herself on her pillows. By nine, she's read most of the early journal entries, which date from the early-2000s. They detail Hobby's skepticism at Backster's experiments and his own attempts to duplicate them in his lab at Berkeley. One entry near the end, *I think the old guy's DNA was short a nucleotide.*

After that, there was nothing until 2015.

Bought the Pudding Creek property. Retirement looms.
September 13, 2017: JJD has asked if I'll take a young man under my wing. First time offender. It's community service or juvenile detention. Against my better judgement, I agreed.

Oddly, Hobby didn't name who the young man was. Kelsey can only assume it was Will, since he'd said, "been there, done that."

The next entry, nearer the middle, she finds the one she read in the greenhouse, marking her arrival on that first day, and another one from a few days earlier.

August 16, 2019: JJD called today. I agreed to take another of their delinquents. I swore after that last one I wouldn't, but this one's a girl with no father and her mother's an alcoholic. Hit me where it hurts. Couldn't say no.

Kelsey puts the journal down. It's odd to read his thoughts about her, and to realize he's known her history all along, though she not sure why that surprises her.

September 3, 2019: My little delinquent is buying a new plant, one that's not tuned into what I do around here the way Phil is. I'm going to try Backster's brine shrimp experiment using earwigs. If it works, it may break through that shell of hers. Trying to get her interested in learning anything hasn't worked so far. She's solely focused on getting her hours over with. She did seem mildly interested in the mimosa experiment.

September 4: Success!!! The girl brought a fresh Dracaena *to the lab. That was the secret. It had no connection to me, or her. It reacted violently to the destruction of the earwigs. I had her empty in the second batch and the response was muted. The third time, you could practically feel the damn thing shrug. She got interested enough to defend the earwigs.*

September 8: I was looking at the day's readout from Phil when something alarmed him. The tracings were all over the page. I turned the light off in my office and watched through the window. I'm sure it was that thug, Will Something and the other guy I took in a couple of years ago. Flipped on the microphone and cranked my siren a couple of times; he and his pal took off like farts in the wind.

Here it is. It *had* been Will and Ryan snooping around.

September 14: It's five and the girl—what's her damn name—one of those modern names—I can't find her paperwork—hasn't shown up for three days.

September 15: Still no girl. I found her paperwork. Kelsey McCully. Wonder if she's related to John? I called her house and left a message. Hate like hell to call JJD on her. She's been pretty reliable 'til now.

September 18: Today's paper had a story about a kid getting killed out on Sherwood Rd. Saturday. Not named McCully, but dollars to donuts that's why my truant is truant.

September 20: Kelsey showed up yesterday. She was mad at me for asking about her friend's death. Phil reacted to her emotional upheaval. That just astonishes me. It is so exciting. Sad for her, of course, but what a test of that theory!

There are more entries, other experiments. A couple of notes about crediting her an hour a day, though he was sure she'd quit coming. Kelsey feels guilty.

September 29: That cop neighbor of Kelsey's, called to tell me she's been picked up for shoplifting again. Later today, a woman called from the police and asked if I'd come pick Kelsey up. Pretty sad state of affairs when the only person she has to call for help is someone she can't stand. Poor kid.

Kelsey reads the line again. *Jerry called him. He arrested me, then tried to find help for me.* A sense of regret sweeps over her. She hopes Hobby doesn't die thinking she hated him.

October 10: I stuck out my neck and told the judge I'd take responsibility for her. I really believe the kid's got a good center. It's pretty clear Phil likes her—his little chlorophyll heart goes pity-pat every time she heads this way. It's gotten so I can set my watch by the blip on the readout and 5 minutes later, here she comes. That's Phil; Gen would desert me in a minute if Kelsey wanted to take him home. If the plants and animals think she's an okay risk, who am I to argue?

October 12: We had a long talk today. She's so confused. I meant to tell her more than I did. We talked about her mending her ways, but, if I'd thought she would understand, I could have told her that on a cellular level we are completely different people every seven to ten years. Not a single cell in our bodies, with the exception of our brain cells, is the same. If our bodies can renew themselves, form cohesion only through cellular memories, then we should be able to heal emotionally, too. I'll try to remember to tell her tomorrow. Between the experiments and this kid, in whose life I might actually make a difference, I feel like I have a new opportunity to feel useful.

That was the last entry. Kelsey closes the journal. More than anything, she wants a chance to tell Hobby he *has* made a difference and she will prove him right for believing in her.

She goes down the hallway to check on her mother. Lydia's watching TV. If Kelsey lets her know she's still awake, her mother will ask to have her feet tickled. Back in her room, Kelsey takes *The Secret Life of Plants* off her bedside table and opens it again to the first chapter. Now that she's finished Hobby's journal, she wants to reread the part she read before. On page seven, she nearly laughs out loud. This Cleve Backster guy showed a group of Yale University students how a plant reacted to a spider's attempt to get away from a human trying to catch it. *I couldn't do a thing around there without Phil squealing on me.*

On page nine, Kelsey's mind starts to race. Backster set up an experiment with two plants. He had his students draw straws. The person with the shortest straw was instructed to go alone into the room with the two plants and kill one of them—rip it out of its pot, tear its leaves off, and stomp it to death. He committed "the crime in secret; neither Backster nor any of the other students knew his identity; only the second plant was a witness."

Kelsey sits up, a white-knuckle grip on the book. In the experiment, Backster marched the students through the room and the surviving plant reacted when the murderer passed by. "Oh, my God," she whispers. "Here it is. I was right. Phil does know who did it. All the plants know." Phil *recognized* Will and Ryan, and thought Kelsey was in danger when they showed up. If Hobby dies, one or both of them is a murderer. What can she do? She closes the book and turns out her light.

Backster coined a term to explain how plants do what Hobby described—attune themselves to us: primary perception. For people, it's a gut-level knowing about things you can't explain or know about in any other way. It's how she knew something was wrong when she came back from the feed store, before she spotted Will and Ryan in the greenhouse. Is it such a stretch to believe plants are capable of releasing chemical warnings, exactly like what humans call our sixth sense?

She lies awake for a long time trying to decide her next step. She doesn't have a very good relationship with the law, but she falls asleep trying to remember that lady detective's name.

CHAPTER 31

On Monday morning, Kelsey rides her bike to the sheriff's office. She chains it to the *Reserved for Sheriff* sign and goes in. There's a dried up, nearly leafless *Ficus* in the corner of a sparsely furnished entry. She goes to the glass window—bullet-proof, no doubt—and speaks to the receptionist through an amplifying grill.

"I need to see a detective."

"Which detective?"

"I don't know. She's a lady. I'll know her name when I see it."

"That would Detective Moran, she's our only female detective." The woman picks up the phone. "Your name?"

"Kelsey McCully."

A pink plastic, solar-flower dances on the other side of the glass as the woman speaks to someone, then hangs up. She nods toward the door and pushes a buzzer when Kelsey's hand is on the knob. The receptionist meets her on the other side. "Leave your backpack here." She points to the corner just inside the door next to another dead plant.

Kelsey shrugs off her pack. "Your plants need water."

"I know. The secretary who takes care of them is on maternity leave."

How frigging hard is it to fill a glass with water?

"Last door on the right." the woman says.

The door to Detective J. Moran's office is ajar and Kelsey sees a hanging basket in the corner by the window with a healthy philodendron cascading nearly to the floor. Kelsey looks back at the receptionist whose arms are crossed over her chest. She nods and Kelsey knocks.

"Come in."

Detective Moran sits at her desk, typing, her face bathed in the light from her computer screen. Behind her, along the windowsill, are a half dozen pots of blooming African violets in various colors, and a *Dracaena* in the corner. Kelsey smiles. If she has a prayer of getting anyone to believe her, she's hit the jackpot.

Detective Moran glances up.

"Do you remember me?" Kelsey stays in the doorway.

The detective studies Kelsey over the top of reading glasses. "You're Dr. Hobbes' court re... you worked for him."

"I still work for him."

"It's been a week, how's he doing?

"He's still in a coma."

"I'm sorry to hear that. Come in. What can I do for you, Miss McCully?" She leans back in her chair and laces her fingers together behind her head.

"You have nice plants." Kelsey stands behind the chair opposite her desk.

"Thanks."

"Do you take care of them yourself?"

"Yep. It relaxes me." Detective Moran's eyes grow curious. "Watching them grow makes me feel better about the world. Know what I mean?"

Kelsey nods. "I think Hobby feels the same way."

"Dr. Hobbes?"

"His friends call him Hobby."

"I see."

Kelsey sees her swallow a smile.

"We haven't made any progress on his case, if that's why you're here. We've got a few partial prints and DNA off the steel door, but no matches so far."

"Do you know who did it?" Kelsey folds her hands over the chair back in front of her.

"We have a couple suspects, but no probable cause to issue warrants."

"I do."

Detective Moran's brow creases. "You do what?"

"Know who did it."

"Greg Wright is the lead detective. Shall I call him?" She leans forward and puts her hand on the phone.

Kelsey shakes her head. "I think it needs to be you."

"What makes you think that?"

Kelsey glances at the African violets. "I just do."

"I'm afraid I need a reason."

"Does Detective Wright like plants?"

Detective Moran closes a file folder on the desk and reaches for another. "I can't say. He doesn't have any in his office, if that's your criteria."

"It needs to be you then."

"Well, Kelsey, I've got a bit of work to do here, so if there is something I can do for you, I think you'd better tell me."

"Have you ever read *The Secret Life of Plants*?"

Detective Moran sighs. "I can't say that I have. No." She puts her elbows on her desk and church-steeples her fingers.

"If I loan it to you, will you read it?"

"Kelsey, I don't have a lot of time, could you come to the point?"

"Just say yes or no. It's important."

"I'll look at it, okay? I can't promise I will read it."

"That's fair enough." Kelsey leans across the desk and sticks her hand out.

Detective Moran smiles and shakes her hand.

"The book is in my backpack at the end of the hall. It will explain how I know who did it. I'll be right back."

"Well, I love a mystery—as you might have guessed—and you've certainly piqued my interest."

"You only have to read as far as page nine."

She laughs. "Well, that will save some time."

·   ·   ·   ·   ·

The phone rings early Saturday morning. Kelsey's in the kitchen and grabs it on the first ring to keep from waking her mother who slept the entire night in her recliner.

"So, you think the plants witnessed the whole thing?" Detective Moran says.

Kelsey smiles. "Yes ma'am, I know they did."

"I made a phone call this morning."

Kelsey picks at the chipped Formica countertop.

"Cleve Backster lives in San Diego. We had quite a talk once he got past his reticence to speak to me. I guess he has taken quite a beating over the years for his theories."

"He's still alive? Wow. What did he say?"

"He said the plants are definitely witnesses."

"I know that—"

Her mother stirs.

Kelsey lowers her voice and walks toward the back door with the phone until she runs out of cord. "One of the plants is still hooked to Hobby's lie detector and it went crazy when these boys from my school came into the greenhouse last week."

"Boys came to the greenhouse?"

"Uh huh. Don't you call that returning to the scene of the crime?"

"What are their names?"

"Will Phelan. I don't know Ryan's last name."

"I do. Did they threaten you?"

"Not really. Will acted a little creepy, and he asked about the equipment in Hobby's bunker. I mean his office."

"It looks like those two are prime candidates, but I can't imagine a judge willing to authorize a warrant based on the testimony of a Ficus." She laughs.

It took all Kelsey's nerve to go to Detective Moran with her theory. She's not giving up now. "It's a philodendron."

"Sorry. I was making a not-too-funny joke. But you get the point, right?"

"Is there coffee on, Honey?" her mother calls. "I could really use my coffee."

Kelsey covers the mouthpiece. "Just a minute, Mom."

"How about I meet you later this afternoon?" Detective Moran says.

"Okay."

"Will 3:30 work?"

"Yes ma'am."

"Want me to pick you up at your house?"

"No," Kelsey says quickly, perhaps too quickly. "I have my bike. I'll meet you at the greenhouse."

"Righto, then."

•   •   •   •   •

Gen shadows Kelsey while she waters, walking to the edge of the plant stand and pushing against her free hand for a tickle. He's at her elbow as she roots in the bran for a mealworm for Carlotta, who waits at the edge of her web.

Even knowing it's Detective Moran arriving, Kelsey's stomach flip-flops when she hears a car door slam. If it had been Will, Gen would have hidden. Instead, he jumps down and runs to meet the detective. Kelsey follows, wondering how he knows, without seeing who it is, that the person is safe. Is it because the plants aren't alarmed?

"Call me, Hannah," Detective Moran says when Kelsey greets her. "Has that cat gotten beefier?" She picks Gen up and cuddles him. Added reassurance that Kelsey has the right person.

"I've got him on a diet, but I think he's bulking up on mice. I'd take him home with me, but my mother's allergic."

"I remember."

Hannah looks around the bunker. "He has quite a set up here, doesn't he? I met him once. Interesting guy. Any improvement?"

"The same. The nurse says he may never come out of the coma." Kelsey ducks her head. "I really like him, but I never told him."

"He knew. Knows. I'm sure he noticed the change in your tone of voice, and that you worked a little harder to please him."

"I hope so."

Hannah settles herself in Hobby's chair, and Kelsey sits on a corner of the desk. "Since we talked, I've checked on Will and Ryan. Will was a court referral a couple years ago. If Dr. Hobbes doesn't come out of this, or can't identify them when he does, there will be no grounds for a warrant. They even have an alibi. Both boys were seen by a cop in the alley outside the Headlands Café twice, first at eight-thirty and again at ten-thirty. The other kids with them will no doubt swear they were there all evening."

"They'd be lying."

"I'm sure that's true." She looks around the room. "There was blood and a bit of skin on the door frame above the lock—"

"It was Ryan's. He was still wearing a Band-aid on his knuckle when they were here."

"That might be so, but without probable cause, we can't require a DNA sample. I'm afraid Detective Wright considers this case cold, or nearly so, at least until Dr. Hobbes wakes up." Her eyes meet Kelsey's. "If he does."

A bubble of anger nearly causes her to say something she would later regret. She's terrified Hobby will die, but inexplicably she doesn't want to hear the same concern from anyone else. "Didn't they fingerprint them when they were arrested before?" Her tone is accusatory.

Hannah, if she notices, gives no sign. "Yes, but their juvenile records are sealed, and we only got partials off the crowbar. They aren't complete enough to make a positive match—even with the computer lacing program."

"Can't you bring them in for questioning and give them a soft drink or something to get a DNA sample."

Hannah smiles. "A CSI fan, huh?"

Kelsey blushes. "My mother is. I watch sometimes."

"Right now, we don't have a legitimate reason to bring them in, and we're still waiting for the DNA results."

"What's taking so long?"

Hannah smiles again. "There's always a back-up, and the forensic lab is in Ukiah."

"See Phil there?" Kelsey taps the glass window. "He's hooked to the polygraph through these wires." Kelsey kneels and begins to reel in the paper until she finds the section she'd marked. "Last week I went to the feed store to get mealworms for Carlotta—"

"Carlotta?"

"She's Hobby's— She's our pet spider."

"Oh." Hannah gives a little shiver. "Not nuts about spiders."

"Neither was I, but she's changed my mind. Anyway, when I got back with Carlotta's worms, Will and Ryan were here, snooping around. I've known them for years. Ryan's a doormat and does whatever Will says." She decides against mentioning how repelled by and attracted to Will she was, like two ends of a magnet. "I wasn't afraid of them until I saw this." She holds out a portion of the printout. "I think this is when they got here. Phil somehow recognized them because this is his reaction." She drops that section and finds the next. "Here's where I rode up a few minutes later. I know this sounds crazy, but Hobby says Phil likes me and was afraid they would hurt me. And this is where Will grabbed me around the neck."

"He assaulted you?"

"Not really. He gave my head a noogie and let me go." She looks up. "This sounds ridiculous, doesn't it?"

"It would have before my talk with Backster."

"I know they did it. Gen's the friendliest cat in the world. He ran out to meet you. He hid from Will and Ryan." Kelsey strokes Gen, who's made himself part of the conversation by sitting alertly on Hobby's desk. He gives a chirpy meow at the mention of his name.

"Kelsey, even if you have interpreted this read-out correctly, a read-out won't get a judge to issue a warrant. I can't believe I'm saying this, but we have to have more than the words of a potted plant and a cat. Right now, that's all we have to go on."

"Only thing I can't figure is, if Ryan was wearing my gloves, how'd he hurt his knuckle?" Kelsey says

"I can only guess. He skinned his knuckle, and then got the gloves. Or Will wore them. You say he's smarter."

"If Will had on gloves, then it must be Ryan's fingerprints on the crowbar."

"Not necessarily. They might be Dr. Hobbes' and they got smeared by the glove-wearer."

"Jeez." Kelsey smacks her forehead and jumps off the table. "Hobby never turned off the polygraph. Phil would have freaked when they hit him. That will tell you what time they were here."

Kelsey begins unfolding the stack the paper has made, that's folded itself as it comes out of the machine. She looks for Hobby's marks, his last date and time. She goes through quite a bit of it and finds nothing, so she starts over. "I know he didn't turn the machine off, so it's got to be here. Here!

Here. Look." She finds a section of paper with violent lines where the pen swept side-to-side for what must have been a full minute, then went absolutely flat. "That's weird."

"He fainted." Hannah says.

"Who fainted?"

"Phil. Backster said they faint, or seem to, at a certain level of stress. Did Hobby always add a date and time?"

Kelsey nods. "I think so. He's pretty fussy."

She only has to go back two pages to find the neatly printed date and time: *October 23 / 2247 Nite, nite Phil.*

"He uses the twenty-four-hour clock," Kelsey explains. "That's 10:47 p.m."

"I know," Hannah says. "I prefer it myself." She kneels and spreads the two-page section out flat on the floor. There's a tape measure among the odds and ends in a tray on Hobby's desk. With it, she measures the distance between where he'd written the date and time and the point where Phil began to react to what was happening. It measures thirty-eight-and-a-half inches. "Now, we need to measure how long it took the paper to get from there to where the prolonged reaction occurred. Turn it on, will you?"

Kelsey draws a line across the paper, writes the time and flips the switch. "At least we know their alibi is dust. Hobby was okay at ten-thirty, the last time the cop said he saw Will and Ryan."

"You've got that right." Hannah watches the clock on the wall. "Still it doesn't give us enough for a warrant."

They stand side-by-side, watching the minutes on the clock tick by and keeping an eye on the pencil line moving slowly toward the floor. "Five minutes. I think that will do it," Hannah says.

Kelsey turns off the lie detector, draws a second line across the paper, and measures between the two lines. Thirteen inches.

Hannah does the math. "Thirteen into thirty-eight-and-a-half is . . . two point nine-seven, so nearly three times our five minute test, or fifteen minutes. That means they probably watched him leave, and then tried to break in. At least the assault wasn't premeditated."

"What makes you say that?"

"Well, they were at the Headlands at ten thirty, and he closed up here at ten forty-seven. The drive here, if they'd left immediately after the cop saw them, is maybe seven minutes—we can check that. That's ten thirty-seven. That leaves a ten-minute gap. If they got here just as Dr. Hobbes was closing up, they must have watched him lock the door. If they wanted to make it easy on themselves, they could have knocked him over the head before he locked it, so I'm guessing they waited ten minutes or so, then went to work." She takes out a notebook and writes down the times.

"He must have heard them, come back, they panicked, and hit him," Kelsey says.

"That would also explain why Phil's reaction—and I'll swear I never said this—only lasted a minute. If he'd sensed, or whatever accounts for this ability, that they were here to harm Dr. Hobbes, he, Phil, would have reacted when they arrived, like he did when you had your encounter with them. The gap between the time Dr. Hobbes made his last observation and the time Phil reacted to the assault was fifteen minutes, nothing in between." Hannah patted her hand. "So, the good news is, we know that he got clobbered at eleven-twelve, and the boys have no alibi."

"He tried to get his pepper spray, you know."

Hannah's eyes become hooded for a second. "How do you know that?"

Kelsey recognizes suspicion when she sees it. "I found a drawer in the potting table and it was in the drawer. He was lying right beneath it. I figure he was going for it when one of them hit him."

"We didn't find a drawer. Show me where it is."

Kelsey leads her outside and shows her the drawer and the pepper spray. "If we can get a sample of their DNA, can you arrest them?"

"Depends on whether it's a match and how it was acquired. All this is circumstantial at best. We can't require either of them to give a sample. If it's gotten without their knowledge or permission, it may work. Depends on the judge."

They go back into the office where Hannah takes the clipboard off the nail on the side of the cupboard. "I want to ask you about this."

"Those are my community service hours."

Hannah runs a finger down the column. "You've been here every day?"

Kelsey nods. "I come to feed Gen and Carlotta and water the plants."

"Well, I'll check with JJD, but I bet they'll accept my signature on this." She initials all of Kelsey's entries and signs at the bottom. "You continue to track your hours and bring them by every week. I'll sign off on them."

"Yes ma'am. Thank you."

"It's very responsible of you to keep up with your obligation. Dr. Hobbes will be pleased and very proud of you."

Kelsey shrugs, and for the first time, feels pride in herself.

CHAPTER 32

As usual, Kelsey stops by the hospital on her way home, chains her bike to the newsstand, and waves to the volunteer behind the desk, who's on the phone. She heads down the hall to ICU, taps lightly on the door, opens it and sticks her head in. Where Hobby had been for twelve days lies an old woman, surrounded by weeping family members.

Kelsey backs into the hall, spins, and runs toward the nurse's station. No one's there. She turns and sees a nurse coming out of one of the rooms.

"I'm looking for my uncle." Her voice cracks. *Did he die?* Tears swim in her eyes.

"His name?"

"John Hobbes. He was in ICU." Kelsey braces herself against the wall.

The nurse smiles.

Kelsey can't tell if the smile is meant to comfort before giving her the bad news.

"He's been moved to room 109. Down the hall on the left."

"Did he wake up?" Kelsey's pulse slows.

"No, but he's better."

"Thank you. Thank you so much." She takes off down the hall.

"You can stop running," the nurse calls after her. "He's not going anywhere."

Hobby lies in the bed closest to the door; there's no one in the bed by the window. Kelsey marches back down the hall to the nurses' station. "You have to move him to the window," she says, when the nurse looks up.

"I'm sorry?"

"He's a botanist. You need to put him by the window."

"I don't understand.'

"He needs to be closer to the plants. When he wakes, I want him to be able to look out and see the yard and the trees. And he needs his fingers wrapped. With electrical tape."

"You're his niece, right?"

Kelsey doesn't flinch. As far as she's concerned, they are now related. "Yes."

"Any other relatives?"

"No."

"He's still hooked up to a lot of machinery—."

"Please move him. It's really important."

"Okay. As soon as I'm free and can find an orderly to help me, we'll move him to the window. Now, what about his fingers?"

"He likes them bound together with electrical tape."

"Can't we just use a bandage?"

Kelsey knows she's being humored. "No. He doesn't like bandages. They show the dirt. He wants electrical tape."

"I'll see if maintenance has some."

A light comes on over a door down the hall. The nurse gets up.

"Can I bring him a plant for his room now?"

"Flowers are okay. Nothing in soil for the time being." The nurse starts down the hall toward the call light, stops, and turns. "When you go in, tell him who you are. Talk about your day, normal things. Assume he can hear you. And holding his hand or stroking his skin can be very comforting."

•   •   •   •   •

Her mother is on the phone in the kitchen, her back to the door when Kelsey comes in. Something about the way she's standing—shoulders humped, head lowered—stops Kelsey cold.

"She's none of your business," Lydia hisses.

Her mother must sense Kelsey's there because she whirls and her eyes widen. "Don't call here again." She slams the phone into the receiver.

"Who was that?"

"Nobody." Lydia runs water on the sponge, and wrings it like a chicken's neck.

"Sounded like somebody."

"A solicitor." She begins to wipe the counter, avoiding Kelsey's eyes.

"Why did a solicitor ask about me?"

"He didn't. Why are you sneaking around?"

"I'm not sneaking anywhere. I live here. You said *I* was none of his business."

"Okay, if you must know," Lydia throws the sponge in the sink. "It was some man checking to see if you're still working for that doctor. I said it was none of his business."

"Jeez, Mom. Was that the JPS? Why were you rude? Detective Moran is going to sign off on my time sheet. We talked about it today." Kelsey crosses the room and takes the phone off the receiver. "I'll use *69—."

"No." Her mother snatches the phone, presses a number, and hangs up.

"Why'd you do that?"

"I don't want you calling and kowtowing to him. He was rude to me."

Kelsey knows her mother's lying, but she can't figure out why. For one thing, the person in charge of her case is a woman. "Okay," she says. "Detective Moran said she'd drop by JJD tomorrow and make sure it's okay for her to take over until Hobby's better."

"Let her handle it, then. That's best." Her mother opens the freezer.

"He's better, by the way."

"Who?"

"Hobby. They've moved him out of ICU." Kelsey takes the vodka bottle from the kitchen counter. "Is this what you're looking for?"

"Don't smirk at me like that. It's after five."

"Did you hear me about Hobby?"

"What about him?"

Kelsey shakes her head. "Never mind."

•　　•　　•　　•　　•

The phone rings at eight the next morning. Kelsey runs from her room to answer it, hoping it won't wake her mother who stayed relatively sober last night, but Lydia's in the kitchen and catches it on the second ring. She says hello, then hangs up.

"Who was that this early?"

"Wrong number. Want some yogurt?"

"I'll take it with me."

It's Saturday, but instead of going to the hospital, Kelsey goes straight to the greenhouse. Gen, as usual, waits in the driveway. Kelsey's no longer surprised that he's there, even when she's early. She picks him up, hugs him, puts him in her basket, and wheels him to the greenhouse.

She's developed a routine: open the office and turn on the polygraph, which makes her feel guarded, feed Gen and Carlotta, then water the plants according to the schedule by the spigot, starting with Phil. She feels trustworthy, reliable, and useful. She's been responsible for her mother for as long as she can remember, but this is different. Taking care of everything for Hobby is her choice and makes her feel like a good person, not the rotten kid who needs her mother to keep her out of foster care no matter what condition her mother's in.

After she finishes, she goes to the office to shut everything down and lock up. The unopened yogurt is on the desk and seeing it reminds her she's hungry. The only spoon she can find is the one she used to serve Gen his wet food. She takes it out to the hose to wash. When she gets back, she sees a blip in the needle tracings. Phil reacted to something. Gen had waddled out to the sink with her, but now lags behind, scratching fleas. He runs to her when she calls him. When he's inside, she slams and locks the door behind him, turns off the lights, and peeks through the window. There's no one there and the needle is calm. Besides, Gen would have hidden if it was Will and Ryan. She turns the lights back on and sits in Hobby's chair to eat her yogurt. Immediately, she hears the scratch of the polygraph needle and jumps up to look out the window. No one.

"What's with you, Phil?"

She finishes her yogurt, puts the container in the trashcan, and starts to turn off the polygraph. Instead, she goes to the door. "Phil, how would you feel about giving up a branch or two for Hobby?" She leans back to see if he reacted. There was a little jerk, but that could be almost anything. She goes on: "He can't have anything with soil, but you'd be in water, and when he comes home, your parts will come back, too. They can grow into little Phils. Whatcha think?" She watches the needle for a moment. "Not much, I guess."

Or did you faint? An image of Phil pops into her head, leaf to his forehead—wherever that is—collapsing like a damsel in distress. She laughs. But when she takes the clippers from the nail by the front door, the polygraph needle whooshes back and forth. When she cuts the first of Phil's leafy tendrils, the needle scratches violently.

"Oh my God, Phil, I'm sorry."

One tendril will have to be enough. She gets the yogurt cup from the trash, rinses and fills it with water, cuts an X in the lid for the stem, and pokes it through.

•   •   •   •   •

Kelsey still breathless from her bike ride, carries the cutting to the nurses' station, and asks if they have something nicer to put the philodendron cutting in. The nurse goes to a storeroom and comes back with a green vase, which Kelsey carries to Hobby's room.

His bed has been moved to the window, but the dandelions the mower left outside ICU are no longer visible from this room. At least there's an arcing pine tree branch framed by the window, giving his room a less fish tank feel. A breeze causes the needles to scrape the glass. Two thoughts come at once: the nurse telling her how healing touch can be and the realization that the only time Kelsey touches her mother is when she's guilt-tripped into tickling her feet. The second was Hobby once telling her that everything an oak tree needs to become mighty is inside an acorn. All she can be is in her.

She turns from the window. Hobby looks the same and his fingers still point off in different directions, but there's a roll of electrical tape on his nightstand. Just then the nurse comes in to check the saline drip connected to the needle in a vein in his hand.

"Thanks." Kelsey holds up the tape.

"You're welcome. I left it for you since you know how he likes them wrapped." The nurse stops at the door. "He's mighty lucky to have a niece like you."

Kelsey looks at her feet. "I'm . . . I'm not really his niece."

"I know."

Her head comes up. "How'd you know?"

"I read the paper. You're the one who found him—maybe even saved his life." She smiles. "He's still very lucky to have you."

The sting of tears nearly makes her sneeze. Kelsey pinches the bridge of her nose.

After the nurse leaves, Kelsey places Phil's offspring on the windowsill and sets to work wrapping Hobby's cold, scaly fingers. It feels odd to touch him. She remembers how she thought he was gross when she first met him with his wild, white hair, wrinkled skin, and crooked yellow teeth. Now, as she binds his broken fingers together, she sees that his face is kind. When she finishes his fingers, she takes the little black comb from the nightstand drawer, and combs the section of his hair that isn't covered by a bandage.

The first entry in his journal pertaining to her was about the chip on her shoulder. Whatever her future holds, she's glad she isn't that person anymore. Hobby's magic worked on her. She doesn't know much about Will, except the rumor that his father's in San Quentin, and his mother's a meth addict. It occurs to her that if it wasn't for Hobby, she might have eventually turned out like Will, or like her mother. That makes her wonder about Will's time with him. Was he just too far gone, or did Hobby's subtle way of exposing her to life beyond the one she's living not work on Will?

"You look nice." She puts the comb away and returns to the window.

"Gen's doing great, Hobby." She centers Phil's vase on the sill. "And I brought a sprig of Phil to keep you company."

"Am I in the hospital?" a gravelly voice says.

Kelsey jumps and spins around. Hobby's eyes are open and he's looking at her.

She nods, for a moment, too stunned to speak. "Don't . . . Don't you remember?"

"Remember what?"

CHAPTER 33

As soon as school's out on Monday, Kelsey rides to the Sheriff's office to give Hannah last week's hours.

"You look like the cat that swallowed the canary," Hannah says when Kelsey puts the time sheet on her desk. "What's up?"

"Hobby's awake."

"That's wonderful. I'll send an officer by to take his statement."

"He doesn't remember anything." Kelsey picks a dead leaf off the African violet on the windowsill. "The last thing he remembers is Gen diving under his bed. Have you made any progress?"

"Not a lick. Well, except the DNA results are back, but the story's the same. No probable cause. No warrant. The boys haven't been back to the greenhouse, have they?" Hannah holds out her hand and Kelsey puts the dead leaf in her palm. Hannah drops it in the trash can under her desk.

"Not while I've been there. Phil *was* acting a little weird Saturday morning, but it didn't turn out to be anything."

"They'll slip up. We may not get them for this, but they'll make a mistake, and we'll get them for something else."

"It's not fair. They shouldn't get away with cracking Hobby's skull."

"Life's not always fair, Kelsey. As you well know." Hannah shuffles papers on her desk.

"I guess." Kelsey stands for a minute with her thumbs in her jeans' pockets. "Well, see ya."

Hannah looks up. "Sorry. I'm a bit overwhelmed here."

"That's okay." Kelsey stops at the door. "Did you talk to JJD?"

"I did. They're fine with me signing off on your hours."

"Good, 'cause the case worker called my mom."

Hannah's eyes narrow. "I don't think so, Kelsey. They didn't know anything about what happened to Hobbes. Why would she call?"

"My mom said it was a man who called."

"Your case worker is Marny Rontero."

"Maybe her boss?"

"She is the boss."

Hannah's phone rings. She answers and waves goodbye to Kelsey.

Kelsey gets a creepy feeling as she walks down the hall. Had her mother really out and out lied, or was there someone calling and pretending to be JJD? *Who would do that?* An instant later: *Will?* "But why?" she says aloud. She turns, walks back to Hannah's office, and taps on the doorframe. "You didn't call and talk to my mom, did you?" she says when Hannah looks up.

"No, why?"

"Nothing."

•   •   •   •   •

At the hospital, Hobby's sitting in a chair by the window. All the tubes and wires have been removed. He's shaved and wearing two clean hospital gowns, one on backwards and one as a robe. When she raps on the door, he opens his eyes, and smiles at her. "I'm told you've been here every day since I got bonked."

"Maybe not every day."

"I also hear you're my niece."

Kelsey blushes. "It was the only way I could visit you in ICU."

"A well-timed fabrication."

"When are they going to let you go home?"

"Not sure. Have to have my head examined again—" he smiles and pats the bandage still covering two-thirds of his scalp.

"How's little Phil doing?" Kelsey goes to the vase, lifts the tendril and lays it along the windowsill so it will get more light.

"I bet he didn't like losing a chunk of himself," Hobby says.

"I warned him, but he still acted like a big baby. I think he knew what I was up to because he was acting weird before I did it."

"How was he acting weird?"

"I don't know." She turns. "Jumpy."

"What were you doing?"

She leans against the window ledge. "Eating yogurt."

"Who knows?" Hobby shrugs. "When the roots develop, you can take it home with you. Phil will like that."

The door opens and a nurse comes in—a different nurse from the one who's been so nice to Kelsey. "Got a shot here for you, Dr. Hobbes." To Kelsey she says, "Do you mind stepping out? This has to go in his backside."

Kelsey has reached the door when she hears Hobby yell, "Stop." Then, "Kelsey, come back here."

"What?" she and the nurse say in unison.

"It was the bacteria."

"What was the bacteria?"

"Go away," he shoos the nurse.

"I have to give you this shot."

"Later. Not now. I'll call you when I'm ready."

"We'll see about this," she says.

Hobby waits until the door closes behind her. "Kelsey, it was the bacteria Phil was reacting to."

"What bacteria?"

"The bacteria in your yogurt."

"Yuck. It didn't taste funny."

"There's supposed to be bacteria in yogurt. Good bacteria. Did he react when you started eating it?"

"I don't know. I went to wash Gen's cat-food spoon, and when I came back the needle had moved. Why would Phil care about bacteria?"

"Don't you see?" Hobby squints like someone looking into the sun. "No, of course you don't. How could you?" He picks at the electrical tape around his fingers. "Life on earth started as single-celled organisms, specifically photosynthetic bacteria. If all life arose from that primordial soup, then the cells of every organism living today carry the memory of their origins. God, this is exciting."

"That was billions of years ago. You said so. And you said we have completely different cells every seven years?" Her heart leaps to her throat. He'd written that in his journal as something he meant to tell her but hadn't gotten the chance. He doesn't seem to notice.

"Different cells yes, but they all carry forward their mitochondrial DNA. Plants have it. We have it. In us it's called the mitochondrial Eve. And mitochondria are thought to be primitive bacteria. It's the DNA that passes only from the female egg. Never mind. I'll explain later."

"Sorry I asked."

Hobby looks at her and smiles. "No, you're not."

"I might be." Kelsey grins, so relieved that he hasn't caught on she read his journal.

Hobby glances over his shoulder at the door. "Where is that damnable woman?" he fumes. "Go tell her I'm ready now."

Kelsey covers a laugh by coughing. "So, now she's also supposed to be at your beck and call?" Who would have ever guessed she'd be thrilled to have Hobby ordering her around again.

The nurse arrives and Kelsey steps out. "What took you so long?" Hobby says.

"I liked you better in a coma," Kelsey hears her say.

"Ouch."

The nurse comes out and winks at Kelsey. "You can go back in."

"I can't wait to get out of here." Hobby picks at the electrical tape again.

"I just wrapped those for you. Stop picking at it." She opens the drawer in the nightstand and holds up the rest of the roll. "See. Hey, did I tell you that Backster lives in San Diego?"

"You're kidding. He must be a hundred."

"Late eighties."

"I'll be dipped. How do you know that?"

"Detective Moran called him after I told her Phil knows who beaned you."

Hobby snorts. "You read the book I gave you."

"Yeah. Well—" Kelsey bites her lip. "Not all of it. Yet."

"Did your detective friend believe you?"

"Not at first, but after she talked to Backster she seems to be considering it. Because of Phil's reaction, we know exactly what time they beat you up."

"Now if I could just remember who?"

"I know that, too."

"You do?"

"Yep."

"Those two delinquents?"

"Uh huh."

"If I can't remember, they're going to get away with it."

Kelsey suddenly has an idea. "I don't think so."

•   •   •   •   •

At school the next day, Josh asks what she's doing Saturday.

"Why?"

He shrugs. "I thought maybe we could go to a movie. Want to?"

Kelsey smiles. "Yeah. Sure. And afterwards, we're going to the Headlands Café to get ourselves some DNA."

CHAPTER 34

"Why did you become a botanist?" It's Saturday morning, and Kelsey stands at Hobby's hospital room window watching misty gray dandelion heads swirl past. There's a wind and clouds of their seeds whirl like ballerinas through the air.

"I was what you kids call a nerd?"

"You still are." She glances over her shoulder and smiles.

He's looking at her. "It's not a bad thing to know what you are."

"I know. And you're my favorite nerd."

His cheeks pink. "Yeah, yeah." He shoos the flattery. "I got curious about plant communication when I read first read *The Secret Life of Plants*. That was back in—"

"It was published in 1974."

"Was it? I guess so. Time flies."

She turns back to the window and sees his smile reflected in the glass. It's the proud-parent kind of smile she's seen on the faces of other kids' moms and dads when they've accomplished something their parents hoped for. A first of it's kind for her.

"At the time," Hobby continues. "I was teaching at Berkeley and doing some experiments of my own with plants. Backster's work spurred a lot of researchers to try to duplicate his experiments without much success, and he took a beating from the scientific community because he was only a lowly polygraph instructor. No credentials, no PhD. No one believed him. But I did. Or at least, I believed Backster was on to something. And he was, of course. It's now common knowledge that plants communicate."

"Why did you believe him?" Kelsey turns, moves little Phil's vase to the corner, and hitches herself up on the windowsill.

Hobby sighs. "Because it made sense. A plant's leaves droop as they lose electrical current. Adding water replenishes the current and the osmotic pressure lifts the leaves. Of course, Backster's polygraph could record that increase. It's called electrotropism. Phototropism turns Phil's leaves toward the light. Geotropism causes roots to grow toward the gravitational pull of the earth.

"What kind of experiments did you do?"

"A species of lupine grew near my house in Berkeley, *Lupinus arboreus*. I decided to try to mimic insect predation. By then, scientists knew that plants can change what they taste like if they're getting eaten by insects. At night, I'd clip a leaf to test its proteins using thin-layer chromatography—"

"What's that?"

"You mash a leaf up and smear it on a piece of glass, plastic, or aluminum foil, and then you apply a solvent. The different chemical elements in the leaf are drawn up blotter paper by capillary action."

"Wait. Slow down. What's capillary action?"

Hobby points a bony finger at the cutting of Phil on the windowsill. "It's how Phil's stem take up water against the pull of gravity." He reaches and pulls a tissue from the box beside his bed, and hands her his water glass. "Pour a little water on the windowsill."

"Why?"

"Just do it." He folds the tissue into a square. "Now, dip the tip of this tissue in the puddle."

Kelsey barely touches the puddle with a corner of the tissue and it sucks up all the water.

"That, my dear, is capillary action. The solvent separates the elements in the leaf soup and they climb the paper at different rates. I found the lupine changed the proteins in its leaves to a toxic alkaloid moments after I made the cut."

"The leaves turned poisonous?"

"Exactly. Then they changed back again by morning when they needed those proteins for growth. I repeated this experiment every night, and here's the thing that blew me away. On the fourth night, the lupine was ready for me and had already changed its proteins to the toxic alkaloid. In other words, it 'remembered'—" Hobby made air quotes—"what happened during the preceding nights and had proactively altered its proteins." He grins. "Doesn't that blow your mind?"

Kelsey glances at the baby Phil, with his leaves turned to the window. "What's this called again?"

"You mean how the leaves face the sun?"

"Uh huh." She nods.

"Phototropism."

"I'm not sure I'm cut out to be a geek, but when you're better, can I help you with some of your experiments?"

Hobby's wrinkled, gray face lights up. "Nothing would make me happier."

•　　•　　•　　•　　•

That evening, after the movie *Ford v Ferrari*, Josh and Kelsey sit side by side at the Headlands Café's counter opposite the picture window that faces the alley. The light from the café shines out onto the wall of the Italian restaurant across the otherwise dark alley.

Kelsey hasn't told Josh about her suspicions, and she certainly hasn't told him about the plants in the greenhouse being witnesses. She totally believes they are, but it still sounds too ridiculous to share with anyone. She tells Josh, "If Will and Ryan show up, we're going to pretend to have a fight and you're to leave."

"Why do we have to have a fight?"

"We just do."

"But why?"

"Josh, I can't tell you right now. I need Will to think I'm mad at you."

He looks genuinely hurt. "You'd think you could tell me. I'm your best—."

"Hush," Kelsey says. "Here they come."

Will, Ryan, and Carlos pass through the light from an apartment farther down the alley, then into shadow again. Ryan spots Kelsey and Josh and elbows Will, then starts to sashay, swinging his hips, one hand bent at the wrist.

Kelsey elbows Josh and laughs, as if she finds Ryan's acting gay funny.

Josh looks stung, which makes Kelsey feel awful. Josh has driven her crazy about Lauren and is too clingy, but she's never before made fun of him. Never would.

"Oh," he says, like what this is about has dawned on him. "Does this have something to do with what you said about getting some—"

"Shut up, Josh," Kelsey snaps. "They can see what you're saying."

Josh glances at boys, turns in his seat, and puts his hand up to shield his mouth. "If this has to do with that old man getting beaten up, it could be dangerous to leave you here with them."

"It's not dangerous. You have to trust me." Kelsey pats his knee. "Act mad at me and leave. Okay?"

"Well, guess what? I *am* mad at you." He scrapes back his stool and stands. "I thought we were friends." He snatches his cellphone off the counter.

Will is leaning against the wall of the building across the alley, watching them.

"I'll see you around." Tears well in Josh's eyes.

Kelsey wants to take his hand and apologize, but she doesn't dare. "Whatever," she says so Will can read her lips.

As Josh weaves his way toward the back door, she grabs her Coke and heads out the front to draw Will's attention.

"I can't take him whining about Lauren another minute," she says when she gets outside. She sits down next to Ryan, with her back to the restaurant wall. "Want to finish this?" She offers Ryan her Coke.

He takes it, drinks some, and shakes the can. "There's a slug left, want it?" He hands it up to Will, who watches Josh walk down the alley. Maybe it's the way the light from the Café casts its shadow, but Will's eyes look hooded like a cobra's. He snatches the can, puts it on the sidewalk and, without taking his eyes off Josh, stomps it under the heel of his boot, and kicks it into the street beneath a car.

Kelsey watches her DNA sample land next to a tire.

"We was thinking of getting some beer and going to Glass Beach." Ryan says. "Wanna go Kels?"

"Nah. I need to get home and check on my old lady. She's sick again."

Will snorts a laugh.

Kelsey looks up at him. "What did that mean?"

"Sick is one way of putting it."

Anger wells. "What do you know about it?"

"Nothing. I was just thinking we've got a lot in common."

"I doubt it." But before she opens her mouth to tell him where to get off, she reminds herself why she's here.

Ryan takes a pouch of tobacco from a jacket pocket, ZigZag papers from another, and begins to roll a cigarette.

Will snaps his fingers. Ryan looks up, then hands him the cigarette he's just made. He rolls another for himself. Kelsey smiles inside as she watches Ryan run his tongue down the edge of the paper. *Even better.*

"Want one, Kels?" Ryan lights it and offers it to her.

She shakes her head. "I get plenty secondhand from my mother."

"You still doing time at ole Doc Hobbes'?" Will says.

"Yep. Feed the cat. Water the plants."

"I saw in Thursday's paper that he was out of the coma and may be going home soon."

Her breath catches. She hadn't figured on Will reading the paper. She glances at him. His tone is nonchalant, but she knows better. He's pumping her for information.

"I went by to see him yesterday, and I don't think he's ever gonna be right in the head again." She purposely looks at Will. "He didn't know where he was or how he got there."

"That's too bad." Will smiles. "Maybe he'll end up drooling and wheeling himself up and down the halls at Sherwood Oaks."

Sherwood Oaks is the local nursing home. Kelsey fists knot inside her jacket pockets, but she forces a laugh. "Could happen."

"He's sure got a lot of neat crap." Will flicks his cigarette butt toward a puddle in the alley. It hits dead center and dies with a hiss.

If Ryan does the same thing, there'll be no DNA.

Will kicks her leg. "Whatcha thinking?"

"Nothing. Why?" Did Will see her look at the cigarette and guess what she's up to?

"I thought maybe you was thinking it's a shame all the expensive stuff of his is going to be sitting there and not get used. I thought maybe you was thinking about getting me and Ryan to help you clean the place up a bit 'fore all the stuff gets estate-sold or something."

"Yeah," Ryan says. "We know a guy who'd buy it from us, don't we?"

Ryan drops his cigarette and steps on it.

Kelsey's heart sinks. This isn't working at all.

Will speaks, startling her. "You know the combination to that lock, don't you, Kels?"

Her heart ping-pongs off her ribs. *What was he thinking?* "Even if I did," she says as calmly as she can, "I'd be the first one the cops would suspect."

"You could accidentally forget to lock up one night." Will takes the tobacco pouch out of Ryan's pocket. He rolls and lights another cigarette, then puts the pouch and papers in his own jacket pocket.

"Give those back." Ryan holds his hand out.

Instead, Will hands him the cigarette he just lit.

"I'll have to think about it." Kelsey's mind is reeling. Has she gotten herself into a trap?

"You better think fast. It'll be gone before you know it. Soon as some relative figures out he's a vegetable, they'll come whipping in here and sell the works."

Kelsey stalls by gnawing on a cuticle. "What would I get out of it?" she says

"A third. All you have to do is leave the lock open. Or, if you ain't interested in being involved, you could just tell me the combination."

Kelsey snorts. "I don't think so. I'd still be the first one they suspected and get nothing for my trouble. How much you think you could get for it all?"

"I ain't sure what he's got, but three hundred give or take."

"It sure would be nice not to have to kiss my mother's butt for every dime."

Ryan takes a final drag on the cigarette and flicks it toward the puddle. It misses and rolls against the Café wall.

"We got a deal?" Will says.

"I said I'd think about it," Kelsey says. "I want to make sure I'm someplace else when you do it." She forces herself to look at Will and the cigarette's tip still glowing in the dark. "Maybe, I could make up with Josh and go to a movie or something."

"When will you let me know?"

"I'll call you. Give me your cell number."

"Gimme yours."

"I don't have a cell phone."

"Poor baby. Maybe with your share of the dough you can cross over into the twenty-first century." Will takes out the book of matches he used to light his cigarette and writes his cell number in it. "Make it soon." He clicks her under the chin with his fist then jerks his head at Ryan. "Let's get some beer."

Ryan scrambles to his feet. "Sure you don't want to come with us?" he says to Kelsey.

"Yeah, I'm sure."

"See ya then." Ryan scurries down the alley after Will.

"Yeah. Later." Kelsey watches them go, acting nonchalant, but heart thumping. The smoldering cigarette has both their DNA. Will rolled it and sealed with his spit. Ryan smoked it.

A girl from her history class comes out of the Café. Kelsey walks over like she's going to strike up a conversation, and stands near the smoldering cigarette.

"Hey," the girl says.

"Hi—." Kelsey can't remember her name. "History, right?"

"Yeah. Have you decided what you're doing that paper on?"

Kelsey glances down at the cigarette. It still glows and might burn right down to her DNA sample. "Something on the 1850 wreck of the *Frolic* and the rise of the timber industry." She squints into the darkness. Will and Ryan could be anywhere—even in the shadows watching her.

The girl starts in about her report. Kelsey can't wait. She grabs the cigarette butt, flicks the last of the embers off the tip and puts it in her pocket. "See ya." She waves to the confused girl and walks away.

CHAPTER 35

The phone rings the next morning at seven. *It's Sunday*, Kelsey thinks as she runs on tiptoes down the hall from her room to answer it before it wakes her mother.

"Kelsey?" A man's voice. Not Hobby's. Not Will's.

Blood whooshes in her ears. She has no idea how she knows who it is, but she does. She's suspected her mother lied about the recent calls being wrong numbers or a man from JJD. Now her lies suddenly makes sense. "Yes?" she whispers.

"This is your dad."

She swallows hard. "I know."

"I'm so . . . " His voice cracks.

"Why call now?"

"There was an article in the *San Francisco Chronicle* about the attack on John Hobbes. I was a student of his at Berkeley. It mentioned you found him."

"How'd you know it was me?"

"Well, you have my last name and Kelsey was your mother's maiden name. Then there's your age. The last time I was in Fort Bragg was fifteen years ago for our tenth high school reunion. It was too much of coincidence."

Kelsey doesn't say anything. Her mother said he left when he found out she was pregnant. Why was he acting like she's a big surprise? She should hang up on him.

"Are you still there?" His voice is deep, soft, and gentle.

"Yes."

"Is this bad timing? Should I call back later?"

"I thought you were dead."

"Well, I'm not."

"Mom said you were."

"It's not true."

Kelsey nods, as if he could see her.

"It's kind of hard to know what to say, isn't it?" He says, softly.

"Uh huh."

"Well, I know. I can't wait to meet you, to hug you—my daughter—" his voice breaks again. "To start getting acquainted."

How she'd longed for a father. She'd convinced herself that her crappy life would be different if he'd stayed. She hates him for leaving, yet wants to forgive. "I've been here all along, you know." Her voice shakes. "I'm the one she was pregnant with when you cut out on us."

She hears a sharp intake of breath, then silence. *Has the blame in her voice made him sorry he called?*

"Honey, until I read the *Chronicle* story, I didn't know you existed."

Kelsey feels her knees buckle and grabs the edge of the sink. "But . . . Mom said—" Maybe she should have known what those calls were all along. Or at least guessed knowing the ease with which her mother lies.

"You have to believe me. I didn't know about you. She never told me."

Kelsey hears the toilet flush. Lydia will soon come to the kitchen for her coffee. She'll walk in thinking it's just another day. She won't know that the door to this cage just swung wide open.

Kelsey feels lightheaded. "Where do you live?"

"Truckee. I'm a United Airlines pilot based in San Francisco. I commute there for my trips and fly to the Orient."

Truckee. He lives six hours away.

"May I come to see you?" he says.

"Yes."

"I'm heading to San Francisco right now. I have a trip starting Tuesday, but I'll be back late Friday. How about I come up Saturday?"

Kelsey can't find her voice.

"Honey, would Saturday be too soon?"

"No."

"I'll be there about noon. Are you in your mom's old house on Maplewood?"

"Yes."

For a moment she thinks he's hung up until she hears him swallow. "Kelsey, tell me, have you been happy?"

She presses the phone hard against her ear. A sob catches in her throat. "Not very," she whispers.

"I promise from now on, things *will* be different. I'll see you Saturday." He hangs up.

Still holding the phone to her ear, she puts an arm across her eyes, and leans against the freezer compartment.

"Are you crying?" Lydia says from the doorway.

Kelsey lowers her arm and turns to look at her mother. The disconnect blares. Lydia's eyes widen as she watches Kelsey walk to the wall and hang up the phone. "Who was that?"

"You know who it was." Kelsey takes a step toward Lydia.

Her mother clutches her robe closed at her neck. "No, I don't."

"Yes, you do." Kelsey jaw muscles tighten. "He's called a bunch of times. Remember the all those wrong numbers?"

"Oh my god." The color drains from her mother's face.

"Not God. Guess again."

"It's not funny."

"You're right. Definitely not funny. How about my dead father."

"There's no such person."

"Stop it," Kelsey screams. "Stop lying to me. He'll be here Saturday."

Lydia changes right before Kelsey's eyes. She shrivels from her full height to something frail and bent. She backs out of the kitchen, flapping a hand blindly behind her until it hits the headrest of her Barcalounger. Using it for support, she shuffles around the armrest and crawls into it like a wounded animal. "I begged him not to call."

"How could you?" Tears streak Kelsey's face. All these years, she been trapped like one of Carlotta's worms in her mother's web.

"He'd have taken you away from me," the spider moans.

•   •   •   •   •

On her way to school on Monday morning, Kelsey stops at the sheriff's department with the cigarette butt in a Ziploc in her pocket. The woman behind the bullet-proof window says, "Detective Moran is on vacation,"

"No," Kelsey cries. "She can't be."

The pink, solar flower dances and waves its leaves behind the bullet-proof glass, mockingly.

"Sorry. Friday was her last day."

"Where'd she go? When will she be back?"

"In two weeks. I don't have the slightest idea where she went, and if I did, I wouldn't be at liberty to say."

"This is life or death." Kelsey clutches her pocket.

"Sorry. I can call one of the other detectives. What's this about?"

"Nothing." Kelsey turns and runs out of the station. Outside, she leans against the wall and tries to think what to do. *Two weeks!* She can't stall Will for two weeks. She's standing there gasping in cold air when the door opens.

"Kelsey?" It's Hannah.

"Oh, my God. You're here."

"I came by to pick up some paperwork. The receptionist said you just left. I'm leaving town for a couple weeks—a little well-earned R & R."

"You can't." Kelsey pulls the cigarette butt from her pocket. "I got Ryan and Will's DNA for you."

"Jesus. How?" She shakes her head. "It doesn't matter. You shouldn't have risked that."

"That wasn't the risky part. I kind of told him the head injury left Hobby a vegetable and agreed to leave the lock open so they can rob the place before some relative sells everything."

"Oh, brother." Hannah takes Kelsey by her coat sleeve. "Come with me." She opens the door and pulls her inside.

"Sit down," she says, when they are in her office. "When is this supposed to happen?" She takes the chair behind her desk.

"We didn't set a day. I told him I'd think about it and call him."

Hannah picks up the phone. "Get me someone from the crime lab," she says, and hangs up.

A few minutes later, a young woman comes in. Hannah hands her the Ziploc. "Send this over to the lab and see if the DNA in the saliva matches the blood and skin we found on the door at the Hobbes' crime scene. I want this yesterday. Please," she adds and smiles. "I'll pay for a courier both ways." She fixes Kelsey with a stare, then says, "I don't want you to do a thing until we find out if it's a match. If it is, only then do you call and tell them you'll to do it. Do you understand?"

"Okay." Kelsey can't help grinning.

"Wipe that grin off your face. You shouldn't have done this." She smiles. "But I have to say, it was damn clever. Now, go home. Don't go to the greenhouse under any circumstances. Is that clear? They could show up and force you to open the lock."

"I have to go feed Gen."

"I'll get the cat and bring him to you."

"My mother's—" Kelsey stops. Maybe her mother's cat-allergy is a lie, too. "Bring him. I'll figure it out. And what about Hobby? He could get out of the hospital any day."

"I'll go to see him this afternoon and tell him what's happening. I doubt they are ready to discharge him, but it they are, I'm sure there is someone he can stay with for a few days."

Kelsey goes to the door and turns. "My father called me. I thought he was dead."

"Oh, honey, that's wonderful, but what made you think he was . . . Your mother?"

Kelsey nods.

"I suspect she was afraid she'd have to share custody," Hannah says.

"If you love your kid, wouldn't you want what's best for her?"

"I'm sure—at first—she was convinced that keeping you a secret *was* best for you." Hannah comes around her desk and puts her arms around Kelsey. "We tell ourselves all sorts of lies."

"He's coming this Saturday."

Hannah lets her go. "That's exciting."

"I'm afraid he'll hate me when he finds out all the bad stuff I did."

"Kelsey, you are his daughter. He's going to love you no matter what you've done. Besides, right now, you're the most upstanding citizen I know."

•   •   •   •   •

Kelsey arrives home from school just as Hannah pulls into the driveway. She gets out a pet-carrier and a paper sack out of the backseat. "You'd better keep him in the house until he gets used to his new digs. Cats tend to lock into a place rather than a person."

"Not Gen. He's acted like I belong to him from the day we met. Do you want to come in?" Kelsey doesn't hold the door open, hoping Hannah will say no.

"No time. I'm headed to the hospital to see Dr. Hobbes. Gen's food is in this bag." She puts the sack on top of a concrete flowerpot full of dry, crusty soil.

"What is that?" Lydia says, when Kelsey comes into the kitchen.

"Our feline houseguest."

"It's a *cat*?" Her mother crushes her cigarette out and covers her nose with both hands. "Put it outside. I'm allergic to cats."

Kelsey puts the carrier on the floor, kneels, and opens the door. Just as he had done that first day, Gen climbs in her lap, locks his paws around her neck, and buries his face against her throat, purring.

"This is Hobby's cat." Like that will matter to her mother.

Lydia flaps a hand toward the door. "Please. Put it out."

Kelsey closes her eyes against the anger and resentment that roils inside her. It doesn't help. "I love this cat. If he goes, I go. Is that clear?" She lifts Gen and presses his head to her shoulder. "He'll be in my room. Don't let anything happen to him." She starts down the hall, then turns. "I'm trying to forgive you for lying to me my whole life, Mom, so don't get in my face for a while. And if you start to sneeze, chase that vodka with a Sudafed."

CHAPTER 36

All week, Kelsey fantasizes about meeting her father. Her mother's yearbook is under her bed. She takes it out and looks at his picture every night before turning out her light, trying to imagine what he'll look like now, twenty-four years later. She does her best to clean the house, even taking the screen off the kitchen window and cleaning out the dead bugs. At night, Gen sleeps with her, their heads together on the pillow. She floats through the days at school, so Will's call Friday afternoon shocks her back to the present.

"What'd you decide?"

For a moment, Kelsey can't think.

"Well?"

She pinches the bridge of her nose to sound stopped up. "I'm sick with a cold, but I'm thinking I'll probably do it. Why should someone else get all the stuff? Give me a couple more days to feel better, and to arrange to meet Josh somewhere so I'll have an alibi."

"Why don't you just give me the combination and I'll take care of this while you're sick. Your mother can be your alibi."

"My mother!" She blurts, then pinches her nose again. "That's a good one. She never knows where I am or what I'm doing. Great witness in my defense she'd make." In an effort to sound more convincing, she adds, "Besides, I'm not giving you the combination and then get left out of the deal."

"Ah Kels, you don't trust me?"

"True," she says.

"What's the difference? You leave the lock open or tell me the combination. You could always turn us in if we don't do a split."

He has her. She hopes her excuse for delaying doesn't make him suspicious. "I—" She pinches her nose again. "I want to make sure my alibi is air-tight, then I'll give you the combination. Take it or leave it."

"Okay. Okay. Get that faggot lined up and let's get this over with. We've got the guy ready to make the buy, but he's getting antsy."

"You were that sure I'd go along?" She realizes her feelings are hurt.

"Kels, from what I hear, you ain't all that honest. Figured you'd eventually move up from shoplifting teddy bears."

"It was an elephant."

The minute Kelsey hangs up, the phone rings again. "We've got a match." Hannah says. "It was Ryan's blood on the door frame."

"Yahoo," Kelsey whoops. "Are you going to arrest him?"

"Not yet. There's a chain of custody problem."

Kelsey watches enough TV to have an idea what this means. "I put it in a Ziploc."

"I know, sweetie, but there's a process we have to follow for it to hold up in court. I have to be able to show where and when the sample was obtained, who secured it, and who had control of it. Without that, I can't issue a warrant."

"Oh."

"Don't feel bad. We would have needed grounds to get our own sample. If the sting works, we can get a legal sample that will hold up in court. What you pulled off gave us the right perp."

"Will called a few minutes ago. He's after me to give him the combination."

"Oh Jesus. What did you say?"

"That I would."

"We don't want to set up a stake-out and just wait. We need to figure out how to know when they're coming."

Kelsey grins. "No problem. I told him I'd be the first person you would suspect when the stuff goes missing, so I have to have an alibi. I told him he has to do it while Josh and I are at the movies."

"Kelsey," Hannah laughs. "I'm glad you decided to go straight."

"Me, too," she says, surprised by how much she means it.

"Okay. Let's plan on Saturday. I haven't seen a movie in so long, what time do they usually start?"

"The matinees start at 1:15, but can we make it Sunday? My dad's coming on Saturday."

"Sunday, it is. We'll have everything in place by noon."

"I want to be there," Kelsey says.

"Sorry, kiddo. No way."

"I'm going to get to testify against them in court, aren't I, so what's the difference? They won't be armed, there'll be plenty of cops nearby, and, Hannah, if you don't let me go, I'll tell him I changed my mind. I want to do this—for Hobby. And for me."

"You're getting pretty good at this blackmail thing. I don't believe for a minute you'd let them get away with beating your friend nearly to death, but I'll talk to Detective Wright. It's his case, though damn if it isn't looking more and more like it's yours and we're just along for the ride."

"We can turn on the lie detector and Phil will let us know when they're coming."

Hannah laughs. "Let's keep that bit between us."

Kelsey hangs up, takes the pack of matches from her pocket, and dials Will. Her stomach roils while she waits for him to answer.

"Yeah?"

"Sunday."

He snorts. "I got church."

"What?" For a split second, Kelsey believes him. "Ha. Ha. Very funny."

CHAPTER 37

After setting a time with Will, Kelsey rides to the hospital and finds Hobby sitting in the chair by the window. The last of the bandages around his head are gone. His white hair sticks up around a shaved, crinkly-looking circle of skin. The rows of black stitches make the backs of Kelsey's knees tingle. She tries not to look.

"Guess what?" She checks baby Phil's water level.

Hobby smiles.

"You already know?"

He nods. "Your dad called me right after he talked to you. I told you I once knew a McCully. He sounds like a fine man. I'm happy for you."

"How'd he know how to find you?"

"We only have one hospital, Kelsey. Not a giant leap."

"Did you . . . you know, tell him how we met?"

After the phone call from her dad, Kelsey went through the stack of newspapers in a box by the woodstove looking for the *Fort Bragg Advocate News* article about the attack on Hobby. She wanted to remind herself the reason it gave for why she was there. In it, she was referred to as "his young volunteer." Her father doesn't know the truth—unless Hobby told him.

"I didn't, but it wouldn't matter if I had. He's your dad." He moves his bony legs off the footstool and pats it. "Come here."

She sits.

"You're the only one with a low opinion of yourself. You're an exposed nerve of a person, Kelsey, with a huge capacity for love. That's what Gen and maybe even Phil recognized right away. We humans have filters. Plants and animals don't. You've learned to protect yourself by pretending not to care about anything, which is the opposite of how you really feel."

Kelsey looks at her hands, palms up in her lap. Tears threaten.

"Here. Here." Hobby takes her hands. "Nothing of your past will mean a single thing to your father except to make him wish he'd been here for you from the beginning. Remember what I said in the truck that day at the police station, about all the bad stuff ending when you wise up?"

She nods, accepts the tissue he pulls from the box on the nightstand, and blows her nose.

"You've done that. When you came to me you were a vacuum, hermetically sealed against all the love just outside. The seal's been broken and the devotion people and animals, and maybe even plants, have for you is pouring in. Excuse the metaphor, but you're about to bloom—" he grins and rubs the stubble on his head. "—thanks to you, I'm still here to see it happen."

•　　•　　•　　•　　•

Kelsey's plans to straighten up, dust, and vacuum again before her father arrives, evaporate. The night before, she stood in the kitchen archway and looked at the ceiling over the woodstove, dark with smoke from the million times her mother has forgotten to open the damper before she added wood to the fire. Kelsey sniffed the air, stale from cigarette butts and spilled drinks. Under her mother's Barcalounger she spots a dried slice of lime. Nothing short of tenting this house, like they do for termites, could possibly disguise the truth. It looks so beyond anything her efforts have so far accomplished or could hope to accomplish, she decides to leave it—including the molding slice of lime. Let him see how we live.

Gen's asleep, stretched out on the kitchen window ledge in a patch of afternoon sun. He's wider than the ledge and holds himself in place with two paws pressed to the table. He begins to purr when Kelsey enters and walks to the sink. He stretches, loses his leverage, and rolls off the ledge onto the table, knocking over the salt and pepper shakers. "Silly." Kelsey rights the shakers and tickles his belly.

Lydia's fallen asleep watching *Judge Judy*. A gin and tonic sweats beside her on the TV tray. The woodstove blasts hot air and makes the house feel like a broiler. Kelsey crosses to the woodstove to adjust the airflow, then goes back into the kitchen, opens and closes the back door, and calls, "I'm home."

Lydia opens her eyes and stretches. "Hi Honey. How was school?"

Kelsey doesn't answer. Lydia doesn't ask again.

She's full of nervous energy. To take her mind off tomorrow, she does the dishes, takes out the garbage, gathers all the recycling, mostly liquor bottles, and takes them to the garage. After all that, she decides this probably counts as cleaning and goes to get the vacuum.

Her mother has dozed off again. Kelsey watches her chest rise and fall. All she wants is to understand how her mother got like this.

She empties the ashtrays and uses half a spray bottle of *Febreze* trying to cover the stink of cigarette butts. When she starts the vacuum, Gen leaps off the table, and runs down the hall to her bedroom.

Lydia bolts upright. "Why are you doing that in the middle of the night?"

"It's six, Mom." Kelsey turns off the vacuum. "Don't you remember? My dead father is coming tomorrow."

The look on her mother's face gives Kelsey a moment of perverse pleasure before she turns the vacuum back on.

Lydia, with bathrobe hanging open, gathers the photo albums off the coffee table and hugs them to her chest. When Kelsey jerks the vacuum plug out of the wall socket and begins to wind up the cord, Lydia says, "These will be all I'll have left after he takes you."

Kelsey doesn't take the bait. She's too excited. All those photos of her grandparents, her mother as a baby, herself as a baby, even her aunt in Nebraska, are all the family she's ever had. Until now. But she imagines the pictures are lies, too—people saying cheese, pretending to be happy while they wait for the flash to go off.

After dinner of tomato soup and a government-issued-cheese sandwich, Kelsey gathers her schoolbooks off the counter and starts for her room. There are loose papers on top—handouts from one of her classes. She hasn't bothered to look at them, but now, one meant to be shared at home, catches her eye. *Ways to <u>Encourage</u> Your Children to Use Drugs*. Kelsey balls it up, opens the cupboard under the sink and throws it into the trashcan. Like a flyer full of advice will make her mother change.

In her room, she tries to focus on her homework, but her mind keeps imagining how tomorrow will go. After an hour of failing to get much done, she takes her mother's yearbook, from under her bed and looks at her dad's picture again. Gen lies beside her, purring, as she outlines his face with a finger. She wonders if they passed on the street, would she recognize him? She wonders if she will see herself in him?

Before she turns off her light, with Gen at her heels, Kelsey goes to check on her mother one last time. Lydia, asleep in her recliner, is snoring with her chin on her chest. Her ugly handmade afghan lies on the floor. Kelsey picks it up and covers her mother, tucking in the sides so it will stay put. She takes her mother's uneaten sandwich and untouched bowl of soup to the kitchen and puts them in the refrigerator. She checks to make sure all the cigarette butts are cold, opens the cupboard, and dumps them into the trash. The handout has un-balled itself. She picks it out and flattens it with the side of her hand.

Number one is, *never eat together as a family*. "That's a good one, huh, Mom?" she says. "And listen to this." Kelsey carries the list to the pass-through window, leans with her elbows on the counter, and begins to read it to the back of her mother's chair. "'*Keep your home atmosphere in a state of chaos.*' No problem there, right? Or how about, '*Never hug them . . .*' or '*Never tell them how much you love them . . .*' Wait, here's the best one, Mom. '*Don't worry about using drugs or alcohol in the presence of your children.*'" Kelsey closes her eyes.

Gen jumps up on the counter, puts his paws on her shoulders, and presses his face against hers. She picks him up and carries him back to bed, turning off all the lights as she goes.

CHAPTER 38

Lydia's been in the bathroom since eleven trying to repair the damage decades of booze have done. Kelsey walked past earlier and saw her mother pushing her sagging skin tight against her ears, which made her mouth look like a wide, red gash.

Before her mother took over the bathroom, Kelsey tried to improve her looks, too. She got up early, showered, and washed her hair. She blew it dry, pulled it into a ponytail, shook it loose, and redid it. Better the second time.

Between eleven-thirty and noon, Kelsey starts going to the front window every few minutes to look out at the driveway. At twelve-ten his car—a black Lexus with a San Francisco Giants license plate frame—turns into the driveway. Her heart races, but instead of rushing to open the door, she steps behind the smoke-saturated drapes to watch him get out of the car. He wears jeans, a blue flannel shirt, sunglasses, and a Giants baseball cap. She can't see his face well, but he's tall and slender. He stands for a minute, looking down the street, probably at the ocean in the distance and what's left of the Georgia-Pacific mill site. When he turns toward the house, what she can see of his expression looks pained.

Maplewood has a lot of sad-looking houses, but theirs is the most dilapidated. It has never—in Kelsey's memory—been painted. Weeds choke the two patches of open ground on either side of the cracked concrete walkway, and one of the front steps is dangerously rotted.

Kelsey's legs feel rubbery. What if he's arrived with expectations and high hopes, only to decide there's no hope for a kid raised in a place like this? Maybe, he'll think he's missed too much to start a relationship now. Only then does it occur to her that he's probably married with other children—a whole family she will never fit in with. She turns and flees through the kitchen and out the back. She hears him knocking on the front door as she creeps down the side of their house.

Lydia shouts for her to answer the door.

Her father raps more insistently. Moments later, she hears the front door hinges creak and Lydia say, "You couldn't leave well enough alone, could you?"

"Nice to see you, too," her father answers.

"He's here." Her mother's voice is harsh and bitter.

Kelsey leans against the wall beneath their bathroom window hugging herself, hands clamped in opposite armpits to keep warm.

"Are you okay, Kelsey?" shouts their next-door neighbor, who is old and deaf. Kelsey's name ricochets between their houses.

No escape now. "I'm fine, Mr. Kemp. Thanks." She retraces her steps, and quietly opens the backdoor in time to hear her mother say, "I knew you'd try to take her from me if you found us."

"You can't know what I would have done, but I had a right to know she existed." Her father stands with his back to the kitchen. He's holding Gen and rubbing his ears. His baseball cap is on the sofa.

Kelsey has a second to stare at his broad shoulders before Gen jumps out of his arms and runs to her. Her father turns. Little about him resembles the picture in the yearbook. The hair that hung in his eyes in his senior picture is now short and graying at the temples. Only his eyes are the same, except wiser and kinder. They stare at each other, saying nothing for a long moment before he opens his arms.

Later, she can't remember if she went to him or he came to her. They were across the room from each other and now he's hugging her. She turns a cheek to rest against his chest, hears his heart thundering, like hers, and feels his lips brush her hair.

Kelsey's senses fill with the freshly ironed smell of her father's shirt, the heat from his body, and the strength of his arms. She resists letting the sounds of her mother crying break through. When she opens her eyes, Lydia's hand reaches for her with tobacco-stained fingers.

Seeing the red splotches of rouge on her mother's dough-colored cheeks, her heavily lined brows, and too thick mascara, Kelsey feels anger instead of sympathy. She looks at the room's cheap dark paneling, ugly shag carpet stained by spilled drinks and cigarette burns, furniture too disgusting for any place but the Caspar dump. How could her mother let them live this way all these years knowing this man was out there somewhere? Why did she hide from him?

"Don't leave me, Kelsey. I don't know what I'd do."

The disgust Kelsey feels must show on her face because a sob full of agony escapes her mother. It's like no sound Kelsey's ever heard before, a wounded animal howl. Lydia slides to the floor, brings her knees up, and covers her head with her arms.

"Oh, God." Kelsey feels stabbed. "Mom, don't."

Her father hugs her tighter, but she slips free. "I can't leave her there like that."

"I know." He closes his eyes for a moment, then walks over, lifts Lydia off the floor, and puts her in the recliner. He crosses the room and takes a seat on the sofa. The expression on his face is pity.

Her mother weeps into her hands. "I'm sorry. I'm so sorry."

"It'll be okay, Mom." Kelsey rakes her fingers through her mother's freshly washed hair, sweeping it away from her face.

CHAPTER 39

After assuring her dad that it will be okay, he agrees to leave long enough to check into his motel and give Kelsey time to calm Lydia.

Kelsey gets her mother to take one of the expired Valium tablets and fixes her a gin and tonic. When she puts the drink on the TV tray, Lydia grabs her wrist. "Promise me." Her voice is screechy. "Promise you won't leave me."

If she promises, the door that has opened on a different life will clang shut. For a moment, she resists the grip her mother has on her wrist. Out of the corner of her eye, she sees Gen, who's once again lying on the kitchen table in a patch of sun. Her heart swells. "I promise."

An hour later, she hears her father's car return. He waits in the driveway until Kelsey slips out.

"Is she okay?"

Kelsey nods. "She's asleep."

"I haven't been here in fourteen years. Would you mind a walk?"

"Sure." Inside she grins, hoping there will be a face in a window of every house they pass, watching her walk by with her father.

They head downhill toward the ocean. Waves, driven by an approaching storm, batter the cliffs on which the relic of the Georgia-Pacific sawmill stands.

Her dad stops and gazes at the mill. "When I was growing up, nearly everyone had a parent working there. The lights were on 24/7, smoke rising night and day. Ash coated everything." He takes a deep breath. "The air is so clean now."

A block farther and they take a right on Cory. "I've always loved this town. I'm not sure what it's like now, but when your mother and I were growing up, it was a place where you weren't defined by what your parents could afford."

Kelsey thinks of Lauren, then Brie. "It still is. Mostly."

"It's amazing how little it's changed in all these years—except the mill closing," her dad says. "That will break my father's heart. He worked there most of his life. I guess that's news to you, too. You have grandparents. They live in a retirement community outside Santa Rosa."

"Are my mother's parents dead? She said they were."

"They are, but you have an aunt."

"I know about her. She lives in Nebraska. She writes at Christmas and on my birthday."

"When is that?"

"February 22nd."

She can see her father making a mental calculation. "You were born a month premature."

"Was I?"

"Not surprising, I suppose. I doubt she quit smoking or drinking while she was pregnant." Her father stops outside a neat, little house on Cory. "This was where I grew up. It's nice to see whoever owns it now has kept it up."

They are four blocks from home. Kelsey feels lightheaded. She's ridden her bike past this house every Saturday on her way to Hobby's. It seems she should have somehow known it was special.

They decide to go to the Headlands Café, where the only empty table is next to the window that looks out on the pay phone. It's been three months since Kelsey used it to call Brie. Two months since she lost her best friend. It's hard to believe so much has happened in such a short time.

Her father orders a chocolate milkshake for Kelsey and the local Scrimshaw beer for himself. The woman at the counter gives them a number for their table so the server will know whose order it is. Kelsey puts their number 9 on the table between them. Her dad moves it and hold his hands out to hers. He smiles. His eyes are green like hers, with the same dark straight lashes. Every time he looks away, she studies him for other features they share. She feels him doing the same when she glances at people coming in, going out, or walking past the window.

"Finish telling me about you and Mom."

"There's not much more to tell." He moves his thumb back and forth across her knuckles in a soothing rhythm. "We were sweethearts in junior high and all through high school, but after graduation, I went into the service. She never wrote to me or answered any of my letters. I was pretty devastated at first." He looks up at one of a dozen paintings on the wall and seems to drift away for a moment. "I never really looked at it from her point of view until now, but I suppose losing her father, then her mother, and me leaving was more than she could handle."

"She told me her dad was a logging truck driver. Was that true?"

"Yes. He died in a rollover on Highway 20. She was thirteen. Four years later, the same month we graduated from high school, her mother died."

"Cancer?"

Her father hesitates. "Alcoholism, Kelsey. She drank herself to death."

Kelsey feels a jolt. It has never occurred to her that drinking could kill a person, except in something like a car accident. "It's in Mom's blood, isn't it? I mean she can't help herself, can she?"

"The predisposition is inherited," he says. "But it can be beaten. Many have done it."

The way he says it makes her wonder if he's one of the many. But if that was true, he probably wouldn't have ordered a beer. "It must be in my blood, too."

"Could be, but you don't have to beat an addiction if you never let it get a grip on you."

"She told me you came back from the Gulf War married to someone else but were divorced by the time she saw you again at your tenth reunion."

"Really?" He shakes his head. "Honey, the Gulf War started in 1990. We were still in high school. I enlisted in the Air Force after high school and was stationed in Germany for a few years. Your mom was my first call when I got back. She told me she was in love with someone else, but when I saw her at the reunion, she was still single. I'd stayed in love with her for a very long time and tried to rekindle our high school romance at the reunion." His cheeks color, and he squeezes Kelsey's hand, releasing it when the girl puts their drinks on the table. "When I tried to see her again, she said it had been a mistake. Now I realize she must have been pregnant and, for whatever reason, wasn't going to tell me. Taking my last name was real smart. I Googled her under her maiden name every year or so, but it was as if she'd disappeared. Since we never married, it would never have occurred to me to try to find information for a Lydia McCully. Very clever."

"She told me you left us when you found out she was pregnant—" Kelsey realizes she's holding her breath. She lets it out in a sigh. "And then you were killed in the Iraq War."

He winces. "Oh, brother."

The milkshake is thick. Kelsey stirs it with her straw. "I can only see Mom the way she is now. What was she like when she was young?"

"Pretty, funny, and fun. She had—maybe she still has—a great sense of humor and was always the life of the party." His eyes soften. "So beautiful. She still had that spark when we met at the reunion. I fell in love with her all over again."

Kelsey feels an ache in her chest. After Lauren died, she'd given up wishing for a real mother, one who remembered important stuff like her daughter's best friend dying. Hearing her dad talk about when Lydia was young brings that forgotten longing back. "I wish I'd known her then."

"I wish you had, too."

"Do you hate her now?"

His brow creases and he shakes his head. "Not at all. Just sad."

"That was you who called a week ago Wednesday, right?"

"I called a few times. The first after I saw the newspaper article about Hobby. Why?"

"She was cooking dinner when I came home from visiting Hobby in the hospital. She said she was turning over a new leaf, going to drink less and start being a real mother."

"Has she been successful?"

"She lasted through *Jeopardy!*" Kelsey smiles, wryly. "That was the night she told me you were dead."

Her dad's lips compress. "How'd you happen to meet Hobby?"

Kelsey works the straw up and down in her milkshake. "It's long story. Can I tell you later?" She wants to give him time to like her first before he finds out how much trouble she's been in.

"Sure. If you'd rather."

"How'd *you* meet him?" Kelsey says.

"When I was discharged from the Air Force, I went to college on the G.I. Bill. I wanted to be a forester. Hobby was my botany professor at Berkeley. After I graduated, I needed money. Jobs for a wet-behind-the-ears forestry major weren't so easy to come by. Since I had all that flight training and the airlines were hiring, I applied, got the job and the rest is history."

"Are you married?"

"For seven years now. My wife, Judy, is a flight attendant. We both fly for United. We don't have any children." He smiles. "Not until now. This is going to take some getting used to—having a daughter."

CHAPTER 40

When Kelsey and her dad come out of the café, the sky is black with rain clouds. Will, Ryan and a few of their friends are in their usual spot in the alley. An acrid weed smell fills the air. "Hey—" Ryan says before Will elbows him. Kelsey feels questioning eyes watching them.

Her father takes her arm and guides her from his right side to his left, putting himself between them and her. When they are out of earshot, he glances over his shoulder then says, "That's a rough looking bunch. Do you know them?" She sees the concern on his face.

"They're the ones who beat up Hobby."

"What?" He catches her arm.

"They're the ones who nearly killed Hobby."

"You're putting me on, right?"

Kelsey shakes her head.

"How do you know that? And why aren't they in jail?"

"The answer to the second question is there's no way to prove it—yet. The answer to the first question is a long story."

They've reached home by the time Kelsey finishes telling her dad about Phil and Backster's experiments and how Hobby's been trying to replicate them. "Sounds crazy, right?" They are side by side leaning against the trunk of his Lexus.

"Not really. I remember that book. It caused quite a stir. As I recall, he had us try to duplicate the test where a plant—air quotes 'witnessed' the destruction of its pot-mate. I think I'd remember if it had worked. But if Hobby still thinks it's possible, there's a good chance he's right. We learn more about this stuff all the time, especially how interdependent all beings are. Just because we don't completely understand the way plants communicate, doesn't mean they don't, and right under our noses."

The moon is momentarily exposed, and then rapidly covered by rushing clouds. There's a sudden loud boom that startles them both. That's followed by a long slow rumbling.

"I don't think it thunders like that anywhere else in the world. It sounds like a plane taking off," her father says.

They move to sit on the front step and watch the moon wink on and off. When it begins to sprinkle, Kelsey gets up. "I should check on Mom."

"Wait." He takes Kelsey's hand. "I'm worried about those boys. If what you say is true, you could be in danger."

"I've been pretending we're friends."

The only thing she left out of the story was the trap planned for tomorrow. Telling him doesn't feel like a good idea.

"What does that accomplish?"

"I'll tell you later, but don't worry, Detective Moran doesn't think they meant to hurt him. They were after his stuff—the computer, stereo, and TV. Hobby caught them and one of them hit him. When Will was a court referral, I don't think Hobby was doing the kind of experiments he's doing now. They don't know there's a greenhouse full of witnesses." She grins.

"Court referral?"

Kelsey's stomach flip-flops. She ducks her head and picks at the cuticle of her thumb. "I got arrested for shoplifting. I'm doing three hundred hours of community service at Hobby's."

He doesn't say anything for a moment—long enough that Kelsey feels a prick of worry. His daughter's a juvenile delinquent. Not someone he'd want to take home to his wife. Would she blame him if he stands, gives her a peck on the cheek, and walks away?

"I'm sorry," he says.

Her heart drops like an anchor. *Here it comes.* "For what?"

"For not being here for you. You've pretty much raised yourself, and you've done a good job. We all get in trouble when we're young, and I'll bet you've learned your lesson."

"Have I ever."

He hugs her. "I'm very proud of you."

Kelsey whispers against his shoulder, "Thank you for finding me."

She tries to keep her dad from walking her inside but fails. The house is dark except for the TV. Lydia's asleep with her head back, mouth open, snoring. The small bag of frozen peas she uses to ease her headaches has slipped and is draped over a shoulder. She's covered herself with an ugly orange, red, and brown afghan, but her crusty, bare feet stick out from beneath it like those of a body in a morgue. All she's missing is a toe-tag. Her overturned drink glass lies on the floor, where the contents have soaked into the stained, cigarette-burned shag carpet. The room reeks of gin.

"Jesus," he says.

This is Kelsey's normal, but seeing it through his eyes embarrasses her.

Kelsey picks up the glass and puts it on the TV tray.

Lydia mostly drinks vodka because it's cheaper, but she loves gin martinis because of the way they make olives taste. A half empty jar of them is on the counter by the sink. If it weren't for olives, most nights she wouldn't eat anything.

Her dad goes to the sink to wash his hands. Kelsey imagines that will have to do until he gets to his motel to shower off the stink of this place.

He looks at her over his shoulder. "I think I know the reason she kept you a secret."

"Why?" Kelsey caps the olives and puts them in the fridge. When she turns around, she recognizes pity in his eyes, maybe even grief, and realizes he's seen the new five-pound block of government-issued processed American cheese, still in its *Donated by the U. S. Department of Agriculture* wrapper.

"So she could drink unencumbered." His face muscles tighten and he turns to gaze out the kitchen window. "She partied a lot in high school. By our tenth reunion, I could tell it had become a problem. I told her the drinking worried me. That might have been the reason she didn't want me in her life."

Kelsey tries to wrap her mind around his theory. She wets a dishtowel, wrings it out, and carries it to the living room. She kneels beside her mother's chair and dabs at the stain on the carpet.

Lydia stirs and shakes a bare foot. "Tickle my feet, will you, honey?"

"Not tonight, Mom."

Lydia opens her eyes, sees John standing in the archway. She covers her face with her hands. "You're going to take her away from me."

"I'm sure as hell going to try." The words seem to surprise him as much as they do Kelsey. He backtracks. "I really mean it. I want you to come live with us, but it's not just me. I have to ask Judy."

Lydia moans.

Kelsey's emotions crash against each other. Escape this house. Be free of her mother. Leave Hobby and Gen. Live with strangers. She'd have a better life with him—a new house, no more coming home to her mother splayed out in the Barcalounger, no filthy kitchen and an empty refrigerator. No stained rugs and overflowing ashtrays. There would be a new school with all that entailed, a stepmother who might try to impose rules, two people to care where she was going and why, but to whom she would be accountable. The truth was, she thought she might be able to leave her mother, but not Hobby and Gen, or even Josh, and Lauren's grave where she goes when she needs a good cry.

Her father watches as her mind churns with the possibilities. "I'll talk to my wife and meanwhile, think about." He looks at Lydia, then glances at Kelsey and winks. "We'll have to make arrangements for her. Find her a rehab facility somewhere."

Lydia's face loses all color. She grabs Kelsey's arm. "Don't let him do that to me. You promised. You can't imagine how they treat people in those places."

Kelsey pulls her arm free. "They can't be all that bad." She tries to smile, but all the years alone with her mother and her lies make it impossible to find any humor in this joke, if it is a joke.

"You can't mean it?" Panic raises her mother's voice.

Maybe it's because she has a safety net, but Kelsey feels suddenly free to let her anger bubble to the surface. Her hands knot into fists, and she leans her face close to her mother's. "Things are going to change around here, Mom. People can stop drinking. Josh's mom did. She went to AA. If you want me to stay, you're going to quit."

"The doctor said I could die if I quit like that."

"Did he?"

Lydia's head bobs. The peas slide off her shoulder and land on the floor.

"I guess we need a new doctor," Kelsey says.

·　　·　　·　　·　　·

It's raining when Kelsey waves goodbye to her father from the doorway. He'd asked to take her to dinner, but Kelsey was afraid he'd pry tomorrow's plans out of her. Now that she has options, she needs time to think.

After her dad leaves, Lydia starts in again with the story of how he left when he found out she was pregnant.

"No more lies, Mom."

"How could you believe him and not me?"

"Easy. He's not a liar and you are. And you know what, 'til today, I've had more affection from a cat and a potted plant than from you. Stay away from me." Her voice shakes. "Start acting like a mother. Quit drinking, then maybe I'll stay. If you don't—" Kelsey's grabs her mother's empty glass and lifts her arm to throw it across the room. Gen is on the pass-through counter in the kitchen, head to one side watching. Kelsey's shoulders sag. "If you don't, I will go live with my father." Kelsey slams the glass back down on the TV tray and runs from the room with Gen on her heels. He shoots into her bedroom and she locks the door behind them.

Since Gen's first night there, he's slept with her. When she crawls under the covers, he jumps up beside her, puts his head on her shoulder, a paw against her cheek, and gazes at her with eyes so full of love it almost breaks her heart.

Lydia rattles the doorknob. "Talk to me."

Kelsey wants this day to end with that hug goodbye from her dad, not listening to her mother whining. "Go away. I don't want to talk."

"Please."

Kelsey doesn't answer. She rolls her head so her cheek is against the top of Gen's head. "I love you, Chunky Chicken," she whispers.

"Kelsey."

"Go away."

"Promise you won't leave me."

"I don't want to talk about it now."

Her mother's scratching on the door sounds like the times they've had rats in the attic.

It takes all Kelsey's will-power to listen to Lydia's pleading whispers and not let her in. Long minutes pass before her mother quiets and Kelsey drifts off to sleep. Her last thoughts are of the walk to town with her dad, his arm around her shoulders.

She isn't sure how long she slept when a sound wakes her. Gen jumps down and runs to the door. The hallway light is on and Kelsey sees the shadow of her mother's feet outside her door. Kelsey gets up, tiptoes over and presses her ear to the wood. For a moment, there's only the sound of her mother's breathing, then she hears the rip of tape. A picture slides under the door. It's from one of her mother's photo albums. A second photo follows.

Kelsey gets on her stomach, with Gen beside her, and tilts each picture to the light as it comes through: her baby picture, another at four or five, her first-grade class picture, and one of Kelsey learning to ride a bike.

"I love you, Kelsey," her mother whispers.

God help me, I love you, too.

CHAPTER 41

Her dad stayed the night at the Harbor Lite Lodge, overlooking Noyo Harbor. Last night's storm, their first of the season, left a blue, blue sky and air like ice water. Kelsey rides her bike down to meet him at the Home Style Café for breakfast and arrives shivering.

When her father orders biscuits and sausage gravy, Kelsey's favorite, she feels a sudden rush of emotion and is as unready for her reaction as she had been last night to her mother sliding snapshots under her door. She hasn't been brave enough, or trusted him enough, to let herself think about loving him. She thinks about how attracted she'd been to Will. She should have listened to her suspicious mind about him. Shouldn't she be wary of the feeling bubbling inside her toward her father? Is it love or wishful thinking?

Unlike those photos from her past, this first breakfast together and the mental snapshots from yesterday are among the first memories of a new life: standing in front of her dad's house on Cory Street—his hand on her shoulder; the two of them at the Headlands, she and her dad sitting on the front steps watching clouds skitter across the moon, the unexpected thunder that made them both jump, and now—as silly as it sounds—the arrival of two identical breakfasts.

"I talked to Judy last night." Her dad looks at her over the rim of the coffee cup he's ready to sip. "We want you to come to Santa Rosa next week for Thanksgiving. And when you're there, we can talk about you coming to live with us."

Leave Mom. Live with him. Live with them. Her mind reels.

"What do you say?" He doesn't wait for her answer, as if he sensing the conflict. "You'll love Judy. She's got a great sense of humor." He waits for Kelsey to say something, then puts his cup down, reaches, and takes her hand. "It's too soon, isn't it?"

"It's not that. Or maybe it is." Just three months ago, she thought going to juvie sounded good. Three hots, a cot, rules to follow. A life with some structure. She takes a bite of the biscuit and rich thick gravy, and has trouble swallowing. She closes her eyes, but can still see his expectant face—waiting. She swallows with effort and puts her fork down. "I don't want to say yes for the wrong reason."

"And I don't want you to. And I'm sure you won't."

Until Lydia told Kelsey her dad was dead, she'd spent her life wishing for this moment. Now here he is and he wants her to come live with him. Before the decision became real, it felt easy. She never had to ask herself if she could really leave her mom. The temptation to say yes nearly overwhelms her. She takes a deep breath before answering and what comes out is, "I can't leave Mom."

Her dad's lips compress. "I said that too abruptly. Of course, you can't just pack up and leave—"

Kelsey smiles. "I promise she's going to think I can. Maybe that will be the motivation she needs."

Her dad nods. "Maybe it will." He pushes an uneaten slice of kiwi around his plate. "I hope so." He puts his fork down. "If it doesn't, the offer stands. Say the word, and I'll come get you. In the meantime, you have to promise me one thing."

"What's that?"

"You'll come for Santa Rosa for Thanksgiving, and to Truckee for Christmas. Deal?"

Tears fill Kelsey's eyes. "I'll try. Okay?"

"Sure. I'm sorry." He puts his hands up. "Too much pressure."

"We haven't had a turkey for Thanksgiving or a Christmas tree since I was seven. A real Christmas, with a real family. I can't even imagine, but I am afraid to leave Mom alone."

Her father reaches across the table and takes her hands in his. "I'm being unreasonable. Things *are* going to change, but let's take this a step at a time." His eyes are moist, too. "You have a father now. And, incidentally, I went to Savings Bank yesterday and opened a savings account in our names. You need to go in on Monday and sign a signature card."

She'd told him about the recipe box, so he knows there isn't any money left over to save. All their days are rainy. "I'm not sure what to say."

His smile tells her he's read her mind.

"I opened it with a deposit of four thousand dollars."

When she bursts into tears, he leans closer and whispers. "Don't cry, sweetheart. We've got fourteen years of catching up to do."

•　　•　　•　　•　　•

Detective Moran and Kelsey sit huddled on the darker side of Hobby's office. Two other cops are hiding in the building with the woodpecker knocker. Hannah's car is parked at the neighbor's house. By the luminous dial of Hannah's watch, it's two-fifteen. The only light comes dimly through the one-way window. They've been here since one. The movie Kelsey is supposed to be at with Josh started at one-thirty. To make sure Will and Ryan didn't show up until she and Josh were in the theater, she told him she'd call him with the combination once they were inside and seated. She'd called thirty minutes ago using the cellphone Hannah bought for the occasion. What was taking them so long?

Kelsey sits on the floor with her arms wrapped around her knees. Hannah has moved from the chair, which squeaks, to a spot she cleared on Hobby's desk. Now the only sound is the soft scratch of the polygraph pen on the rolling paper.

While they've been waiting, Kelsey has talked herself hoarse telling Hannah every detail of her father's visit: how she hid at first, what he looks like, what they talked about, his house on Cory Street, him wanting her to come live with them, how conflicted she feels. As time wears on, she's gotten quiet, but the stillness makes Kelsey tense, as if every nerve is exposed to the air. She can't help reliving the moment she found Hobby, his head cracked open, seeing all the blood, and thinking he was dead. "What do you think happens to us when we die?" she whispers.

"I don't have a clue," Hannah whispers back.

"Hobby doesn't either, at least not what happens to the soul, if we even have one. He says he can only account for the body."

"What does he mean?"

"He says we're big bags of atoms, and that atoms disassemble and reassemble all the time. They become part of something else. It's reincarnation in a sense. They don't hold together after we die. They drift off in different directions, and become part of other things."

"Shh." Hannah presses a finger to her lips.

A car with a booming stereo passes.

"It's not them," Kelsey says. "Phil will tell us when they get here."

"Dr. Hobbes is a scientist," Hannah says, "so I'm sure he's right, but that's kind of a sad end, isn't it?"

"I don't know. I guess it depends on what all we become." Kelsey falls silent for a minute. "I went to church after Lauren died."

"Did it help?"

"I wrote a note on one of those envelopes in with the hymnals telling the minister my best friend had died and I'd like to maybe talk. No one answered."

"Maybe he never saw it."

"Somebody saw it. They wrote asking for money. Sent me a pledge card."

"I— " Hannah puts her hand on top of Kelsey's head. The polygraph needle sweeps frantically back and forth across the paper. Hannah slides off the desk and pulls Kelsey to her feet. She opens the cupboard door and makes Kelsey stand behind it. "Stay there!"

Will and Ryan may not hear the racket her heart is making when they open the door, but they will definitely hear the pen scratching out Phil's reaction to their approach. She darts from behind the cupboard door and flips the polygraph off.

"Good," Hannah whispers, then pushes Kelsey back into the cupboard, turns and draws her gun. Seeing Hannah in her bulletproof vest, gun drawn, makes Kelsey realize how serious the situation really is. Her stomach does a flip flop.

They hear someone fumble with the padlock, then Will's voice. He laughs. "She didn't lie. It's frigging four zeros. The old fart never made up a new code." He removes the lock and pulls open the door. A burst of sunlight throws a door-shaped rectangle of brightness across Hobby's chair, his desk, and up the wall making where Hannah stands seem darker. Kelsey's eyes adjust. Through the crack in the cupboard door, she watches a hand feel the wall inside for a light switch.

The switch isn't on that side. Will steps inside and feels the other wall. A blaze of fluorescent light fills the room.

"Damn," Will says over his shoulder. "There's great shit in here."

His back is to the gun. "Police," Hannah hisses. "Put your hands on your head."

A stunned Will whirls and falls back against the lie detector. "Shit!"

"You bitch," he snarls when Kelsey peeks out from behind the cupboard door.

Ryan makes a run for it, but the doorway of the greenhouse is blocked by two more cops, guns drawn.

"You set me up." Will's lips curl in a familiar sneer. "I'll get you for this."

"Good luck with that." Hannah spins him around, shoves him against the desk, kicks his legs apart, and pulls his hands around to snap the cuffs on. "You just threatened a witness in front of a police officer. Want to add anything else to the charges?"

"Hobby's my friend," Kelsey says. "You and Ryan nearly killed him."

"They got no proof. You got nothing on us."

Kelsey smiles. "You two should give up smoking, Will. Ryan's DNA was on the *spit* he left rolling your cigarette. It matched what he left skinning his knuckles on the door."

"That don't prove I hit him. Ryan did it."

"I did not," Ryan wails from the greenhouse.

Hannah puts a hand behind her back, palm up and Kelsey slaps it lightly. "You have the right to remain silent—." She begins to read off the Miranda card.

•　•　•　•　•

Hannah waits to drive Kelsey home while she turns off the light and locks Hobby's bunker. She pauses outside the door and looks up at Phil. "You did good."

"Giving him my thanks, too." Hannah's in the doorway.

"He'll go into cardiac arrest, but would you like a chunk of Phil for your office?"

"Absolutely."

"Want to see his reaction when I take a cutting?"

"You bet." Hannah joins her at the door, while Kelsey dials the combination on the padlock.

Inside, Kelsey turns on the polygraph and takes the clippers from a nail in the wall. Outside, she speaks softly to Phil while she decides where to make the cut. She can hear the polygraph needle begin to make jerky scratches. "Here goes." She cuts off the longest tendril.

The needle blackens the paper.

"Well, I'll be dipped." Hannah laughs. "Phil is a sissy of the first order."

•   •   •   •   •

It's raining again when Hannah and Kelsey pull up in front of the hospital. Hobby paces back and forth under the canopy. A peeved-looking orderly points to the empty wheelchair. "He's supposed to be sitting in this, not storming up and down."

Kelsey laughs and hugs Hobby.

"I've been sitting or lying down for weeks," he says.

"My point exactly," says the orderly. "You need to get your legs under you again."

"Piffle. They are under me."

The orderly throws up his hands, spins the wheelchair, and heads for the door.

"Thanks," Hobby calls after him.

"How'd the arrest go?" he asks, settling in the front seat of Hannah's VW after Kelsey crawls in the back.

"Great," they answer in unison. "The boys turned on each other and spilled their guts."

Kelsey removes the towel hiding Gen's travel cage and opens the door. He comes out, sticks his head through the gap between the seats and bumps Hobby's arm.

"What the— Well, hey there old man." Hobby pulls Gen into his lap and hugs him. He turns to look at Kelsey. "Thank you."

CHAPTER 42

Two days after Will and Ryan's arrest, a package arrives for Kelsey. Inside is a Samsung cell phone and a card that reads: *So we can keep in touch, Love Dad.* His home number, email address, and cell number are programmed in. She uses it to call and say thank you. Her second call is to set a make-amends date with Josh. He welcomes her into the 21ˢᵗ century and makes her give him every detail about the arrest and meeting her father.

•   •   •   •   •

Kelsey waits until the Monday before Thanksgiving to tell her mother she is going to Santa Rosa for the holiday. Lydia sobs out all her failings, how this is her fault, then gets falling down drunk, and stays that way. Knowing that her grandmother drank herself to death plays on Kelsey's mind until, by Wednesday, she's too afraid to leave Lydia alone.

She calls her father, crying. "I can't leave. I'm too afraid of what she'll do if I'm not here."

"We'll come to you," he says. "Mom and Dad would love to see Fort Bragg again, and Judy's never been that far up the coast."

"Please don't."

There's silence at the other end. A full minute ticks by on the cat clock, eyes slipping side to side, tail twitching, Kelsey crying on one end of the phone line, her father breathing on the other. The truth is, she isn't ready to meet her stepmother, or her grandparents, and certainly not ready for them to see how she's been living. But she's afraid backing out on this promise will destroy things before they've had a chance to begin. "Please give me a little more time," she whispers. "This is killing Mom."

Her father sighs. "I don't have the right to pressure you. You have to do what you think is best. Just know that we want you with us. Can we hope for Christmas?"

"Yes. I promise. Thank you."

Kelsey may not be ready to be absorbed into a family of strangers, but she's determined not to spend another Thanksgiving like last year's. She'd gotten a small turkey from the Food Bank and her mother—always weepy at holidays—held herself together enough to get it into the oven. Along with the free turkey, Kelsey'd grabbed the last box of Stove Top stuffing and a box of Betty Crocker instant mashed potatoes. Her mother was sleeping off her morning Bloody Marys and her midday vodka and tonic when the turkey came out of the oven. Hoping Lydia might wake up sober, Kelsey quietly made the stuffing and the potatoes, but when she carved into the turkey, she found her mother hadn't removed the package of giblets and the neck, which had been inside the bird in a plastic bag. The bag had melted and spread heaven only knows what toxic chemicals through the meat. She was too afraid to even put it out for the ravens. She dumped it into the trash and ate potatoes, stuffing and a bologna sandwich for dinner, sitting alone at the kitchen table.

This year she'll use the debit card that came with her savings account, go to Safeway and buy a turkey, or maybe a small ham. She'll use her phone to Google a recipe.

A few minutes after hanging up with her father, Hobby calls to invite her to have Thanksgiving dinner with him. The timing feels suspicious, but she accepts. He picks her up in his old truck and takes her to Silver's at the Wharf. She wears the new dress she bought last week when she still thought she'd go to Santa Rosa for Thanksgiving. It's holiday red with long sleeves and a flared skirt.

"I'm definitely going to Truckee for Christmas. No matter what," she tells Hobby over turkey with real stuffing and real mashed potatoes. "If she dies, while I'm gone, she dies." It comes out sounding much more cavalier than she feels.

Hobby's hair has grown in and sticks straight up like a crop-circle on the side of his head. "There's some new research out on dodder," he says.

"Are you even listening to me?"

"Keep your britches on." He pokes the air between them with his fork. "I'm making a point here. Do you remember that dodder experiment?"

She rolls her eyes. "It's a parasitic vine. It has no roots of its own and it can't produce its own food. Its favorite hosts are tomatoes and wheat, but if given a choice, it prefers tomatoes." She takes a bite of mashed potatoes and lets her eyes follow a fishing boat headed out to sea. She wonders if that boat captain, along with the other people eating their Thanksgiving dinners here, have no families, like Hobby, or families like hers.

"Good, you remembered. Pay attention, now. This is important." He puts his fork down and wipes his mouth. "Botanists thought dodder seedlings grew in random directions and happened upon their prey by chance. Recently, they did experiments and found that, when the seeds germinate, they rotate until they sense the direction from which the chemical they're attracted to is strongest." He takes a breath. "This is the important part. Are you listening?"

"I'm listening." She stirs the pool of gravy in the hollow of her mashed potatoes.

"Wheat produces a chemical to repel dodder, so if given the choice, dodder grows toward the tomato, which has no such defense." He picks up his fork. "They even put the tomato scent on a slab of rubber and the dodder seedling headed right for it."

Kelsey's confused. What does this have to do with her mother? What's so important that he wants to tell her right this minute? "So?"

"Think about it." He begins to eat again.

For whatever reason, she remembers the class handout: *Ways to Encourage Your Children to Use Drugs* list. *"Always pick up after them and don't ask them to accept responsibility."* It dawns on her that the list cuts both ways. She's making it easier for her mother to drink. "Are you saying I'm my mother's tomato?"

"Absolutely, I am." Hobby raises the hand with the electrical-taped fingers. They high-five. "In humans, the parasitic relationship is called co-dependency and it's a nasty habit to get into. By taking care of things for your mother, you make it possible for her to take no responsibility for herself or for you. You allow her to continue to drink, but what's worse, it's setting you up for a lifetime playing that role. You are a giving person, but there have to be limits. Be wheat, Kelsey. Crank out the repellent. By all means, go to Truckee for Christmas."

*   *   *   *   *

Hobby's old truck rattles to a stop in front of Kelsey's house. She starts to get out, then leans and kisses his cheek. "Thank you."

A faint, pink flush creeps up his cheeks. "Ump." He clears his throat. "Your hours are done you know. You don't have to come anymore."

She can't imagine life without Hobby and Gen. Old feelings surface: Anger—easily tamped down. Then hurt that he might be glad to be rid of her. "Don't you want my help?"

"Of course, I do. I'm just giving you an out, if you want it."

She stares at the ocean through the dirty windshield. "I don't."

"Good, I bought a Venus Fly trap and a bottle of chloroform. I want to see if a plant can be anesthetized."

"Boring." She grins and hops out, then leans in the open window. "Thank you for the best Thanksgiving ever. See you tomorrow."

Kelsey waits by the front door to watch Hobby drive away, then turns. This morning, she'd hung the cloth reindeer head on the front. She takes it down. No more pretending for the neighbors that they celebrate Christmas like normal people.

CHAPTER 43

Two days before Christmas, Kelsey waters the sprig of little Phil she brought home from the hospital. The pot hangs from a hook she screwed into the wall above the kitchen window. "You look good there, Junior." She rubs a leaf between her thumb and forefinger and smiles, feeling silly. She glances over her shoulder, then whispers, "Keep an eye on Mom while I'm gone, will you?" Her stomach churns.

Hannah delayed her vacation for a second time to deal with Will and Ryan's arraignment, but she is finally heading to her friend's cabin near Yosemite. She offers to give Kelsey a ride to Truckee on Christmas Eve—swearing it isn't that far out of her way. She'll pick her up again on New Year's Day.

On Christmas Eve morning, Kelsey puts a few final things in her suitcase. She smells her mother's first cigarette of the day and turns to find Lydia standing in the doorway staring at her.

Kelsey's heart starts to flutter. "Hannah will be here in a few minutes."

Lydia's expression doesn't change; her gaze is unblinking and level, even when she taps the hot cigarette ash into her other palm.

"It's only for a week, Mom." Kelsey zips her bag closed and lifts it off the bed. When she turns, her mother's gone. Kelsey faces the empty doorway for a moment, before flipping off her ceiling light and wheeling her suitcase down the hall.

She'd used her new debit card to buy a stack of frozen dinners—all things her mother can microwave. She leaves her suitcase by the door and goes into the kitchen where Lydia is stirring a Bloody Mary with a stick of celery.

"If you need anything while I'm gone, call Mr. Kemp next door. I asked him to check on you."

"I don't need checking on."

Kelsey looks pointedly at the drink in her mother's hand. "In case you do." She opens the freezer compartment. "There's plenty to eat in here."

"Don't need that crap either." Lydia takes out the celery stick and bites off a chunk. "I don't need *his* charity—or yours."

Anger flares in Kelsey like a match head. "Really? That's a switch. What do you think the Food Bank, food stamps, and your disability checks are? Earned income?"

"Leave! Go ahead. What do you care if I spend Christmas alone?" Her mother throws an arm across her eyes.

Kelsey fights down the instinct to say she'll stay. "Don't cry, Mom," she says then, with an ache in her heart, she walks to the window to watch for Hannah.

•   •   •   •   •

By the time Hannah beeps for her, Lydia's most of the way through a second Bloody Mary.

There's nothing left to do but cross her fingers and pray. At the door, Kelsey glances back at her mother in her Barcalounger, looking as if she'd been slung there, crumpled and wet-faced. Kelsey stares at the hook where the reindeer head should be and does the hardest thing she's ever done: she closes the door and goes down the front steps, avoiding the rotten one in the middle.

"You okay?" Hannah says.

"I've never left her for more than a few hours."

"Kelsey, this will sound cold, but you *are* the kid here. She is the only one who can decide to quit drinking and begin taking responsibility for herself and for you."

"I know that, but it doesn't make leaving any easier."

Hannah pats her hand, shifts into first, and pulls away from the curb. As they drive away, Kelsey sees the curtains part and her mother's face at the window.

By the time they get through the mountains to the little town of Cloverdale, an hour and a half later, Kelsey's stomach is in knots. "I don't know if I can go through with this. What if she burns down the house?"

Hannah pulls over. "Didn't you tell me you have a friend whose mother is in AA?"

Kelsey nods.

"Call her. If I'm not mistaken, she will welcome the chance to check on your mom. She might even be able to get her to go to a meeting while you're gone."

Kelsey takes out her cell phone, but holds it, looking out the window.

After a minute, Hannah said: "Call her, honey. This is not a situation you can handle by yourself. AA is about reaching out to others. Your friend's mother will know exactly what to do."

Kelsey dials Josh's number.

EPILOGUE

On the drive back home to Fort Bragg, Kelsey first asks about Hannah's vacation, and listens politely, before launching into her own amazing Christmas. She talks non-stop about seeing snow for the first time, learning to ski with her dad at Alpine Meadows, shopping with Judy for clothes, and eating chocolate fondue. "It was the most wonderful week of my life. I never wanted it to end." Her voice trails off.

Hannah glances over. "I know what you're thinking, but no matter how you find your mother when you get home, you now have an entire family in your corner."

"The first couple days were hard. Everyone was so nice—too nice. I felt like a total misfit and that they all pitied me. I almost made a fool of myself, too."

"I doubt that."

"It's true. Have you ever eaten an artichoke?"

"Every chance I get."

"I'd never even seen one. I sat there with this gray-green prickly bulb on my plate, wishing I was home where I belonged. Judy cleared her throat to get my attention, and I saw her peel off a leaf, and dip it in the mayonnaise-y sauce she'd made. I copied the way she scraped the bottom soft bit off with her teeth. I liked it, okay but it's a lot of work for very little reward."

"I make a stuffed artichoke with crab meat. I'll have you to dinner one night." They go around the bend in Highway One in time to see the sun settling into the ocean. "Did you hear from your mom?"

"That's the best news. Well, no, I didn't, but Josh called. His mom took my mom to an AA meeting."

"I told you." Hannah lifts her hand to high-five Kelsey. "Did you know there is a version of AA for family members affected by alcoholism? It's call

Al-Anon. They meet Mondays and Wednesdays downtown at 6 p.m. We could go together."

"Why would you go?"

"Two reasons. Both my father and my ex-husband are alcoholics. And because we're friends."

Kelsey's eyes tear.

•   •   •   •   •

The closer they get to Fort Bragg and Maplewood Street, the quieter Kelsey becomes. As the car rolls to a stop at the curb in front of her house, she glances at Hannah. "Thank you for driving me. It really was wonderful."

"Whatever you have to face here, Kelsey," Hannah says. "You can do it. You are one strong kid."

Kelsey nods and turns to open the car door. "Look." She grabs Hannah's hand.

The colorful, cloth reindeer head hangs on the front door.

"What?"

"The reindeer head."

"Okay."

"It's hard to explain." Kelsey smiles. "I'll tell you the whole story when I come over for that stuffed artichoke."

ACKNOWLEDGEMENTS

Nothing gets written without the help and guidance of my writers' group, the Mixed Pickles: Norma Watkins, Katherine Brown, Nona Smith, Kate Erickson, Lynn Courtney, and Virginia Reed. Thanks also to Susan Chang, Susan Bono, and Kathy Dawson for their encouragement and for their sharp-eyed edits of this book in all its iterations. The book is dedicated to Teresa Sholars, botanist, mentor, and friend. She's taught generations of Mendocino County college students to love and value our unique environs, at the same time fighting for the preservation of our redwoods and the pygmy forest. I'm also grateful to the Fort Bragg Police and especially Sgt. Mary Miller for taking me through the arrest procedures, and then not keeping me. Thanks to Kelly Nichols, independent designer for finding Kelsey and David King, Design Director, for working so diligently to create a captivating cover. Lastly, thanks to Black Rose Writing and Reagan Rothe for believing in the book that's been lodged in my craw for decades.

SUGGESTED READINGS

The Revolutionary Genius of Plants by Stefana Mancuso. Particularly Vision in plants, pg. 49

Cleve Backster experiments
https://www.youtube.com/watch?v=M2ezqEAG_vA

The Botany of Desire Young Readers Edition: Our Surprising Relationship with Plants by Michael Pollan

What a Plant Knows: A Field Guide to the Senses: Daniel Chamovitz

Finding the Mother Tree: Discovering the Wisdom of the Forest by Suzanne Simard

ABOUT THE AUTHOR

Ginny Rorby is the author of six novels for Middle Grade/Young Adult readers. Prior publications include *How to Speak Dolphin* (Scholastic), *Lost in the River of Grass,* 2013 winner of the Sunshine State Young Readers Award, *Hurt Go Happy*, 2008 winner of the Schneider Family Book Award, *The Outside of a Horse, Dolphin Sky*, and *Freeing Finch* (2019). Her 7th novel, *Like Dust, I Rise* (Dec 2021) is Coming of Age, historical fiction set in Dalhart, Texas, the epicenter of the Dust Bowl.

Like Dust, I Rise
INDE
BOOK
AWARDS
NEXT GENERATION
FINALIST
From award-winning author
Ginny Rorby

NOTE FROM GINNY RORBY

Word-of-mouth is crucial for any author to succeed. If you enjoyed *Girl Under Glass*, please leave a review online—anywhere you are able. Even if it's just a sentence or two. It would make all the difference and would be very much appreciated.

Thanks!
Ginny Rorby

www.ingramcontent.com/pod-product-compliance
Lightning Source LLC
Chambersburg PA
CBHW060709190726
48289CB00002B/604

We hope you enjoyed reading this title from:

www.blackrosewriting.com

Subscribe to our mailing list – *The Rosevine* – and receive **FREE** books, daily
deals, and stay current with news about upcoming
releases and our hottest authors.
Scan the QR code below to sign up.

Already a subscriber? Please accept a sincere thank you for being a fan of
Black Rose Writing authors.

View other Black Rose Writing titles at
www.blackrosewriting.com/books and use promo code
PRINT to receive a **20% discount** when purchasing.